HOLLY SMALE wanted to write from the age of five when she discovered that books didn't grow on trees like apples. Her passion for stories led her on a number of adventures, including modelling, teaching children in Japan, PR and backpacking across dozens of countries around the world. She has a degree in English literature and an MA in Shakespeare from Bristol University.

The Valentines series is the much anticipated follow-up to the number-one, internationally bestselling Geek Girl series, which sold over 3 million copies in thirty languages and won the Teen and Young Adult category of the Waterstones Children's Book Prize.

*Far From Perfect* is the second in a brand-new series that follows the famous Valentine sisters.

This is Faith's story.

Follow Holly on Twitter and Instagram @holsmale.
Follow Geek Girl on Facebook/GeekGirlSeries.

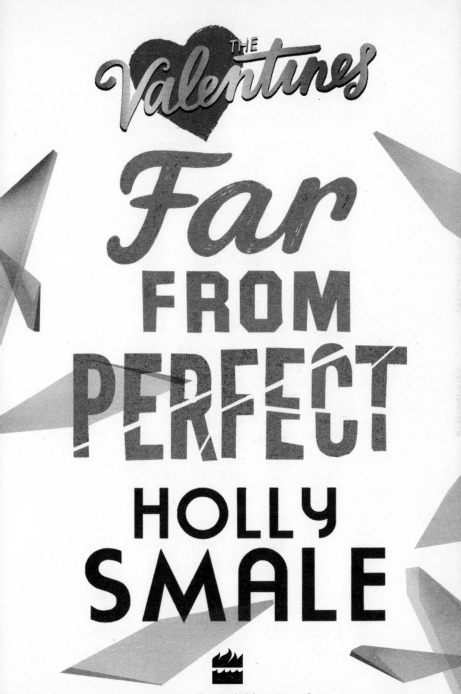

# THE Valentines

# Far FROM PERFECT

# HOLLY SMALE

HarperCollins *Children's Books*

First published in Great Britain by
HarperCollins *Children's Books* in 2020
HarperCollins *Children's Books* is a division of HarperCollins*Publishers* Ltd,
HarperCollins Publishers
1 London Bridge Street
London SE1 9GF

The HarperCollins website address is
www.harpercollins.co.uk

1

ISBN 978–0–00–825417–9

Holly Smale asserts the moral right
to be identified as the author of the work.

Typeset in Plantin Std by
Palimpsest Book Production Ltd, Falkirk, Stirlingshire
Printed and bound in Great Britain by
CPI Group (UK) Ltd, Croydon CR0 4YY

**MIX**
Paper from
responsible sources
**FSC™ C007454**

*For Judith,*
*who will always be with me*

# VALENTIME FOR A CHANGE?

**Leggy beauty Faith Valentine sported a brand-new hairstyle last night. Seen leaving The Ivy alone (left), her curly locks were worn straight, prompting immediate questions about her relationship status with pop star Noah Anthony.**

Blasting straight into the FITTY FIFTY at number eleven is brand-new entry, FAITH VALENTINE (16). Tall, slim, with caramel skin and angel eyes, she's 100 per cent modern bombshell. Online influencer, up-and-coming movie star and YES, part of THAT family, we want her as OUR Valentine come February!

'I'm an early riser,' Faith admits during our interview in the sun-dappled sitting room of their impressive family mansion. 'I wake to the sound of dawn birds singing. The first thing I do is drink water - it perks up the digestive system - and practise ballet.' Her exquisite face dimples. 'I've been dancing since I was little. It really keeps me grounded.'

1

## WELCOME TO THE T-ZONE! YOUR ONE-STOP SHOP FOR EXCLUSIVE SLEB ACCESS!

The Valentines have fame, hotness, *soooo* much money (like lend me a fiver already LOL!) and THIS award-winning blogger (links below, no I didn't make them up, they're totally real, KEVIN) has a PRIVATE INTERVIEW with FAITH VALENTINE, the best one. The T is about to be served!

**Take a closer look at this year's hottest couple – all is not well in paradise. Sources claim they are struggling to find time for each other. With Noah's touring and Faith's film career, there's no opportunity to connect. She's definitely feeling it more than he is, though. Experts agree: 'Their body language shows that she's holding on to this relationship with both hands.' Will it be enough?**

# 1

Snoring.

That's the first thing I hear. Loud snoring, followed by the realisation that I'm the only person in the room so it has to be me. Outside, wood pigeons coo and sparrows chirp, but I've just managed to wake myself up with the machine-gun rattling of my floppy air cavities.

Hot stuff, Faith Valentine.

Eyes shut, I unstick my furry tongue with a *clack*. Then I sit up, yawn with breath like forgotten laundry, swig from a glass on my bedside table and promptly spit melted toothpaste and paprika all over my duvet.

Stuck to the bottom of the glass:

*Bet your intestines are super PERKY now*
*LOL. Max xxx*

With a small grimace – my brother needs a hobby – I open my curtains. Sunlight streams in; I sleepily swing my legs to the floor, scratch my knee and turn the radio on. Then I head straight to my mat.

There's an entire six-metre wall of glass covering one side of my bedroom – in this light, my pores look like potholes: you could get a rope and a tiny hard hat and climb down into one of them – so I quickly unfocus my eyes and grab hold of the wooden barre. Then I bend my knees deeply.

Lifting my heels off the floor, I yawn through my nostrils and gesture to the side with my left hand: *grand plié*. Flatten my foot and hold my leg up and back: arabesque. A single-leg *relevé* to stretch my foot. *A la sec—*

I'm going to have to step up my exfoliation routine or Grandma's going to kill me.

*Battement fondu, battement frappé; quatrième devant.*

Perhaps we could just use Polyfilla?

*Gliss—*

'Coming up,' an overexcited woman on the radio trills, 'the latest hit by Noah Anthony! This one's got *all* the romantic feels, hitting me right in the chest cav.'

'Yeah,' a guy deadpans. 'I'm, like, a mess.'

'My heart's all over the floor!' she agrees, neatly ignoring his sarcasm. 'And here it is! The UK's newest Number One, pouring straight from our ears into yours!'

I stop mid-spin. What does that even *mean*?

With a quick leap, I make it to the radio just in time to catch the opening guitar chords. Guilt tugging at me, I turn the volume down before my boyfriend starts *mmmmm*ing and *do-do-do*ing.

*Sorry, baby. Love you.*

Then – hamstrings still tight from yesterday – I head back to my mat, breathe deeply, close my eyes, stretch upwards, touch my toes and then plank peacefully for a few minutes. Pushing further up, I arrange myself into a deep V shape: feet and arms on the floor, head hanging down, knees flexing and—

'You're a total freak, Effie. You know that, right?'

I open my eyes. My big sister's face is thirty centimetres from mine, lying on the floor, directly below me. She must have silently slipped in and squiggled under my downward dog.

'Something's definitely wrong with you,' Mercy

5

continues, dead-pan. 'Do you think it's, like, medical, or psychological, or genetic, or just the latent impact of a general cultural inequality? I'm legit curious.'

Mer's so close I can see the fibres of her mascara. There's melted black eyeliner streaking from each corner of her eyes towards her hairline as if she's wearing a mask, her foundation is separating around her nose and her lips are patchy with what was burgundy lipstick. The short pink wig she's wearing is slightly knotted and wonky, the fringe lopsided.

My sister looks defiant and exhausted. My heart twangs.

'Good morning,' I say, leaning down and kissing her slightly greasy forehead. 'How was the party? What poor yet totally suspecting soul did you make cry this time?'

Then I stand up, take a long step forward and perform a wide lunge over my sister's reclining black-Lycra'd body.

'Oh my God,' Mercy snaps crossly. '*Stop exercising on me.*'

She shuffles across the wooden floor, sliming up

and on to my bed one muscle at a time like a disgruntled deep-sea creature.

'Hell, *no*,' she adds, punching the OFF button on my radio. 'I'm not listening to your basic boyfriend's lame warbling, either. Nuh-uh.'

I frown at her. '*Mercy.*'

'What? Oh, please. He sucks at writing music and you know it.' She scowls at the light. 'And you can turn *that* off too.'

'The sun?' I pirouette carefully.

'Yes.' Mer watches me spin in disgust. 'It's doing my head in. As are you, Faith Valentine. Stop being so bendy and twisty. It's not even six am. Such a psycho.'

Then – ritual insults completed – Mer puts an arm over her face, closes her dark eyes and picks up snoring where I just left off, vibrating like a drill into a solid brick wall.

I watch my big sister, angry even in her sleep.

Sometimes I think of my bed as a timeshare, like a cheap flat in Majorca. I get the night, and my seventeen-year-old sibling gets the 5am till 2pm post-party slot. I'm not completely convinced Mercy even remembers where her own bed is. There's only a year between us, but if I ever locked my door I'm pretty sure she'd just curl up and sleep on a damp towel in the hallway like a puppy.

Gently – well, quite gently – I pull my minty-paprika duvet over her. Then I refill the glass with non-Maxified water, put it back on the table and step out of my white silk shorts and cami. Hopping, I tug on neon-green leggings and an orange T-shirt. Carefully – God forbid I crush them – I tie my curls into a loose bun, then tug on a cap and sunglasses.

Finally, I lace up my trainers, click on my fitness monitor and slip out of the room. For a moment, I pause in the hallway.

Hope is making cute squeaking sounds – no ugly drilling noises for my little sister – Max is still out as usual and, at the far end of the huge corridor, Mum's door (and the door next to it) is pointedly shut. Noah was playing Wembley last night and Dad is on a flight here from California: they're both definitely unconscious too.

Which means – I take a long, deep breath and stretch – everybody in my life is fast asleep and everything the sun touches is mine. Today is important, and as soon as the rest of the world wakes up I'm going to have to be at my brightest, shiniest, most utterly flawless.

I'll have to be Faith Valentine. But I've got two hours left before that happens.

I'm going for a run.

What kind of sports car does a cat drive?

A Furr-ari.

I'm nobody when I run.

When I run, I'm not a Valentine or a girlfriend or a big sister or a little sister; I'm not a daughter or a granddaughter; I'm not Fitty Number Eleven or a movie-star-in-the-making or The One To Watch or a *girl on the verge of womanhood* (vomit).

I'm not the inspiration for a love song.

As I pound down the long driveway and through the electronic gates – as sweat starts to collect on my top lip like a tiny, salty moustache – I begin to disappear into the familiar, piston-like in-and-out of my lungs.

Richmond Park is so beautiful at dawn. Damp

and rose-gold, the path winds round the huge lake, past the ducks – partying in the early sunshine – and the white swans gliding blankly towards nothing.

I speed up, enjoying the burn in my legs, the heat in my chest and the sweat soaking into my T-shirt. Grimacing slightly – better crack out the razor as soon as I get home or my prickly underarms are going to get their very own head-lines – I take a right turn and run even harder. I pump my arms back and forth, keeping my head down and—

'Faith Valentine?'

*Not yet not yet not—*

'Faith? Faith Valentine? It is, isn't it?'

A boy is jogging next to me, acne shimmering in the sunshine. He jumps forward and leans round so he can peer under the brim of my cap, breathing right into my face.

Why does he smell of prawn-cocktail crisps? At *6am*?

'Nope,' I say, pulling my cap down and running faster. 'Sorry, I think you've got the wrong person.'

'I haven't,' he insists cheerfully, speeding up too.

'You're Effie Valentine. I read that you run every morning and you live in this area, so I got up super early for a whole week in a row and caught the Piccadilly then the District to Richmond and here you are!'

He's running casually alongside me, as if we're voluntary jogging partners discussing tricky daily commutes.

Quickly, I weigh up my options. I could *probably* run faster – although I'm more of a long-distance type – or I could stop, but that might look like an invitation to chat. Or I could dive off the path into the trees, but that's definitely one of the most idiotic suggestions I've ever given myself.

Instead, I veer subtly across the grass so we're headed back towards the main path. I don't want to hurt his feelings.

'I can't believe it's you!' the boy continues chirpily. He can only be about thirteen. Why isn't he playing video games or missing the toilet bowl while he pees or something? 'This is awesome! Wow, I was right, you *are* really hot. I mean, like, naturally, you know? Not a smidge of make-up. That's my favourite kind of hot.'

His favourite *kind* of hot? As if there are multiple genres of hotness available to a prepubescent boy with a ripe pimple between his eyebrows.

'Thank you.' I smile. 'That's so sweet.'

'Do you come here often? This exact route, I mean?' He lankily matches my pace. 'Also, what are your feelings about parks in general?'

'Umm.' This must be some new, obscure kind of flirting. 'I don't run this route normally, no.' *This route is now dead to me.* 'And, mmm, parks are . . . nice?'

'*Nice!*' The boy sounds thrilled. A quick glance around. 'So what's your favourite . . . tree?'

'Oak.' I'm well trained in quick-fire questions, which is good because I'm not even properly awake yet.

'Favourite food?'

*Cornish pasty.* 'Sushi.'

'Colour?'

*Grey.* 'Green.'

'Epic!' We're still running pretty fast and a drip of sweat runs off the end of his chin. 'Can I have your autograph, then?' A Sharpie is thrust under my nose. 'You can write on my arm!'

13

Stopping, I put a hand on my waist, wipe my forehead and grab the pen with my damp hand.

*Faith V—*

'All my love,' he prompts. 'Write all my love.'

*All my love, Faith Valentine.*

Then he shoves an arm round me, tugs me into his Lynx-saturated side, plasters wet lips to my cheek and holds a phone up in front of our sweaty faces. My stomach lurches: there's a little red light flashing at the top: *4:36, 4:37, 4:38—*

He wasn't flirting with me. This was an *interview*.

'And *you*,' the boy announces to the camera, making an awkward T with his free hand, 'have just been T-zoned!' He beams at me triumphantly. 'Thanks for the exclusive, Eff. Eleven *schmeven*. You're *my* Number One! Or, like, Number Two. Behind Lily Aldridge. She's a Victoria's Secret Angel and I'm going to marry her.'

And he's off, running back into the trees.


I may need to rethink my exercise routine.

Maybe I should get up earlier, start at 4am instead. I could sprint in circles round the lake in our garden. If only running on the treadmill in our basement gym didn't make me feel like a giant neon hamster.

Pushing through the front door, I wipe my forehead, check the time, then pick my phone up off the table. It's already flashing with notifications and Google alerts.

Stretching, I send Noah his daily wake-up text.

**Morning, handsome! How did the show go? I watched some on YouTube last night – it looked amazing! So proud of you xxxx**

Then, loosening my shoulders, I email my agent:

Hi, Persephone! Thanks for the update! Is this the last version of the script or will there be another one? x

Mum:

Can I fix you any breakfast? How about some nice healthy porridge? Let me know! xx

15

Dad:

What's your ETA? Need me to leave you a key? Can't wait to see you xxx

Max:

Where are you? You OK? xx

The morning feels like it's unravelling already, so I drop to the floor of the hallway for thirty push-ups. Thirty crouch-star-jumps. Thirty lifts on a nearby chair. Twenty-seven squats with weights above my head (I'll squeeze in the last three after brushing my teeth).

Grabbing my phone, I open today's messages from Genevieve, my grandmother's assistant. The first photo is of a bright green smoothie bowl with a gold spoon on a marble worktop, raspberries and coconut shavings in a beautifully arranged heart shape. It's been filtered to look rosy and nostalgic.

I bet it tastes like the contents of a lawnmower bag.

Frowning, I copy and paste:

*Nothing starts the day like a full heart (and tummy)! Good morning, lovelies :)* ❤ ❤ *xxx*

And . . . POST.

Then I steal a rubbery slice of Mercy's cold takeaway pizza from a box on the kitchen table, wolf it down and burp greasily as I climb the stairs. At the top, I quickly scribble my cat joke down on a Post-it and cock my head to the side. *Furr-ari/Ferrari*. Is that funny? I think it's quite funny. Cats can't even drive! LOL.

Finally, I slip into the empty room, kiss the Post-it and stick it on the wall. *Done.* Then I glance at my watch and breathe out slowly: 8.23am.

Just one more thing left to do.

# 3

My little sister sleeps so easily.

Whereas Mercy confronts darkness like an enemy to be clawed at, fought with and be finally over-whelmed by – and Max fires up and burns straight through it – Hope simply shuts her eyes and ignores it completely.

Softly, I slip into Po's room. She's still passed out in a knotted heap, sunshine pouring through her wide-open red velvet curtains, fluffy black curls in chaos, arms wrapped tightly round her brand-new camcorder. Her left foot is kicking and she's murmuring, '*Cut! Cut! Cut!!*'

Love streams through me, uncomplicated and bright, entirely without shadows.

'Po.' I put a hand gently on top of her head. An alarm is beeping next to her, to no avail. 'Wake up, baby.' I promised I'd stop calling her that now she's nearly sixteen, but . . . 'It's your big day.'

Hope wiggles, murmurs, '*Action!*', then opens her eyes and beams at me. Unlike the rest of us, it takes the youngest Valentine exactly zero time to wake up. She's switched on and suddenly she's all there, like a film starting.

'And so the dream begins!' Hope sits upright, stretches her toes and holds her arms out like a starfish. 'Let the day pray seed.'

I laugh fondly. '*Proceed.*'

'Exactly.' With a quick hop, Po bounces out of bed and starts spinning in dreamy circles with her arms above her head. It's Initiation Day at her new school before she starts properly in September, and she's been preparing since she got back from California last week.

And, when I say 'preparing', I mean 'practising elaborate speeches as Head Girl/Most Popular Person/Chief Party-thrower' (it varies).

My phone *pings*.

Morning, beautiful. Wish you'd been there. The crowd was wild! Am I seeing you later? Love you N xxxx

'Faith and Noah,' Po sings as I smile and type
back:

Of course! Can't wait! When works for you?
xxx

'Snogging in a tree. *S-N-O-G-I-N-G.*'

Then my baby sister starts floating round the
room, clutching all the bright new clothes I bought
her a few days ago. 'Everyone is going to see me
coming a mile off,' she sighs happily, waving them
like flags. 'Cancer's a naturally popular star sign,
Eff. We're built very sociable. I strongly inspect
everybody's going to *adore* me.'

Smiling, I take a pencil case off the mantelpiece.
Hope has always been a happy soul, but ever since
she came back from Los Angeles she's been bouncier
than ever. Except every time I ask her *exactly* what
happened out there – especially with that boy – she
adopts a weirdly secretive expression.

'Oh,' she grins. 'You know, Eff. Just some driving.'

She's also taken to slamming doors and yelling
at inappropriate moments, which is out of character

and kind of adorable. Although I'm not entirely sure what Dad was doing, letting a fifteen-year-old control a car.

'Maybe take something to help with the non-social side of school?' I shake the pencil case. It's totally empty, the little mousebear. 'You know, for luck?'

'Luck *schmuck*.' Po shrugs. 'We make our *own* destinies, Eff. Also, it's a *house of education*. A *church of learning*. There must be a spare pencil lying about somewhere.'

Then she shouts, 'Ooh!' and opens the window.

'Ben!' she yells through cupped hands. 'Benjamin! Ben-jamin-o! We're up here! Can you climb the drainpipe *au* itsy bitsy spider or do we need to come down and let you in?'

Po turns and wiggles her eyebrows at me.

I have a long-term boyfriend and I love him very much, and he isn't the boy currently standing on our doorstep. Not that this small technicality makes any difference to my matchmaking sister.

'Go and say hello.' Hope starts pushing me towards her bedroom door. 'Ben's come all the way back from Edinburgh, Faith. That's just good manners.'

I'm nudged another few steps. 'I don't think—'

'Also,' my sister continues brightly, tapping my shoulders, 'can we take *uno momento* to acknowledge how cute he's got, Eff? Don't you think Ben's kind of gorgeous? He's like a –' she considers her options – 'final-season Harry Potter or something.'

There's excitement all over her sweet little face. My sister loves me very much – and she likes Noah – but she loves a good romance story more. And Benjamin has been killing daisies and leaving them for me on the kitchen table since we were six years old. In her eyes, this is a *solid* love triangle.

'Umm,' I say hesitantly as I'm pushed on to the landing. 'Baby, I honestly need a shower before I see another human. I'm all stinky and sweaty, and I think I ran through some duck poop, so—'

Hope leans towards me and sniffs. 'Roses,' she says matter-of-factly, spinning me round to face the stairs. 'Roses and dewdrops and macaroons and kittens. It doesn't matter what you do, Faith Valentine. You are always *perfection*.'

4

Why did the robber take a bath?

He wanted to make a clean getaway.

'Just a second!' I call through the keyhole.

A clean getaway. HA! *I wish.*

Quickly, I rub a posh scented candle on my neck, wipe my sweaty face on my T-shirt and try to arrange it into an *I'm-just-an-old-friend-almost-like-a-sister-and-not-a-romantic-prospect-who-will-suddenly-see-you-in-a-new-light-stop-looking-at-me-like-that* expression. Ben has obviously watched *way* too many romcoms.

Then I fling the door open and my nonchalant, 'Oh hello,' is appropriately truncated to an, 'Oh *hell.*'

There's a long silence.

'Faith,' Dame Sylvia Valentine says eventually,

looking me up and down in steely-faced horror. 'Is this some kind of . . . joke?'

Blinking, I glance down the driveway. There's no sign of Ben. Obviously, he saw my famous grandmother and her even more famous walking stick coming and dived into a bush. Smart boy.

'Is . . . what a joke?'

'This.' Grandma waves her stick at me and sniffs like a scandalised bloodhound. 'When I said *prepare a natural look*, I did not mean that of a long-term vagrant with –' she leans forward – 'undertones of bitter orange peel and lavender.'

My nose twitches: this is a woman who knows her Liberty candles.

'I thought you said ten o'clock and it's only—'

'You are a *Valentine*.' She holds up a pale, heavily diamond-spangled hand. 'We do *not* open doors in a dishevelled state, regardless of the relative position of the sun. What would you have done if I were a journalist? What if I were a crazed member of the public? What if I had a video-log?'

I hold my head down so she doesn't see my nostrils flicker again. *Video-log?* 'Sorry, Grandma.'

'We must *always* be in a state of readiness.' I

glance up. Grandma has begun projecting in her small-theatre voice. 'There is no intermission, Faith. For us, the curtains are always up.'

I dip my head further. 'Sorry, Grandma.'

'Get in the car, please,' she says curtly. 'I expect irreverent behaviour from your siblings, not from you.'

Then she turns and marches towards the silver limo, disappointment radiating from her shoulders.

Sudden guilt rushes through me. Those two hours weren't mine at all. I should have been washing, scrubbing, shaving, plucking, conditioning, masking, moisturising, face-packing, contouring. I should have been filling in all the holes in me so that nobody else could see them.

'Sorry, Grandma,' I say for the third time. *Three bags full, Grandma.*

Then I do exactly as I'm told.

'. . . potential,' Grandma reads as I lean back in the limo and scrub my face with a cloth that smells of cucumber. 'With the coruscating beauty of a modern movie legend –' she looks pointedly at me – 'and half of this year's hottest teen couple, Faith Valentine is poised to make her mark on the film industry.

Movie offers are already flooding in from around the globe.'

Genevieve hands me another wet towel from an enormous straw bag that appears to contain the entire contents of a day spa. She may at some point produce a hot tub and steam room. I start rubbing hard at my neck.

'On which note, have you submitted your first post to the World Wide Web today?' My grandmother raises her eyebrows. 'Suitably aspirational and *brand appropriate*, I hope?'

She makes social media sound like you have to send an application form with your passport and a stamped-addressed envelope to the tiny robots that run 'The Internet'.

'Yes, Grandma.' I smile at Genevieve gratefully, then absent-mindedly poke the inside of my ear with a finger. 'Over a hundred and thirty-two thousand likes in half an hour.'

'Good girl.' She turns a page in my gold scrapbook of media clippings (aka my Book of Shame). 'Though the tabloids continue to focus on your difficulties with young Noah Anthony. This is not a good look for you, Faith.'

She holds up a papped photo of me scowling at my boyfriend, a large glob of mayonnaise positioned neatly on my chin like a white goatee.

'I was hungry,' I say, flushing. 'We're doing brilliantly, I promise.'

Also I'm not entirely sure how to eat a burger in a way that says *We Are Madly In Love But You Said No To Chips – Get Your Hands Off My Skinny Fries.*

'Valentines don't wash their dirty laundry in public,' Dame Sylvia reminds me severely. 'We pay other people to do it in a secret and exclusive celebrity Launderette facility, preferably on the other side of town. Have I made myself clear?'

I nod humbly.

All millions of people can see is Noah – adoring and attentive – and me: a grumpy, greedy cow with no idea where my mouth is.

*Must do better, Eff.*

'On which note, I saw the *Variety* proofs this morning.' The scrapbook page is turned. 'You look very pretty, but say very little, Faith. Please do try to make an interesting comment. Nobody wants to interview a statue, even if it's of a goddess.'

'But Mercy and Max were taking all the—'

'Then find a way to make yourself heard.' Grandma flips another page, scans, then sighs. 'The *Daily Mail* has once more referred to you as *aloof* and an *Ice Queen*. Darling, if you were a man, that would be a way of saying *enigmatic*. As a woman, it just means *nightmare*. You *must* try to come across as warmer. But not so warm that you look desperate, obviously.'

Genevieve and I make eye contact.

My grandmother's assistant is in her early twenties, but she's wearing a velvet jacket, midiskirt and ruffled blouse. It's like an identical version of my grandmother has sprouted – the way you can take cuttings from plants and put them in small pots to make new ones.

She nods with raised eyebrows. *Warm up, Faith.*

'Sure. Sorry.'

Our limo glides to a stop in the middle of the road – imperiously ignoring the frustrated beeps of the cars stuck behind us – and a wave of nausea whips through me.

Maybe if I vomit all over myself they'll send me home. Although something tells me I'll just be handed another wet wipe, sprayed with pine-scented car freshener and sent on my way.

My phone *pings*.

Ohmygodohmygod, I forgot to say GOOD
LUCK! You're going to NAIL IT. YOU'RE A
TOTAL PARASITE OF FEMININITY! Hxxx

'Umm.' Smiling briefly, I tug the white floaty dress
I've been handed over my damp orange sports bra.
'Grandma, can we . . . Do you think . . . Perhaps
we could quickly *go over* what I'm supposed to—'

'We've been studying drama every Wednesday for
nearly a year, Faith.' My grandmother frowns. 'Have
you not been listening? Did we not cover every key
point?'

'Yes, I've read Stanislavski and Chekhov and
Meisner and Adler – I know every word – I
just—'

'Then I do not understand the problem.'

A short silence.

'Acting is in your blood,' clarifies Dame Sylvia
Valentine, five-time Oscar winner, recipient of the
BAFTA lifetime achievement award and British
National Treasure. 'A rare, valuable gift passed from
my mother to me, to your mother to you.'

The door is opened by the chauffeur as Genevieve hands me a printed script.

A few more irritated beeps from behind us.

'You are a *Valentine*, darling,' my grandmother concludes with a tight smile. 'The entire world has been handed to you on a plate. All *you* have to do is not screw it up.'

## 5

*Don't screw it up, Faith.*

Don't screw it up, screw it up, screw it up, screw it, screw—

The door gets simultaneously kicked from the

other side as I pull on it, nearly smacking me in the face.

'*Whoa! Sorry.*' A short girl with cropped blonde hair and freckles rolls green eyes at me. 'Cat on a pink bicycle, it's *you*? What a waste of my flaming morning. Have fun with the unearned leg-up, Valentine. Must be nice.'

Then she stomps out through the front door: dungarees, thick silver boots, little but somehow taking up so much space. Blinking, I watch her go.

'Faith *Valentine*?' the receptionist squeaks as I turn round. 'OMG, you've *arrived*! And you're even *more beautiful* than in your headshots! How's your poor *mother*? I've been *heartbroken* about Juliet's –' she lifts her voice into a whisper-shout – '*TRAGIC DECLINE.*'

At my name, every girl in the room looks up, narrows their eyes and looks back down again.

'She's—'

'That's just so great!' The receptionist stands up and waves away the actress waiting nervously outside the casting room. 'You, sit down. I'm under *strict instructions* to send Faith Valentine straight in. Please, Faith, do let me!'

She opens the door and bows slightly, as if she can see I might need professional help getting in and out of rooms. Humiliated, I swallow and step forward.

Be *warm*, Faith, but not *too warm*.

*Enthusiastic but not desperate; calm but not dull; funny but not try-hard; quirky but not crazy; feisty but not aggressive; beautiful but relatable; elegant but not icy; confident but not arrogant; feminine but not girly; nice but not boring.*

*Yourself but – you know . . . someone else.*

My grandmother and I have spent the first ten minutes of each Wednesday lesson practising the Stanislavski method. You draw an imaginary circle round yourself and block everything else out, keeping you safe and private, no matter what's happening.

Yeah, I can't do it.

I'm standing in front of an entire roomful of strangers who are assessing me carefully. Taking me apart so they can evaluate the individual components: my mother's eyes, grandmother's nose, father's mouth and height . . . Until I'm just little pieces of people who aren't even me. A composite of recycled beauty handed down by others and instructed to look after carefully, like an old clock or a vintage handbag.

'The middle Valentine,' an older woman with tortoiseshell glasses announces to the room. 'Mike and Juliet's girl!'

'Remarkable,' somebody says, taking notes. 'Exotic but also classic. The camera's going to *love* her.'

On cue, I switch myself on.

'Hello!' Walking forward, I smile with a dimple in my left cheek. 'It's so *very* nice to meet you.' I've learnt to subtly bite the inside of my mouth without anyone noticing. Nobody knows my dimple is fake. Not even Noah.

'Hi,' I say to each person in turn. *Dimple.* 'Hi there.' *Dimple.* 'Hey.' *Dimple. Dimple. Dimple. Dimple.* The inside of my mouth has started bleeding.

'Hello.' I've reached the famous casting director, Teddy Winthrop. He's so old and crumpled he makes my grandma look like a Manhattan debutante. 'It's a privilege to meet you.'

Dimpling again – *ow!* – I hold out my hand.

'Established.' Teddy nods, unimpressed. 'We're all very much greeted now. Shall we get on with it?'

He flicks rheumy blue eyes at the empty chair in the middle of the room and I glance down at my script.

'Off-page,' the casting director demands in an icy voice. 'Please.'

I look up in horror. 'But my agent said—'

'Yes, but as I have been informed, repeatedly and relentlessly, you are one of the *Valentines*. I think you can manage a single short scene, don't you?'

I'm suddenly not so sure that my family connections are working in my favour. He may have already met Mercy.

'Of course.' I obediently drop the script on the floor. 'Yes. No problem.'

Then I sit in the chair as two enormous lights abruptly switch on. I flinch. *Find the circle, Eff.* It feels like I'm some kind of rare lizard in a bright terrarium.

'Where would you like me to—'

'Bang,' the woman wearing glasses abruptly says. 'Crackle. Ooooh-eee-oooooh. Woo. Woo. Woooooooooooooo. Yeeeeeha. Yeeeha. Woof woof meow oink arroooooooooga.'

I stare at her blankly. What the—

*35*

'Oh!' I glance to the side and see that the green light on the camera is blinking. 'Have we started? We've started. Umm. *Fred!* What was that? I heard something – there's someone outside!'

'There'snobodythere,' the woman reads in monotone.

'We've made a mistake,' I say, voice trembling carefully. 'We should g-go – we should l-l-leave. Wait, I think I've got enough battery in my—'

'It'sjustasheeporsomething.'

'But sheep don't sound like that.'

'Acowthen.' The woman peers at me with raised eyebrows. 'AgoatwhatevertheyhaveouthereI'llgoout justwaitforme—'

Wait. Do I . . . *know* her?

A memory clicks. A party my parents threw nearly a decade ago. Music, laughter, flowers, a large white tent in the garden, and we were all sitting on the stairs together, listening to the—

'. . . Kiss.'

My parents were standing on the lawn, making a toast, and—

'Kiss.'

A clink of glasses and I looked round and—

36

'*Kiss.*'

*Wait, is that my cue?*

'Ah.' I blink at the woman from the party, and then at Teddy. I don't remember kissing in the original script. 'Kiss? What – who am I supposed to . . . kiss exactly?'

Confused, I look round the room.

'I'll do it!' A young guy at the back jumps up. 'If you need someone to make out with Faith Valentine, I can do it! Just . . . you know. For now. To practise. Or whatever.'

Teddy stares at the poor boy until he sits down again.

I lick my lips. *Do something, Faith.*

Impulsively, I close my eyes and start to make out passionately with the back of my own hand. I taste of sweat and fear and disinfectant cucumber wipes.

'F-F-Fred!' *Kiss.* 'Don't go!' *Kiss.* 'Please! I love you! Don't leave me in here on my own!' *Kiss.* 'What will happen if— Oh no. Oh no, he's gone. He's gone. He's gone, he's—'

'And stop,' says Teddy Winthrop.

I stop.

'What are you doing?' The casting director frowns. 'Do you not want this role? Do you find television *beneath* the illustrious Valentines?'

'No!' I flush in alarm. 'Of *course* not. I *really* want this role, sir. Acting is my life.'

'You could have fooled me.' Mr Winthrop looks at the woman in glasses, then back at me. 'You're the only character left alive. For the audience, you *are* the film. You're alone, you're scared, something deeply unpleasant is happening and you need to *hold the show. Command* it.'

'Would it help if I . . . move, do you think?'

'I don't care if you cartwheel, darling, just play this role with more charisma than a rotten wooden spoon.'

Ouch. *Be the Orange, Faith.*

Straightening my shoulders, I stand up; change my mind and sit down again; change it again and stand back up. I turn my head; turn it back again. My body feels like it's being driven by somebody who hasn't got their licence yet.

Try *harder*, Faith. You are not trying hard enough. Give them *more*.

Taking a deep breath, I scream: '*NOOOOOOOO!*'

One hand in a fist clutched to my chest, I fall to my knees and close my eyes. 'Fred! FREDDDDDD!!!!'

*More.* 'FREEDDDDDDDDDDDDDDDD!!!!'

'Yes, I think we've seen enough.'

I open my eyes, cheeks flaming.

'Please, Mr Winthrop.' *Don't be desperate. Don't be desperate.* 'Is there anything else I can—'

'No, thank you,' Teddy says curtly. 'Please send the next girl in.'

Blinking, I clear my throat and calmly stand up. Then I dust off my dress, brush back my hair and smile. Because the curtain is always up, the audience is always watching and you must always take your bow, even if nobody is clapping.

'Thank you for taking the time to see me,' I say politely, dipping my head. 'I hope to see you all again in the future. Goodbye.'

I slip out of the room.


The door is way too thin.

'Well,' Teddy Winthrop grunts from the other side, 'the infamous Ice Queen might have the looks, but I'd rather hire my kitchen worktop.'

I close my eyes once more.

'Shame,' agrees my parents' old friend. 'Such a *nice* girl. Can't act for toffee, but my goodness: *what a face.*'

# 6

So, that was fun.

My grandmother's chauffeur climbs out of the car, tips his hat and opens the door for me as I launch into: 'Gosh, that went *so* well! I'm not entirely sure I'm what they're looking for –' maybe a human who can convincingly portray another identical human – 'but I really *connected* with the director and next time I think that—'

The back of the car is totally empty.

'They went shopping in Fortnum and Mason, miss,' the driver says as my smile collapses in relief. 'Then I believe your grandmother took a sudden liking for afternoon tea at the Hilton.'

My grandmother is such a cartoon character. At some point, she took on the role of timeless Great British Dame – walking stick, imperious attitude, haughty expression, *sudden likings for afternoon tea* – and just never took it off again. It's important to remind myself I'm half American and only half Downton Abbey.

My phone *pings*.

Baby, this album is kicking my butt. Come make it all better? :( Nx

'Where now, miss?' The driver climbs back into his seat. 'Dame Sylvia said you're welcome to join them.'

I politely pretend to consider this for a few seconds.

Umm, eating scones in a busy, gilt-embossed room ('Oh, *have* you met my granddaughter Faith? She's the *future* of the Valentines, you know. Darling . . . not so much jam!') or watching my cute boyfriend excitedly twiddle buttons on a huge control system like it's a spaceship he's only just learnt how to fly?

With a wave of relief, I rummage around in the car door for my secret make-up bag and hold a tiny mirror up to my face. I look tired. But a few more dabs of carefully positioned pore-filler, highlighter, foundation, concealer, blush, mascara, eyeliner, bronzer and everyone will think I'm fine.

I start expertly applying the make-up nobody knows about but me.

Thank goodness for boyfriends.

'Take me to Abbey Road, please, John.'

Noah is waiting outside.

As the limo pulls up to the world-famous recording studio, I see my sweet guy. He's perched on a bollard, long legs bent, big black eyes narrowed in concentration while he taps a tune on his jeans with his fingers. You know that moment when you climb into a warm bath, and everything goes tingly and floaty, and you worry you're going to melt and disappear, but you're also kind of cool with it if you do?

That's how I feel every single time I see Noah Anthony. As if I'm disappearing and I don't mind in the slightest.

'Eff!' He looks up as I step out of the car, and I finally feel myself beam without dimples. 'Oh, thank chicken nuggets you're here! I've been playing the same three chords all morning and I was *literally* about to rip my fingers out at the joints.'

Noah's nose is a tiny bit crooked from a brother's punch when he was small, there's a scar above his left eyebrow and his front teeth are a little misaligned from the braces he refused to get. But it's the imperfections that make my boyfriend so gorgeous, that leave the eyes with somewhere interesting to land.

My smile widens as I get closer. He shaved his hair off two days ago – an attempt to look 'edgier' – but it actually makes him look soft and vulnerable, like a tiny lamb.

'Hey.' I give him a gentle kiss and study his face carefully. 'Is it going *very* badly?'

He grimaces.

Noah pretends to find the roller coaster of success overwhelming, but every dip and swerve excites him.

He loves the pressure, but he also needs to play the reluctant, overburdened artist, so I pretend not to see it.

'*Dire*,' he sighs, rolling his eyes. 'Sometimes I wonder what I do it for, you know? I miss the days of sitting in my bedroom, just me and my guitar. The chords aren't working for me today.'

He makes a sad-emoji face, so I quickly search for an appropriate joke. 'What do you get when you, er, drop a piano down a mineshaft?'

Noah frowns. 'Huh?'

I hold my hands out, palms facing him. '*A flat miner.*'

There's a pause.

'A Flat *Min*-or,' I say again, with slightly different emphasis. 'It's . . . a joke about chords, I think?'

My boyfriend gives one short laugh – 'Ha!' – and kisses me on the nose, although frankly he might as well pat me on the head. 'Who says girls can't be beautiful *and* funny?'

Relieved, I kiss him back. 'Pretty much everyone.'

He grins. 'Sad times.'

'Noah?' Out of nowhere, embarrassment wallops me in the stomach. 'This morning . . .' I wince. 'The audition . . . it didn't . . . go . . . brilliantly.'

45

*Charisma of a rotten wooden spoon.* 'I don't think I . . . exactly nailed it. I . . . might have come across as a bit . . . wooden.'

*I'd rather hire my kitchen worktop.*

'Don't be daft, baby.' Noah smiles proudly. 'You're always so hard on yourself, Eff. You need to believe in yourself as much as I believe in you.' Here comes the inevitable wordplay. 'Have a little *faith* in yourself, know what I mean?'

He laughs. He always laughs at that.

'No, I really mean it, Noah.' My eyes are suddenly wet. 'It was horrendous. Grandma's going to be so cross with me, my agent will be furious and I'm not sure what to do if—'

'Oh, please, as if anyone could turn *this* down.' He steps back and gestures at me as if I'm a new goddess rising from the sea foam. 'You're literally the most beautiful girl in the world. And the sweetest. I mean, *look* at you, Eff. These eyes? This hair? This *mouth*. Those—'

I roll my eyes and smack him gently. 'Yes. Thank you, Noah.'

'All I'm saying –' he puts his hands gently on either side of my face – 'is they're not *blind*.'

46

We gaze at each other affectionately.

For a brief moment, I see my boyfriend as he was the night I met him at the BRITs after-party. He was celebrating his first big win, while I was crouched on the floor, helping the waiters clean up spilt hors d'oeuvres.

I kind of had to. It was Mercy who'd knocked them over.

'Noah,' I start, then abruptly stop. His big dark eyes have got a slightly glazed expression and I can feel his fingertips twitching. 'Noah, are you practising the piano on my face?'

'What?' He jumps back. 'No. What?'

'You are.'

'I'm not! We are *talking* about your career, Eff, your destiny, your life path, the—' A scratch of the shaved head. 'Yeah, I was, but I think your little "joke" just fixed my chord problem! It's an A minor, not a C. *A minor!* I cannot believe I didn't realise that earlier!'

I laugh, even if he did just mime bunny ears around my attempt at humour.

It's impossible to be angry with Noah. He has incredibly long eyelashes and a freakish ability to make his eyes look so huge and round you feel like you're snapping at a baby cow.

'Go.' I playfully push him towards the studio. 'Go get that note. Hit inspiration over the head with a baseball bat or whatever.'

Noah tries very hard to look reluctant. 'Sure?'

'I'm sure.'

'Because, you know . . .' He grabs my hand and pulls me closer to give me a kiss. I can feel his breath on my lips: sweet, warm, rich. He's been drinking coffee with three sugars in it again. 'You came all this way and the new album's not *that* important. I *could* always settle for Number Two in the charts and stay out here a bit longer . . .'

Nose twitching, I try to look stern. 'Go record that song.'

'Maybe even Number Three –' he kisses my eyebrow – 'or perhaps I could chuck my guitar in the bin and we could—'

I push him away again. 'Go.'

He kisses my eyelid. 'Make out all—'

'Noah Anthony, *go*.'

And that's when I hear the clicks.

7

I spin round. Cameras are trained on us like guns.

'FAITH! NOAH!' Paparazzi are bursting from every direction. Behind walls and bins, round the sides of cars, yelling, jostling, pushing: 'THIS WAY! DOES THIS MEAN YOU'RE OFFICIALLY BACK TOGETHER?'

'STILL ON THE ROCKS?' More pushing. 'ARE YOU SEEKING COUPLES COUNSELLING? HOW ABOUT A RELATIONSHIP PSYCHIC?'

'ANYTHING TO SAY ON THE AVERY RUMOURS?'

'FEELINGS ON THE SHIP NAME FOAH? FAINOAH? OR JOITH? JAITH?'

'WHAT ABOUT NOITH? NITH?'

Noah laughs. 'Fainoah, that's my favourite one – sounds like something hipsters eat with avocado,' but my brain is already starting to spin, replaying

49

the last few minutes on a frantic loop. How long were they there? What did they see? Could they tell I was nearly in tears? Did it look like we were fighting?

I kept pushing Noah away, and he kept grabbing my hand.

Oh my days, I *smacked him*.

'COME ON, FAITH! GIVE THE POOR GUY A BREAK!' somebody yells as a handy reminder.

Horrified, I turn to stare at my boyfriend.

'Whoops,' Noah grins nonchalantly. 'My PR people must have told them we were here. My bad.'

My eyes are flickering wildly, seeking an exit.

'Hey, hey.' Noah grabs my hands. 'Don't get upset, baby. I mean, it's all part of the fame game, right? I mean, I hate it too, with every bone in my body –' he does not – 'but what can we do?'

I dunno – how about *not* give the paparazzi details of our every single move?

What I really, *really* want is to give my boyfriend a quick hug on his break without millions of people casually assessing *what it means* over their cornflakes the next day. Without judging the minutiae of my facial expressions or hair or outfit; without entire articles analysing our body language. *She pulled away: it's a fractured relationship. Their feet facing away from each other? Lack of intimacy, right there. Did you see her eyes well up?*

*This couple are in deep trouble. Pray for them, readers! Pray for FOAH!*

Except now I sound surly and ungrateful – super unattractive – so I quickly dimple as hard as possible.

'Can we—'

'*Unless*,' Noah interrupts thoughtfully, eyes starting to shine again. 'I mean, if they're going to write about us, Eff, we might as well give them something to write, yeah? Have some fun?'

'Absolutely.' I nod enthusiastically. 'Good idea!'

My boyfriend gives me a wink and whispers, 'Ready?'

I nod.

And he kisses me, hard. One hand on the small of my back, the other entwined in my hair, bending me backwards until I physically have to cling to him. I'm warm and breathless and curiously weak.

It's a movie kiss. A poster kiss. A front-page kiss.

*Click click click click click click.*

Flustered, I kiss him back.

'Now be gone!' Noah shouts when we finally stop. 'Off with you, pap-ouschkas! Shoo! Give us some privacy! Look how beautiful she is, dagnammit! I need some alone time!'

The paparazzi laugh. Noah loves fame – courts it, woos it, flirts with it – and so it loves him straight back. Whereas I carry my fame on my back like a reluctant snail and, no matter how hard I dimple, the paps can see that too.

'Love you very much,' Noah whispers under his breath, squeezing my hand. 'You know that, Eff. OK?'

'Yes.' I relax and smile. 'I love you too.'

'I'll ring you tonight? After the gig?'

Better set my alarm for midnight: he's so hyper and coffee-fuelled, it's going to be another very late video call. 'Yes. Am I still seeing you—'

'Tomorrow?' Noah grins. 'Of course, baby. The date's engraved right here.'

He taps my hand on his chest, then drops a soft little kiss on my forehead. Nobody takes a single photo. A forehead kiss is of no interest, unless it's to illustrate: *Has Fainoah Lost Its Spark?*

'Good luck,' I say to my boyfriend's back as he

disappears into the studio, fingers already twitching with invisible music.

Taking a deep breath, I hold my head high. Not too high. Not arrogant high; not snotty high; not I'm-better-than-you high. Just high enough to look like a confident, grounded girl who is secure and happy in her long-term relationship.

The limo door is opened for me.

*Head up, head up, head up, smile, smile, confident, confident* – I climb in, the door clicks shut and I slump into an exhausted heap behind the blacked-out windows.

'Home?' John the driver asks.

'Yes, please.' I close my eyes. 'Home.'

8

I'm still wearing white.

Except now it's a bedsheet, knotted at the back of my neck, a large white hat of Mum's flopping too far forward and battered white tennis shoes that are much too big for me. I'm standing on an upturned cardboard box in the centre of the room, partly hidden – partly hiding – behind the hat's huge brim.

Holding a . . . candlestick?

'And *where* –' the boy straightens his bright emerald scarf – '*were you* at six thirty-eight pm last night? It's a very simple question, *madam*.'

'I—'

'Don't answer that!' A small girl in a huge turquoise sweater jumps to her blue-socked feet and waves a vacuum-cleaner pipe in the air. 'It's an atrosicky! You don't need to answer anything!'

'You're not this good lady's *lawyer*, Mrs P.' A small chuckle. 'You're another suspect.'

'Well . . . so are you! Also your . . . spanner sucks . . . donkey ears, *so there*.'

'Brutal, birdy. Get him.'

I tilt the brim with one finger to see better as a small pink tongue gets stuck out at the other boy wearing bright yellow fur, holding a mustard skipping rope.

'Can we get on with it?' Under an extravagant red hat, a plastic dagger is studied casually by glowing eyes. 'The show's tonight and *everybody who's anybody* is coming.'

'I was . . .' I clear my throat and look round the dusty attic. Everyone is staring at me. Familiar panic is rising. Where *was* I at six thirty-eight last night? Who does this candlestick belong to? What's it doing in my hands?

*Was it me? Did I do it?*

'I was . . . I was . . . I . . .' My breath is getting faster, my cheeks hot. Abruptly, my hands go over my face. 'I didn't . . . I don't . . . *I don't remember!*'

A short silence.

'She knows she didn't actually do it, right? Like,

55

it's written down in the script. Is she about to confess to a gruesome murder she didn't even commit?'

'Oh, great, she's going to ruin *everything*.'

Muddy purple trainers appear at the edge of my vision. 'Hey, you, get off the stage.'

Overwhelmed, I clamber down.

'Curl in a ball on the floor and breathe.'

I do as I'm told.

'Now close your eyes and concentrate, OK?' The voice is low and husky, a laugh bouncing across it like a pebble. 'You're perfectly round. You're bright and bumpy. You're sweet and you come in segments. You've got pips and taste delicious with chocolate. Got it?'

I close my eyes and strain. 'No. What?'

'If you can convince yourself you're an orange, you can convince anyone you're anything.' A familiar dry laugh. 'Now get up and try again.'

Slowly, I stand up and clear my throat.

*Be the Orange.*

'I-AM-INNOCENT!' I yell, pushing Mum's floppy hat away from my face as my lines come flooding back. 'It was him, with a spanner, in the conservatory! I saw him! *You* are the killer, sir! Confess!'

There's a ripple of relieved applause – finally, that'll do, you can get down now – then it's the girl in scarlet's turn. She pulls me off the box with an elaborate eye-roll and commences her three-page, self-written monologue.

I turn to my purple saviour.

The professor winks – so proud, so loving – and then, slowly, starts to crumble into powder.

Into paint.

Into watercolours of lilac, violet and lavender: melting into the air, swirling in a bright amethyst circle before drifting towards the window, and I realise it's open and I jump, I jump as high as I can, trying to close it, trying to hold the colour in my hands, but the purple's running over my fingers and down my arms and it's seeping through me and into me and I can't, I don't know how to, I can't keep it—

I can't keep it—

I can't—

I—

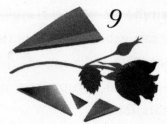

# 9

With a start, I lurch upwards.

'Where am I? No, no, what *time is it*?'

Alarmed, I stare at my hands. Twisting round – I'm still in the back of the limo – I peer out of the blackened window.

We're parked at the end of my driveway, but the sun is rosy and low. How *long* did I sleep for? This can't be happening. I've missed the schedule for posting the rest of Genevieve's photos, I need to shower, face-mask, wash my hair, diffuse it, dress, prepare, apply make-up, learn another script, phone Noah, plan for tomorrow—

Oh no. Oh no. No, no, no—

'I was told to let you sleep, miss.' The driver puts his newspaper down and gives me a kind glance over his shoulder. 'Your grandmother said you looked like you needed it.'

Flushing, I grab my phone: 17.30. It's flashing furiously, the little blue light blinking like an indignant eye.

**MISSED CALL: Hope**

**MISSED CALL: Hope**

**MISSED CALL: Hope**

**MISSED CALL: Hope**

**MISSED CALL: Hope**

Where r u? COME HOME NOW!!! Po :)
XXX

Yo, sis, you with the BF? Your needed here!
Max x

LOL I mean *you're. Don't judge. Max x

**MISSED CALL: Hope**

**MISSED CALL: Hope**

**MISSED CALL: Hope**

Hi, Faith,

I've had feedback from the audition.

They've decided to go in a different direction, but wanted to thank you for your time. They did mention that you struggled somewhat, so again I would like to suggest that we look at smaller roles, with a view to building up to more prominent characters gradually. This is an established way of developing a long-term acting career, and allows you to hone your talents steadily.

I do hope you are not too disappointed.

I have attached another script for auditions next month.

Persephone

**MISSED CALL: Hope**

**MISSED CALL: Mercy**

My eyebrows shoot up. *Mercy?*

I wasn't even sure she had my phone number. Every time we argue, she holds her phone in the air and pointedly deletes me.

Quickly, I thank John, leap out of the car and start running towards the house. I can worry about the audition later. I've already allocated a full hour at around 3am to lying awake, staring anxiously at the ceiling, so that email will fit right in.

Then I push through the front door and—

'. . . HOUSE! HOW DARE YOU SWAN IN AND—'

'—MORTGAGE. AND BILLS. AND THE—'

'—THIS FAMILY FOR A HUNDRED YEARS, AND YOU WANT TO BRING YOUR BIT OF FLUFF INTO MY—'

'ROZ IS NOT A—'

'*SQUEEZE. FLING.* BETTER?'

'STOP BEING CHILDISH, JULIET! I DIDN'T SUGGEST THAT—'

'DON'T YOU *DARE* "STOP BEING CHILDISH, JULIET" ME! I WON'T BE SPOKEN TO AS IF I'M—'

'THEN DON'T ACT SO—'

Biting my lip, I enter the living room.

It's like being in an aeroplane. One minute you're calmly reading *Variety* and eating your dinner; the next you've flown into a storm cloud so thick and dark you can't see anything. All you can feel are the shudders, the spiralling, while everything starts rattling and your beef stroganoff ends up in your lap.

My mother and father are the storm.

Mum, thin and beautiful and silver and electric – crackling in her collarbones, knuckles, the point of her chin – while Dad roars, low and loud, rumbling a few seconds later.

To my right, Max is lying on a sofa: faux-casually eating an apple, long legs stretched out, sunglasses on, pretending to read a book. Hope is sitting on another sofa, eyes on the ceiling, fingers clutched tightly. Mercy is hovering on her feet, an unnatural brightness in her eyes and a strange flush to her cheeks.

So much for the 'amicable divorce', guys. Why do actors and directors need an audience for *everything*?

'WE DISCUSSED THIS!' Dad booms. 'JULIET, WE DISCUSSED THIS, IN DEPTH, FIVE DAYS

AGO! WHAT IS THIS? WHY MUST YOU ALWAYS TURN EVERYTHING INTO A—'

'—BRING *THAT WOMAN* AND *REPLACE* ME AS IF I'M SOME—'

'—*NOT* WHAT I'M SUGGESTING. THIS IS NOT HOW ADULTS BEHAVE—'

'—DARE TELL ME HOW ADULTS—'

Po sees me and jumps up like an overwound jack-in-the-box.

'Eff!' She runs over, holding out a fabric tote with an embossed school crest on it. 'Look! They gave me a *full* branded pencil case like I told you and there's a drama club and I met this girl called Olivia! Insane, right? She's a Pisces just like you so we're *super* compatible. I think she's going to be my best friend forever, how cool is that?'

Umm, I'm not Pisces. My birthday's in October, I'm Libra. But now is not the time to make that correction.

My little sister's cheeks are also pink and she's bobbing up and down on her tiptoes, which is what she does when she's trying to be anywhere else. When she's trying her hardest to not be *here*.

I glance at my other siblings. I'm not sure how

long this fight has been going on, but Max's eyes have glazed over under his sunglasses and a small muscle in Mercy's jaw is ticking like the second hand of a clock.

This needs to stop, and I mean *immediately*. Quickly, I snap into action.

'Dad!' I walk calmly through the thick storm cloud and kiss his cheek. 'How was the flight? I've missed you! How's California? Did the film wrap up well? Is Roz OK?'

Then I turn to my mother. 'Mum! I met one of your *biggest* fans today. She was saying how much she enjoyed *Pinnacle*, and how incredibly talented you are.'

'Po?' I turn to my baby sister, who's staring at me with wide eyes, waiting for instructions. 'Could you make us all a cup of tea? Max, why don't you take Dad's bags upstairs? Mercy—' My sister scowls, but there's relief on her face too – as if I've just pulled the plug on a TV show she hated, but couldn't stop watching. 'Could you get some . . . biscuits?'

My parents are slowly coming back to themselves. Looking around in bewilderment, like small children waking up. Dad's embarrassed and Mum is shutting down again.

They're not really fighting – we know that – but sometimes you have to step in before they rip themselves apart just to make sense of the pieces.

'Biscuits?' Mer scowls. 'Get *biscuits*? I'm not a *dog*.' But she flashes me a glance of gratitude and makes a swift exit.

The tension is draining out of the room.

'Juliet,' Dad says in a much lower voice, turning to Mum with beseeching eyes. 'Please. Obviously, I wasn't going to bring Roz here. It would be hugely inappropriate. She's staying at a hotel in town. I just thought it would be a good idea for everyone to meet before the paps find out. You know we still haven't made the divorce public yet.'

My mother holds her lovely head up.

'Well.' Her grey eyes are remote and distant: Elvis has left the building. 'You *could* have just said so, Michael. It's a misunderstanding. We just don't have the *space* for visitors, I'm afraid.'

We have fifteen bedrooms.

'Mmm.' Dad coughs. 'I thought the kids might

want to come out for a quiet dinner with Roz. Maybe they can get to know her.'

'Yippee for us,' Mer says flatly, returning with empty hands and a mouth full of cookie. 'Your brand-new side order sounds an absolute *treat*, Dad.'

'She is!' Po squeaks behind her, splashing three cups of tea on the white carpet. 'Roz is amazing, Mer! She's *soooo* kind and *sooooo* clever and she has these shorts that have, like, a *million* pockets in them and oh my Ryan *goshlings*, I can't *wait* for her to psychologise you all. Especially *you*, Max.'

'Good-oh,' Max laughs. 'In fairness, I *am* possibly the most fascinating Valentine character.'

'You're not,' Mercy snaps. 'You just think you are.'

And I feel my family slowly recalibrating: finding our places, remembering our lines, resuming our positions.

'Obviously, I'd love to join you,' Mum says icily. 'But the American shrink with zero fashion sense will have to get my signature another time.'

With a stiff back, she leaves the room.

'Blimey,' Max whispers as we slip into the silent hallway. 'Nice one, Eff. Five more minutes and we'd have ended up with our own reality show. On which note—'

Honestly, I don't feel very well. It's as if the black cloud in the room had to go somewhere, so I breathed it all in. And now it's lodged in my chest like thick tar, squelching and sticky.

My phone *pings* and I scan the pop-up.

'Faith,' my brother says as I abruptly sit down on the bottom stair and tighten the laces on my trainers. 'Sis . . . please tell me you're not going for *another* run.'

I frown. Exercise is good for you – everybody knows that.

'I just need some fresh air.'

10

Breathing hard, I follow the river.

Pounding the footpath that winds from the bottom of our garden, I try to focus on the air in my lungs and the soft thud of my trainers in the mud. On the muted colours of the day, the beautiful silvers and greys and the – I mean *what the actual*—?

Focus on the pumping of your blood, Faith. On the warmth in your legs, the heat in your cheeks.

Breathe. Breathe. Brea—

I mean, are they freaking *kidding* me? I turned up at the studio because Noah *asked* me to. I told him to focus on writing.

Dipping round a tree, I hop over a log.

We have never been 'on-off'. *He was on tour.*

With a sharp burst of angry energy, I run faster. I cannot *believe* they've misquoted him on purpose yet again – I take a left turn deeper into the wood – his *I need alone time* might be totally out of context, but they've found evidence for it anyway. Unflattering pictures of me looking hostile, Noah exhausted and oh-so-very-patient.

Breathe. Breathe, br—

That movie-star kiss was never getting printed, was it?

*Boring Couple Snogs For The Three Thousandth Time* doesn't sell papers. And I know it doesn't matter, it doesn't matter – they're just photos, it doesn't matter, it doesn't matter—

Except it *does*.

I'm going to see these photos again and again: when they're cut out and stuck in my scrapbook, when they're analysed in magazines, when one of his fans yells, 'WHY CAN'T YOU JUST BE NICE TO HIM!' outside a restaurant. When '*chilling with laid-back Avery*' is published next to a photo of Noah and a pretty backing dancer on tour; when a big role comes up and they pass me over for someone who's apparently less of a diva.

It'll be there every time I reach for Noah's hand in public, then pull back in case I look pathetic; when I lean in for a kiss, but stop in case I seem desperate.

And every article, every photo, every headline will slip between us. Writing a version that *isn't* us, but that on some level we both start to believe anyway. Until the gap between reality and fiction is too big to cross any more, just like it's become with my parents.

Scowling, I brush past a branch and feel it tug and rip my stupid floaty dress.

I'll give *them* freaking 'furious'.

Except I won't, obviously.

Instead, I draw to an abrupt halt, wipe my nose on my wrist and grab my phone again. Screw Genevieve's cute pug photo, I need to post a selfie quickly or the world will think I've gone into humiliated hiding.

Holding it over my head, I dimple and smile brightly.

*Click.*

I examine the shot. There's a random crisp packet on the ground behind me so I pick it up, stick it in my dress pocket and try again, tilting my chin down and angling it.

*Click.*

Now my forehead looks massive.

*Click.*

My left eye is squinting.

*Click.*

*Waaaaay* too much boob. Let's keep this clean and on brand, people.

*Click.*

Strained and desperate.

*Click.*

Controlling?

*Click.*

Crazy as a box of badgers.

*Click.*

You know how if you say a word over and over again it starts to lose all meaning and just sounds like a random noise? That's kind of what's happening to my face.

*Click.*

It's started looking like a collection of weird shapes.

*Click.*

A couple of hazel blobs, a sticky-out nobble, two pink puffy flaps, a scattering of brown splodges and some random fluff.

*Click.*

Until it feels like I could reach a hand out and rearrange my features: stick my lips on my forehead and push my eyes straight into my ears, turn my nose upside down like Mrs Potato Head.

*Click.*

How d'ya like that, Instagram?

*Beautiful evening! It's times like this my heart wants to burst with happiness!! Have a lovely night, everyone xxx*

And . . . POST.

Another two pop-ups bounce on to my screen:

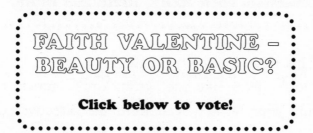

## HELLO FROM THE T-STER! GREAT NEWS!

Our favourite gal-sleb, EFFIE VALENTINE, is gonna be on the single market real soon! Pop star idiots can't HANDLE a REAL WOMAN. Everyone knows HAAAAWTIES are hard work. If he can't be bothered, I'll step in! Call me, Effie! Number on CONTACT ME page.

## FAITH VALENTINE – BEAUTY OR BASIC?

**Click below to vote!**

For the love of—

It's like I'm an impulsively purchased convertible car – attractive in the showroom, but so high-maintenance I end up stuffed in a garage and covered with a dust sheet.

A bolt of nausea pulses through me. Swallowing, I drop Noah a quick text.

Hey. These headlines, huh? Gah! LOL xx

There's another pop-up:

### NEON IS BACK!

**White dress and neon sports bra? We're here for it! Unlucky in love, Faith V, was the latest celeb spotted showing off her underwear. For a more affordable version, click HERE, HERE and HERE.**

This time, I actually laugh.

Don't dress like me, guys. You're unwittingly taking your fashion lead from the directives of a

seventy-year-old woman in a chiffon scarf and a girl
who regularly showers with wet wipes.

*Ping.*

*IKR?!* You look gorgeous though, don't worry!
N xx

I stare at Noah's text blankly – *umm, not exactly
where I was going with that one* – then type back:

Awww. Thanks :) :) :) xx

Then – with no smile on my face, let alone three
– I slip the phone back into my pocket.

And I keep running.

## 11

**MISSED CALL:** Persephone

**MISSED CALL:** Grandmother

**MISSED CALL:** Persephone

Hi Faith,
Please call me as soon as you can. Persephone

**MISSED CALL:** Persephone

**MISSED CALL:** Persephone

Faith, noted film journalist is desperate to talk
to you. Please contact me ASAP. Persephone

**MISSED CALL:** Grandmother

**MISSED CALL: Noah**

Hey baby, just seen the papers!! TOLD YOU
SO. You're the greatest Nxxxx

Umm, DUDE. Max

Yes yes yes yes yes yes yes yes yes yes yes yes
yes yes yes yes yes yes yes yes yes yes!!! Po
xxxxxx

WT actual

Mercy considers her narrative voice instantly
recognisable so she rarely signs off her text messages.
Blinking in confusion, I sit up abruptly in bed and
stare at my alarm clock.

It's *10am*. I must have run so hard for so long
yesterday that I managed to sleep through my alarm,
my body clock, the birds outside, my phone going
crazy. It's flashing so hard it looks like it's about to
take off like a firework.

I roll over – the left side of my bed is crumpled
and there's black eyeliner smudged all over the

pillow. Mercy must have fallen asleep and got up again without me even noticing.

Hair in a cloud, I grab my dressing gown and fly down the stairs with it streaming behind me like a fluffy cape.

'Here she comes!' Max appears cheerfully in the kitchen doorway, eating strawberry jam directly from the jar. 'Faith Valentine. Megastar, icon, siren. A morning vision, complete with greasy forehead and a booger in her left nostril.'

Distractedly, I pick my nose and flick it away.

'What's happened?' Alarmed, I grab my brother by the T-shirt. 'Will you stop the persistent mockery and just tell me *what's happening*?'

'Don't touch me with your crusty booger hand,' he laughs, moving away. 'You know, apparently people consider you vaguely attractive, Eff. A true mystery I cannot understand.'

I'm clearly getting no answers from my idiot brother so I turn to my remaining siblings. Po is impatiently bouncing up and down at the kitchen table – dimpled and glowing – and Mercy's face is literally the stormiest I've ever seen it. You can practically see the dark thoughts skidding across it like clouds.

'What?' I stare at them. '*What??!*'

It's extremely frustrating – I'm normally the one who actually knows what's going on around me.

'Oh my *days*!' I shout to the ceiling. 'WILL SOMEBODY PLEASE TELL ME WHY MY PHONE IS ON FIRE!!!'

Beaming, Hope opens a newspaper. Then she dramatically lays it down with an elaborate flourish; opens another one and does the same; and another; and another. My face is plastered over all of them, except this time I'm not scowling. This time I don't have food on my chin.

I'm poised, poreless – photoshopped to oblivion and Grandma-verified – and the headlines read:

**VALENTINE FOR**
**ROLE OF THE DECADE**

**HAVE A LITTLE FAITH!**
**ICE QUEEN SET TO STAR**

**BRITISH BEAUTY PIPS**
**AMERICANS TO POST**

I stare at them, eyes wide.

'You did it!' Hope jumps up and wraps her arms round my midriff. 'You nailed your *very first audition*. Effie, I'm so *proud I could rupturify on the spot*. I *knew* you'd be a Hollywood star on the floor, and now you're one step closer! After you've won your Best Newcomer Oscar, will you be in my debut film? *Please?* I promise *there will be top-notch sandwiches*.'

I glance at Mercy.

'Well,' she says darkly. 'Genuine skill means nothing to the industry any more.'

'*Mercy.*' Max puts a protective hand on my shoulder. 'For the love of unicorns, can you take a break from being a total monster? Just, like, five minutes to be happy for your little sister? Consider it a short recess. Give us a time-out so we can collectively regenerate.'

'Fine.' Mer scowls and stares at the table. 'Well done, very exciting, what a well-deserved achievement, et cetera.'

My head feels like I've stuffed it with a cashmere sock.

'I don't understand.' My voice sounds foggy.

'What role? Are they talking about *Fright Fortnight*? But I screwed that audition up. They *said* I did. I *heard* them.'

'You heard wrong,' my brother says jubilantly, holding out his jam jar. 'Sugar? For the shock?'

I pick up a tabloid and scan it.

Knockout stunner, Faith Valentine, is confirmed as front runner for 'the biggest teen role ever'. 'It's huge,' a source confirms. '*Fright Fortnight* had buzz, but this launches it to the next level.'

Daughter of A-lister Juliet Valentine and BAFTA-winning director Michael Rivers . . .

I scan faster. Yes, we know my pedigree, thank you. I'm not a dog at Crufts.

Hang on—

'She's a true talent,' delighted boyfriend, Noah Anthony, confirms. 'She thinks she's a terrible actress! She worries she lacks what it takes. Crazy, right? Plus, she's so beautiful. They're lucky to have her.'

When did they speak to *Noah*?

'I see your charming boyfriend is at it again,' Mercy says sharply. 'How *sweet* of him to have an opinion before you did.'

I frown at her – *stop it* – pick up my phone and hit DIAL.

'Persephone?' I turn away and stick a finger in my free ear so I can't hear Max noisily flicking Mercy on the forehead. 'Hi. Is this real? Did I get another audition?'

*Crackle, crackle, crackle.*

'. . . yes.' My agent is brusque. There's an air of army sergeant about her: small talk permanently unwelcome. '*Crackle* – administrative error – *crackle* – final round – *crackle* – tomorrow morning. *Crackle, crackle* – details.'

The reception in this kitchen is truly terrible.

Holding my phone in the air, I try to climb in the gap between the fridge and the wall so I can hear Persephone better.

'*Yes,*' Po insists in the background. 'I'm gonna film all the people I meet on my first day at school—'

'But . . .' I *must* have misunderstood the casting director. Did I hear a few key words and fill in the rest with my own negativity? 'Do you really think I can—'

'They've sent – *crackle* – different scene.' Persephone hasn't got time to stroke my ego. 'Off-script – *crackle* – time to learn it.'

'Actually, tonight is—' I stop. 'Sure. Of course.'

'You're not auditioning for buddies!' Max is laughing at Po.

'Of course I am,' she indignantly replies. 'How else will I know how they'll work out when they star in the film of my life?'

Louder laughter. 'Not enough bubble wrap, little sis.'

With a pointed glance over my shoulder – *shhhhh* – I tuck myself further into the fridge-gap.

'. . . number of requests – *crackle* – interviews,' Persephone is saying, 'but – *crackle* – exclusive.' A burst of phones ringing in the background. 'So – *crackle* – with you in half an hour.'

My eyes widen in alarm. 'Wait, what?'

'Traffic depending.'

'With me?' I glance round the kitchen: there's peanut butter on the floor. 'In my house? Like, *here*?'

'Yes. To see how you live – *crackle*— Inside track on Faith Valentine.'

My throat feels like it's closing.

'Ah. I—'

'Faith, we can't afford to pass this exposure up – *crackle* – you want to work in film. Formal profile pieces – *crackle* – right people pay attention. Just be yourself and the world's your oyster.'

I open my mouth.

'Got to go,' Persephone concludes briskly. 'Tom's on the other line, you know what he's like – *crackle* – later!'

The phone goes dead.

## 12

*Just be yourself.*

As if I don't have a physical folder of pre-approved media question answers written by Grandma and rehearsed to perfection every single Wednesday for practically an entire year.

Favourite colour.

Favourite food.

Favourite film.

Favourite ice cream.

Favourite dog breed.

Favourite music.

Favourite season.

*Being myself* requires a huge amount of memory power, focus and hole-punched paper.

Jittery, I glance at my watch.

There's no time to ring Noah so I quickly bash out a text:

Crazy!!! Mad here but I'm meeting you later, right? What time, where?? xx

Thirty seconds later:

Sure, good-looking! See you 4pm, Covent Garden. Can't wait. Love love love you xxx

I smile and breathe out.

Love love love you too xxx

Then I firmly recommence panicking. Our housekeeper Maggie has been off all week while her son Ben's visiting, and the result is . . .
Well. I can see the resulting piece already:

**Inside their glamorous multimillion-pound mansion, the Valentines are slowly festering in a stew of their own filth.**

'Up!' I say as Max flops on the sofa with his hands behind his head and watches me spiral frantically round the living room. 'Get *up*!'

He digs in, like a belligerent dog.

'Oh, Max, *please.*' With considerable effort, I haul my lanky brother on to the floor. There's dried pesto pasta stuck between the cushions. 'A journalist is turning up any second! They can't see that we live like this!'

'Why not?' He laughs. 'We might be famous, rich, beautiful – me in particular – but we're actually teenagers, we don't really like cleaning up after ourselves that much, hold the front page.'

'*No.*' I rummage again: a shrivelled carrot stick. 'That's *not* what I want us to be known for, Max. And Mum's still upstairs. Remember? Do we *really* want to make it public that she's clearly not OK when Dad's not living here, either? That we're essentially home alone?'

There's a short silence.

'Valid point.' Max jumps up and claps his hands. 'Don't want social services sending you guys to Celebrity Masterchef or whatever. I shall . . . go . . . do whatever it is people do with a vacuum cleaner.'

Meanwhile, Po is drifting round the room, trailing her hand along dusty surfaces. 'I *know* it's not my interview, Eff, but do you think you could mention my upcoming projects? Just drop it in casually. Like, My Sister, Important Director Hope, or maybe: *My Sister, Future Genre-defining—*'

'Hope.' I grab her by the shoulders. 'Sweetheart. I love you and I promise I will mention you, but *please* can you go and lock the kitchen door?'

'*May wee!*' she agrees cheerfully. 'That's French for *I'm so excited, I might wee.*'

When she's gone, I look up.

Mercy is on her knees, quietly cleaning up the tea stains Hope made yesterday. My heart twangs again. This is how my big sister apologises. She doesn't say sorry for insulting your boyfriend or being nasty about your abilities, looks, personality.

She's careful not to wake you when you're fast asleep. She gets to work with a damp J-cloth.

Mer glances up from under her dark brows and glowers.

I throw her a grateful smile. Then I run into the hallway, rip off my dressing gown, stick on a tailored shift dress from the designer freebies cupboard, let my curls down, bite my lips and pinch my cheeks like I'm in *Gone With the Wind*.

I'm at the front door just in time for the bell to

chime. Swallowing, I pause with my hand on the door.

*Remember, Faith. You are the future of the Valentines. It's a relay race a hundred years in the making, and now it's your turn to take the baton.*

*Just. Don't. Drop. It.*

Pulling my shoulders back, I ease the door open. Today's journalist, Rani Basu, is a fierce-looking woman with thick-rimmed black glasses, a blue-black bob and an earnest expression. She looks nice. Serious. More importantly, she looks – I realise with a sudden burst of optimism – like someone who's actually going to listen.

*This could be my chance.* No more quotes from Noah, or assumptions, or 'honest' photos that get it all wrong. It's my interview and I get to say what's written. This is what I've been *trained* for.

*Finally.*

'Hello,' I beam triumphantly. 'I'm Faith Valentine.'


'. . . And *this* is the lower hallway,' I say, holding a graceful hand out. 'Over here is a grandfather clock bought by my great-grandmother Pauline back in—'

The kitchen door creaks open and Hope's

expectant face peers out. I take a few quick steps so I'm behind the journalist and give Po a little nod. She disappears again.

'—1920, just after she won the first of her multiple Academy Awards.' Smoothly, I lead Rani towards the living room. Grandma was very clear about the order in which I should present the rooms: there's a highlighted map and everything. 'Over here we have the formal parlour. This is where the Valentine family gathers for Christmases, birthdays,' *screaming matches*, 'celebrations and so on.'

'Oh yes,' the journalist nods, making a note. 'I *did* want to ask about that. Your mother is recently out of rehab. But as far as I can tell she hasn't been seen in public since – is she still very ill? And your father is in America, correct? With rumours of an affair and upcoming divorce?'

I smile brightly. *Thanks for that.*

'My mother is doing splendidly.' *Lie One.* 'She's been considering upcoming scripts.' *Lie Two.* 'There has been no affair and there will be no divorce –' *Lie Three* – 'and everything is absolutely fabulous.' *HahahahahaHAHAHAH.*

With my head held high, I glide towards the

cinema room and open the door. 'As one of the most celebrated *movie dynasties* in the world –' Grandma will be pleased I got that in – 'the Valentines have an entire room dedicated to our love of theatrical arts, in particular—'

'It can't have been an easy time,' Rani insists belligerently. 'Isn't it exactly two years since—'

'In *particular*,' I repeat firmly, waving my hand around, 'our home cinema, where we often congregate to review performances together . . .'

I shut the cinema-room door. Ugh, I hate it in there.

'And here we have the *library*,' I say, opening another door. 'As artists, our love of books and plays—'

*WOOF WOOF ARRROOOOOOOO!*

'You have a . . . dog?' The journalist looks round sharply. 'I don't think I knew that.'

*I don't think I did, either.*

'Yes,' I nod quickly. That was actually Max's 'secret' alarm call – has been since he was about five years old. 'Two dogs. Huskies. Ah—' I glance behind her. 'Rocket and . . . Book.' *A dog called Book. Nice one, Eff.* 'They're . . . very private dogs, I'm afraid.'

Max is halfway up the stairs.

He *WOOFs* again, then points upwards: *Mum's on the move.* Mum – one of the most famous women on the planet, in her grubby nightie, with dishevelled hair, empty eyes and fun new habit of randomly screaming at people – is about to come into direct, unprepared contact with a member of the national press.

'*Private* dogs?' Rani says doubtfully.

'Ah,' I say, spinning her round to face the other way. 'Yes. Keep themselves to themselves. Antisocial, bordering on misanthropic. Do you know what? I think you really need to see—'

There's a noise at the top of the stairs.

**Juliet Valentine, Oscar-winner and beloved star of *The Heart of Us*, has officially gone bat-poop crazy - here's the evidence!**

'My bedroom!' I finish desperately. It's completely against the rules – Grandma says it's *highly inappropriate* to take journalists into our private quarters – but what choice do I have? It's that or giving a tour of the laundry room. 'Why don't you come and see my bedroom! It's an exclusive! Never seen before!'

Mum appears, so frail she has to hold on to the bannister.

'Darlings,' she calls in a voice as light as a feather. 'Is somebody—'

'Come with me!' Panicking, I grab Rani's shoulders just as she turns to look upwards and twist her in the opposite direction. 'Via the exciting *secret servants' staircase*!'

And I pull her away as fast as I can.

13

Softly, I close my bedroom door behind me and exhale in relief. Then I pretend to fiddle with the lock while I reorganise my panicked face into a serene, calm, placid smile.

This journalist very nearly saw the madwoman in our attic.

I turn round.

'So.' I beam warmly at Rani. 'Welcome to my sanctuary. My haven. My retreat. This is where I come to process the demands of my day and just . . . be me.'

The journalist glances around and sits down by my dressing table.

'I like to dance,' I continue. 'My parents had this mirror and barre fitted when I was a little girl, and I practise every morning. My bedroom faces the garden so I wake to the sound of dawn birds singing. It really helps keep me—'

'Lovely.' She's not listening. 'So . . . this new role.'

I nod and perch slowly on my pillow in an attempt to hide Mercy's eyeliner stains. '*Yeeeees.*'

'It's set to be one of the most expensive shows ever made. We're talking *billions.*' I'm suddenly uncomfortably aware of how piercing this journalist's eyes are. 'How does it feel to be considered for such a prominent role? Your first-ever job, right?'

'Yes.' I need to be humble. Grateful. But also confident. A girl who values herself. But doesn't *overvalue* herself. The perfect amount of self-value. 'It . . . would be my first job. It's lovely. I'm very happy.'

I breathe out: *safe.*

'And you're trained by your grandmother, Dame Sylvia Valentine?'

*Don't sound entitled. Do sound appreciative.* 'Yes. I am.'

There's a long pause.

Suddenly it feels like I'm playing Battleships: one wrong quote and – *BOOM!* – game over.

'So what appeals to you about the world of acting?' The journalist frowns. 'Obviously, you're born into it, but what tempts you to follow the family line?'

*Ooh, I know this one.* 'Acting is a path I've been eager to tread since I was a child.' I dimple sweetly. 'To be so many people, to live so many lives, to tell so many stories . . . there is a kind of –' I pretend to search for the right word – '*magic* in it.'

Silence.

'I see.' Rani frowns again. 'You're sixteen years old, Faith, yet I don't think I've opened up a media source in the last year where you haven't been featured somewhere. What's that like?'

I nod, keeping my expression as flat as possible. *Horrendous.*

'I've been well prepared so it feels natural.' I maintain steady eye contact like Grandma taught me to. 'I have an incredibly supportive network of friends and family. My boyfriend, Noah Anthony, is such an important part of my life. We're very close – unshakable, rock solid – and lucky to share the experience of rising fame together.'

Rani writes something down and I relax a touch. Go ahead and print *that*, lady.

Maybe a few extra details will help with the headlines. 'In fact, today is our one-year anniversary!

Noah's planning a big romantic date. He's very sweet, and does that sort of thing a lot.'

Do I sound like a demanding princess?

'I do nice things too, of course,' I add quickly. 'Our relationship is *very* equal. Balanced. Evenly matched. I love him very much. Very, very much. He's my whole world.'

*Too far, Faith. Way too far.*

'Not my whole world,' I correct, swallowing. *Oh, for goodness' sake. This is why you've been told to stick to the script.* 'Just a . . . healthy chunk of it. Like, ah . . . Russia. Or maybe China.'

Silence.

'So. You've been described by *Vogue* as one of the most beautiful women on the planet.' Rani looks at her notes without expression. 'The *face of an angel*, another magazine states. Does that level of attractiveness feel like a burden or a privilege?'

I stare at her in amazement. What does she think I do? Stand in front of a mirror every morning and high-five myself? I look like me – a range of features and body parts I tend to ignore unless I'm picking at them or colouring them in.

It's also a trick question. If I acknowledge it, I'm

publicly accepting that I think I'm beautiful – huge no-no – but, if I protest, I look like I'm fishing for more compliments: also pretty unlikable.

So I smile and shrug. 'Not sure really.'

We stare at each other for a few seconds.

'Noah Anthony is quoted as saying you don't think you're a good actress.' The journalist is unblinking; I sit up a little straighter. 'A "*terrible* actress" are the words he used. "Lacks what it takes." Is that true?'

Oh, for the love of – Grandma will *kill* me.

'Well.' I make my expression affectionate yet mildly frustrated – *Boyfriends, What Are We Gonna Do With Them?* – and laugh. 'There's so much talent in the Valentine family, it's hard not to feel humbled now and then.'

I'm sure I'm missing something.

'Like, for instance, my sister Hope,' I add quickly. 'She's going to be a famous film director, just like Dad. Watch this space.'

Nothing is written down. *Sorry, Po.*

'But –' Rani is leaning back in the chair, watching me carefully – 'what makes you *you*? That's what our readers are keen to understand.'

'Well.' I smile serenely. 'My favourite food is sushi, my favourite ice cream is salted caramel, my favourite season is summer and my favourite colour is—'

'That's not what I'm asking,' the journalist interrupts.

My throat has started closing.

This woman I have known for literally nineteen minutes leans forward, directly into my personal space, and suddenly I deeply regret bringing her into my bedroom. This is where I *sleep*.

'I'm wondering who the *real* Faith is?' Rani continues. 'Away from the spotlight and the headlines and the red carpets and the smoothie bowls inspo and the running selfies? Who *is* Faith Valentine?'

Fury whips through me. And – for a fraction of a second – I want to headbutt her. I want to pull this total stranger off her bottom and literally nut her in the face.

*How dare she ask me that?*

Instead, I dimple. 'Oh,' I say, biting the inside of my cheek as hard as I can. 'I guess I'm just a very normal girl.'

14

What do you give a sick bird?

Tweetment.

Nailed it.

As soon as the journalist has gone, I return to my room and run through the myriad ways my answers could be construed, quoted and interpreted.

I'm pretty sure I didn't say anything too dumb or controversial or fascinating. I wasn't too warm or too cold. And I didn't commit grievous bodily harm – hooray! – so maybe those Wednesdays with my grandmother were worth it after all.

Although my favourite ice cream is mint-choc-chip. And my favourite season is autumn.

Just saying.

Now I've got less than two hours to learn my

new script for tomorrow, finish customising Noah's anniversary present, shower, do my make-up, change into my anniversary outfit and get across London.

Genevieve – aware of the date – has sent (for my third post today) an image of me and Noah in Paris at Christmas. We're standing underneath the glittering lights of the Champs Elysées, cheeks pressed together, grinning giddily – cold, dripping snot artfully photoshopped out.

She's written a caption, but I ignore it and write my own.

And POST:

*Happy anniversary! One amazing year with my bae. All the adventures we've shared! Can't wait to share the next one with you xxxx*

Within seconds, the hearts are going crazy.

**OMG! This is just. So. Cute!!**

**Couple goals!**

**You guys are giving me LIFE. FAINOAH FOREVAAAA!**

A photo pops up on my feed. Noah and I are on a blue VIP carpet, arms tightly round each other. We look glossy and smooth, me resting my head gently on his suited shoulder pad. I can't help wondering if he got it from his PR too.

*One year today with my beautiful girl. I'm the luckiest guy in the world. Love you so so much. Xxx*

I hit the heart button.

**Aaaagh. I can't even!**

**YOU TWWWWOOOOOOOOOOOOO. Congrats!!!!**

**All. The. Heart. Eyes.**

We were at Mum's premiere for blockbuster weepie *Pinnacle*. Noah fell asleep about five minutes in and stayed that way until I prodded him awake at the closing credits.

Which reminds me—

Sighing, I print out Persephone's email attachment and try not to panic as the pages start reeling out: *one, two, three, four, five, six, seven, eight* – hello, *War and Peace*.

Then I Sellotape all eleven pages of my new scene to the tiles of my en-suite and attempt to exfoliate, shave my legs, mask my face, condition my hair, dry it, apply primer, foundation, bronzer, illuminator, eyeliner, mascara, shadow, eyebrow gel . . . while reading out lines like:

'Which way are we going? I'm sure the map said it was the other way—' and:

'What do you mean, *my destiny*?'

And: 'No! Stop the car! This is madness!'

At least my character sounds confused and out of her depth. These are emotions I should be able to emulate.

Finally – scrubbed and gleaming – I grab the floor-length, tight, iridescent-white, sequinned Valentino dress Noah sent me a few days ago, tug it on, lower myself uncomfortably to the floor and attempt to finish his gift. One year is supposed to be *paper*, so I bought us a First Class trip to New

103

York, for when his current tour is over. Except I'm realising that handing my beloved boyfriend a travel-agent's envelope is a little bit . . . impersonal. So I'm quickly covering it in hand-drawn hearts.

Heart. Heart. Heart.

'No!' I murmur, doodling another one. Heart. 'Stop the car! *No*, stop the *car*?' Heart. '*This is MADNESS*. No.' Heart. 'STOP THE C—'

*Ping.*

**Running late but should make it for 4:20!! Xxx**

Maybe I can use those extra minutes exploring a way to pee while wearing this dress.

**No probs! See you there! What are we doing?! Dying to know! Xxx**

**Haha. That would be telling ;) xx**

With a final scribble – *heart* – I pop the envelope in my handbag. Grabbing my pack of Post-its, I stiffly rustle down the corridor and stick the bird one on the wall. Then I inch woodenly down the stairs.

'*Awwww.*' Hope is sitting on the landing by the window. She's so desperate to start the glamorous Valentine life when she turns sixteen that my heart hurts for her. Even if part of me desperately wishes we could swap over. 'Happy anniversary! You look *exquisite*, Eff.'

'Thank you.' I smile, spinning with my arms out. I feel weird, rigid and scratchy, like a doll. 'It's amazing what a twelve-thousand-pound dress and a pair of *suuuuper*-tight hold-in pants will do, huh? My internal organs are packaged like sausages.'

'You should wear proper clothes more often,' my sister says, dreamily skipping down the stairs as I hobble after her. I open the freebie cupboard again and grab a burgundy velvet Gucci coat and gold Prada heels. 'Noah's going to be *stoked*. It's such a beautiful thing, mouldy sandwich love.'

I pause, holding one foot aloft. 'What?'

'Remember?' Her eyes are bright as she beams at me. 'You said a few weeks ago that your love for Noah was like mould. That it grows best in the right conditions. I didn't understand at the time, but now I think maybe I do.'

I blink at my baby sister. *Mouldy sandwich love?*

Is that how I actually feel about him? Like a piece of damp bread with *fungus* on it?

What an eternal romantic.

'Mmmm.' I kiss her cheek affectionately. 'Sweetheart, are you sure you're going to be all right on your own tonight? You won't be too lonely?'

'Oh no, Ben's coming over to watch videos,' Po says cheerfully. 'I'm going to make him watch each one *three* times. Once on their own, once with the official director commentary and once with *my* commentary. And *what do you know*!' A theatrical, wide-eyed glance over my shoulder. 'Here comes your not-so-secret love-triangle paramour *now*.'

My sister wiggles her eyebrows.

Something tells me she coordinated this on purpose, the little romance-obsessed ratbag.

'Is that the time?' I say, giving her a wry look. *Nice try, sis, but no dice.* 'My goodness! Gotta go! Have fun!'

And I dive, glittering, into the waiting limo.

## HEY, T-DRINKERS! NEWS!

*After careful RESEARCH, I have discovered FAITH VALENTINE'S agent! I'm sending a letter of comfort before she is dumped, then asking Faith out on a ROMANTIC ICE-CREAM date! No, KEVIN, the age gap is NOT a problem. Boys mature faster, dumbo. WATCH THIS SPACE!*

My kingdom for some leggings and an XL hoodie.

White sequins scream *look at me* – I might as well be dressed in a bright yellow chicken suit, spinning a *THIS WAY* banner. No less than fifteen tourists stop to take my photo, looking for all the world like an ice skater about to get married.

It was sweet of Noah to send me something special to wear, but I'd be infinitely happier in a onesie and odd socks.

Exhausted, I hide behind a pillar and text:

Hey, babe! I'm here! Where are you? x

Then I check online again. I'm kind of hoping that this morning's journalist might have somehow posted her copy already. Maybe—

Faith Valentine is a very normal, nice girl who is totally in love with her boyfriend and not a nightmare at all!

Or:

We are amazed by how non-diva-y Faith Valentine actually is!

I'd even take:

NEWS FLASH! Faith Valentine IS NOT A MONSTER!!

But the only new article showing up is the blogger from the park.

I mean, I appreciate the creepy, invasive support – who wouldn't? – but I'm hoping Persephone doesn't forward his ice-cream invitation. Also, I'm not entirely sure that his entire readership isn't one boy called Kevin.

*Ping.*

Running late! Go in without me!
Sorry! xx

This is so Noah.

Where? You haven't told me where we're going! ;) x

Oh! Yeah. My bad!! Ballet! The one about the ducks!! xx

A whoosh of happiness shoots through me, lifting me on to my tiptoes.

Mouldy sandwich, *schmouldy bandwich.*

Swan Lake?!!!! You're kidding me!! That's my favourite! xx

IK! Nearly there! Catch you in a tick! Love you! x

Heart soaring, I raise my head. The Royal Opera House is just round the corner, so – with another jolt of excitement – I mince scratchily towards it with squished kidneys, beaming all over.

When I reach the huge, elegant white building, my heart leaps even further.

*Oh, Noah.*

I've adored this ballet since Mum took me to it when I was four years old. It was what made me love dancing in the first place. I can't think of a more thoughtful gift.

Glittering inappropriately (it's an afternoon matinee – everyone else is in jeans), I pick up my ticket from the gilded foyer and hobble up the stairs to wait in private.

Noah's booked us a *box*. An entire six-person box. Right at the front of the stage. *Wow.*

It's only when I get there that I realise what this

means – until he arrives, it's just me.

Sitting alone, in the most prominent seat in the whole building. Hanging not so subtly in the sky inside a gold container, with a million white sequins catching every bright light in the theatre each time I move, like a human disco ball.

*Hi, guys! It's me! Faith Valentine!*

Sure enough, curious faces are already turning towards me. I hear whispers, giggles, see photo flashes. I hunker down and try to stay as still as possible.

My phone vibrates.

Traffic TERRIBLE. Will sneak in super quiet, I promise! Sorry! Love you! xx

I bite my lips.

Sure thing! No worries! xx

Almost immediately, my phone vibrates again.

Sooooooo, how's the big romantic date going? x

Mercy must be feeling super guilty about what she said this morning. She *never* signs off with a kiss. Also, I guess it's the only way to visually indicate that her text isn't entirely sarcastic.

I type back:

**Amazing! We're watching Swan Lake!! :) x**

Then I delete the last bit.

**Amazing! N's taken me to see Swan Lake!! :) x**

Try again.

**Amazing! N's bought tickets to Swan Lake!! :) x**

That's technically accurate. SEND. A few seconds later:

**He's not there, is he**

You know what? A lot of nice things are said about the sister bond. That special connection which allows you to see into each other's hearts, to know each other's minds, to read each other without words.

I think it's massively overrated.

Not yet, but he's on his way!!! X

Sure he is. What a flaming douchebaguette.

Just because Noah is held up in traffic doesn't make him a douchebaguette, Mer. He'll be here.

You're so gullible. He isn't showing. Fact. You know he hates ballet – it's B O R I N G.

Scowling, I shove my phone in my bag.
*Get lost, Merciless.*
Then I quickly rearrange my face into a bright, happy expression of anticipation. A wide-eyed, appreciative gaze that says: *I love ballet, I love my boyfriend and I swear he will be here ANY MINUTE.*

The last thing I need is a stray photo of me glaring grumpily at some poor ballerinas.

### Loner Faith Valentine
## HATES WOMEN AND ALSO JOY

The lights steadily dim until a rosy, candle-lit glow fills the hushed auditorium and I finally relax. An orchestra appears from the side of the stage and sits down. The conductor bows, baton held aloft. Sweet, mournful tones fill the air and I lean forward hungrily.

Darkness falls and the curtains open.

## 16

FYI, ballet is not *boring*.

It's storytelling at its most athletic: strength and grace set to music. Prince Siegfried appears on stage – leaping and twisting as colourful courtiers and guests spin round him. It's magic.

Though I *will* concede that a large proportion of *Swan Lake* seems to be the prince partying. Like, at least three-quarters of it.

My phone lights up.

**Nearly there! How are the ducks doing? x**

I smile. *See, Mercy?*

**They don't usually show for the first half-hour! You've got time! The prince is still trying to**

find a wife at the party. Something tells me he won't manage it. LOL x

Isn't that the plot of every fairy tale ever? x

Yup. This is essentially The Little Mermaid with wings x

Cool! xx

Relieved, I glance over the balcony. Frowns are pointed up at me, shining vividly in my blue phone light. *Young celebs, so disrespectful, think the rules don't apply to them, etc. etc.*

I flush – *sorry, sorry* – put my phone back in my bag and focus on the stage again. Half an hour in, the music crescendoes and the curtains close: party over.

There's dark silence. I subtly glance at my phone. Nothing.

Then the music starts again – gentle, more soulful – and the curtains open on a lake. It's misty and blue, backed with beautiful painted mountains. A tide of thick cloud rolls across the floor.

116

The lights dim and, from behind the curtains, two rows of swans dance in smoothly and form a neat circle. Arms over their heads like necks, moving in perfect symmetry.

And there she is, the White Swan, Odette. A beautiful princess, cursed to spend her days as a swan, revealing her true human form only at night. She glides seamlessly on to the stage and we all breathe out in collective relief.

*Finally.*

As always, she's wearing a white tutu, white shoes and a white feather headdress. Through minuscule, graceful movements she somehow *is* a bird: feathers ruffling, neck long and elegant.

Slowly, Odette pivots on one tiptoe in the pale blue light and I wrap my arms tightly round my stomach.

My phone vibrates:

Well?? Any sign?

I frown in frustration.

He's going to be here any minute.

117

Sure he is.

For God's sake, Mer, I'm at the ballet. Can you just let me enjoy it?

I'm doing you a favour. You're such an old lady, Eff. How are the prince's MANLY TIGHTS holding up?? LOL.

I look up to see Siegfried dancing with Odette. They're wrapped round each other, infatuated and absorbed. There is *nothing* 'old lady' about this. It is *hot*.

You're obsessed with his tights, weirdo. Is he another douchebaguette too?

Dunno. Never seen the ending.
ZZZZZZZZZ.

I'm typing an indignant reply when the music crashes, the curtains close, the lights go up and I realise I've just missed the first half of my anniversary present, texting my sister.

*Cheers, Mer.*

Below me, the auditorium is buzzing and, with a sharp pang of envy, I briefly consider joining them. Use the toilet, grab an ice cream, maybe purchase a swan T-shirt and programme and chat about how glorious it is.

Except—

*Faith Valentine! OMG! So cool to run into you! Can I have your photo? I'll wait RIGHT HERE outside the cubicle while you pee. Don't worry – I won't listen!*

Maybe I'll just hold it.

*Ping.*

Nearly there! Have the ducks arrived? x

A small wave of irritation. *You've been 'nearly there' for over an hour, Noah. And stop calling them ducks – it stopped being funny at least two texts ago.*

Yup! It's the interval! x

Good good! Hope you're having fun! xx

119

I glance round at the bustling auditorium, then at my lonely box.

Very much! Thanks! x

The interval bell rings and the audience return to their seats. My eyes keep flicking towards the back curtains of our box. Noah is going to arrive *any minute now*, and I can drop my stiff-backed, *isn't-this-wonderful!* expression and get on with enjoying the ballet without all the pitying glances.

## FAITH V – OVERDRESSED
## AND ALONE AGAIN!

The lights finally go down, thank goodness. Yet another ball commences, but this time there's an unexpected guest: the *Black Swan*. She's identical to Odette, however (surprise!) she's dressed entirely in black. Where the White Swan is soft and sweet, the Black Swan is sharp and fiery. Spinning in a series of dizzying circles, she entrances the prince. He immediately marries her.

And – projected on to the back of the stage – is a real white swan, beating her heartbroken wings against a stained-glass window. The curse is fulfilled, the end is coming, get your tissues ready, it's going to be a *corker*.

*Ping.*

**Well?**

I look up with a lump in my throat. We're back at the lake. Swans are filling the stage and Odette is performing her stunning, tragic solo: *The Dying Swan.*

Noah's not coming. He's not even on his way, and I think a part of me knew he never really was. My anniversary gift is sitting alone, watching a swan energetically drown herself.

**Shut the hell up, Mercy.**

Onstage, the mists rise and Siegfried disappears forever with the princess into the blue lake. *The End.*

Blinking back tears, I swallow and reach into my

handbag. I turn my phone off. Then I lean forward over the balcony and clap as hard as I can.

*Happy anniversary, Effie.*

17

I'm halfway out of the doors before I spot him. Standing in the foyer in a black suit, holding an enormous bouquet of white roses.

Noah's driver bows deeply.

'Faith Valentine? Would you like to come with me?'

*Don't cry don't cry don't cry—*

My heart is lurching against my ribcage.

Was this all part of some bigger romantic plan of Noah's, and *Swan Lake* was just something lovely to keep me entertained while he got our real anniversary evening ready?

I cannot believe I let *Mercy* make me doubt my own boyfriend.

Quickly, I wipe my eyes and straighten up. Collapsing on the floor of a public lobby and bawling in relief isn't Valentine Behaviour.

'Mister Anthony has something *very* special

123

planned for you,' the driver says as I smile tentatively at him. 'You're a very, *very* lucky girl.'

Then he gently wraps a black scarf over my eyes.

'Where are we going?' I laugh. Noah's always so *extra*. 'Surely I don't have to be blindfolded?'

'I've been given my instructions. Sorry, miss. Hold on.'

I'm led into what I presume is the back seat of a limousine.

The engine starts and we drive in silence as I try to work out what direction we're going in. I mean, it could be *anywhere*. A private dining-room restaurant? A members-only art gallery? A yacht? Where?!

Noah and I have spent so little time together recently. I bet he's taking me somewhere beautiful, just the two of us. And, as an hour ticks by, I feel my spirits lifting even further. With all those headlines circulating, what we really need is *us time*.

Finally, the limo stops. Gently, I'm helped out of the car and awkwardly led up some steep steps.

A door opens with a click and I hear a noise: quiet at first, then building as we walk towards it. A low rumble, a roar, a clamour, until it's a giant wall of solid sound. Aeroplanes? A private jet revving up? Except it sounds like . . .

*Screaming?*

My hands reach up to my blindfold.

'Just a few more seconds,' the driver says cheerfully, taking my hands away. 'Tell you something, my daughter would *kill* to be in your shoes.'

Then I'm nudged forward. The air changes, becoming hot, cloying and kind of . . . smelly. The screaming is so loud my dress is literally shaking. It feels like the whole world is on the brink of exploding. As if somebody's tapped the edge and now there's too much vibration and it's going to shatter like a glass. Then it all abruptly goes silent.

With one smooth movement, my blindfold is removed.

I blink. I'm at the side of an enormous stage, half hidden behind the curtains. Under the spotlights is Noah, his favourite guitar slung across his back. The floor is scattered with flower petals, there are pink fairy lights everywhere and he's at the centre of it all, wearing a dazzling white shirt and designer blue jeans.

My beautiful boyfriend turns to smile at me.

My eyes fill. My heart glows and rockets straight through the ceiling.

I smile back at him: *Hello, you.*

Then he turns to the arena crowd and holds one hand up like a conductor.

'FAITH!' they screech-chant. 'FAITH! FAITH! FAITH! FAITH! FAITH! FAITH FAITH FAITH FAITH FAITH FAITH FAITH!'

All of the light abruptly drains out of me.

*No. No. No—*

'Wh-what—' I stammer, but strong hands are on my shoulders and I'm being pushed on to the stage, into the spotlights. 'Please, no— I don't want to—'

'AND HERE SHE IS!' Noah beams again and holds out his hand. 'THE MOST BEAUTIFUL GIRL IN THE WHOLE WORLD! EVERYONE, GIVE A *HUUUUUGE* WELCOME TO MY INSPIRATION, MY SOULMATE AND THE LOVE OF MY LIFE, FAITH VALENTINE!'

I can't breathe. Instinctively, I turn to run, but I can't in this stupid dress.

The screams get louder and an orchestra starts up and a neon light pulsing FAITH VALENTINE has been switched on and I'm being pushed pushed pushed pushed pushed—

'Go on, love!' The huge hands firmly shove me to centre stage. 'Don't be shy, sweetheart! Get out there and enjoy it!'

Stiffly, I turn.

Ninety thousand people have broken into raucous cheers.

That's 90,000.

Nine, four zeros and a comma.

'GUYS!' Noah calls over the top of the screams. 'GUYS, GUYS! WAIT A MINUTE! I'VE GOT SOMETHING TO SAY! COME OVER HERE, BABE! COME ON!'

Drowning in screams, my boyfriend grabs my hand, pulls me towards him and spins me round like a trophy. Then he picks me up and puts me on a narrow high chair, the kind boy bands step off when they have to change octave.

My entire body is shaking, like I'm a tapped glass too.

Noah faces the audience again.

'TODAY!' My boyfriend holds a hand up and there's sudden silence. 'TODAY IS OUR

ONE-YEAR ANNIVERSARY! ONE YEAR SINCE I MET THIS GODDESS AT AN AWARDS PARTY! ISN'T THAT RIGHT, EFF?'

He turns to me, radiant in his spotlight. Trembling, I swallow and nod.

'GET THIS!' Noah turns to the sea of tiny faces. 'THIS STUNNER WAS ON THE FLOOR, CLEANING UP WITH THE WAITERS! WHAT A TOTAL SWEETHEART, HUH?'

I open my mouth.

'AND, FROM THE VERY FIRST SECOND, I KNEW.' Noah puts an arm round me. 'I KNEW THIS GIRL WAS EVERYTHING I HAD BEEN LOOKING FOR. YOU ALL KNOW SHE WAS THE INSPIRATION FOR MY SMASH HIT, "FOR YOU I WAS WAITING", BUT TONIGHT I WANT TO PLAY HER SOMETHING VERY SPECIAL.'

With a slight nod from Noah, they all start roaring: 'WE LOVE YOU, NOAH, YOU'RE SO ROMANTIC, NOAH!'

My boyfriend takes my hand, kisses it, then grabs his guitar and plays an opening A minor chord.

My stomach knots tightly.

'THIS IS CALLED "FAITH IN ME".' Noah grins at me, then at them. 'IT'S THE FIRST TRACK OF MY BRAND-NEW ALBUM, *ON THE RISE*! OUT TOMORROW! HOPE YOU LIKE IT!'

My mouth opens—

'*Mmmmmm,*' he hums earnestly into his microphone. 'Ooooh. *Do-do-do. Mmmmm.*' Chord. 'You're state of the art/The song in my heart/You've read some Descartes/It sets you apart . . .'

And this is it.

The Big Dream.

The Grand Romantic Gesture.

The Moment I Will Remember For The Rest Of My Life.

I am on an enormous stage in a glittering designer dress, being serenaded by my famous, gorgeous boyfriend with my very own song, my name being screamed by thousands, the luckiest, most cherished girl in the entire world.

So why do I want to run away so badly? What's *wrong* with me?

'*Mmmmmmm* . . . You're the joy in my soul/The fish in my shoal/I'd meet you in Seoul . . .'

129

My nose abruptly twitches – Noah's been at the Online Rhyming Dictionary again – and I dip my head so he can't see my expression.

'. . . Because, babe, you're my goal . . .'

Torch apps are being turned on all round the stadium and waved in the air, twinkling like techno stars.

*Love this, Faith. Please, just be normal and love it. Love it love it love it love it love it love it love it love it—*

Out of the shadows steps a young violinist, walking towards the front of the stage, long blonde hair shining. With a flourish, she starts playing.

'*IIIIIIIIIII HAVE FAITH IN YOU.*' Noah turns towards me. I'm guessing it's the chorus. 'AND YOUUUUUU'RE THE FAITH IN MEEEEEEEEE.'

I have no idea where to look.

'THAAAATTTT'S HOW THIS LOVE GRREEEWWWWW, AND, BABY, YOU'RE MY KEYYYYYY.' A grand piano is being wheeled on. Noah smiles, hands his guitar to a crew member and then sits down at the keys. 'You're the light in

my chest/Above all the rest/I think you're the best/
I'll see you in . . .'

*Budapest.*

'Bucharest.'

A tiny bubble of snot pops out of my nose and
I don't know whether to laugh or cry. This is so
sweet, so special, so huge.

But all I wanted was for Noah to be there
when he said he would, and not say he was on his
way when he wasn't. For him to come and see
a boring ballet just *once* because he knows I'd love
it.

Instead, I smile as hard as I can, hold a hand to
my chest and make my eyes shiny.

*Blessed, guys. So blessed.*

He keeps singing – a verse of *life/knife/strife/wildlife*
and another chorus – then Noah bursts into a long
high note and finally stops, breathless.

I open my mouth.

'GIVE FAITH VALENTINE ANOTHER BIG
CHEER!' he shouts, jumping up from the piano,
pulling me off my seat and spinning me yet again
in an elaborate, sparkling white circle. My dress/gift

131

suddenly makes a hell of a lot more sense. 'LOVE YOU SO MUCH, BABY! HAPPY ONE-YEAR ANNIVERSARY!'

Noah tilts me backwards and kisses me.

With a loud bang, silver glitter and pink petals fill the air, shooting from every direction, straight into my face. The crowd erupts.

I open my mouth again—

'OK, that's done now, babe,' my boyfriend whispers in my ear, straightening me up again. 'Stay for the after-party, yeah? It's going to be good.'

And I'm ushered back offstage.

*18*

## SHE'S HIS VALENTINE

Last night, Noah Anthony delighted a packed-out Wembley crowd with his new Number One single, 'Faith in Me', dedicated to girlfriend, Faith Valentine. Heart-throb Noah serenaded his lucky lady, who remained composed throughout, dressed for the limelight in sparkling Valentino (left).

I wake up alone.

Honestly, I would have put money on Mercy rocking up at 5am purely to mock me – a YouTube video of last night's show has gone viral and my sister could live off the *chest/Bucharest* rhyme for days – but the next morning it's just me.

I stare at the ceiling for a few seconds. Last night was . . .

Quickly, I roll over, grab my phone and send Noah his daily wake-up text:

Good morning! Last night was REALLY
SOMETHING. Thank you for an amazing
evening, sorry I couldn't stay, LOVED it!
See you tonight so I can give you YOUR gift!
Eff xx

My doodled-on travel-agent's envelope just isn't going to cut it any more. Jay-Z bought Beyoncé a twenty-million-dollar desert island off the coast of Florida; maybe I could find a cheaper beach hut somewhere in Scotland?

I get dressed in my Grandma-approved audition outfit, dutifully post the image of Noah's gig Genevieve sent me last night with a 'to-copy-and-paste quote' – *Luckiest girlfriend ever!!!* ♥ ♥ – and grab the papers from the front doormat. Then I go back upstairs and quietly tiptoe down the corridor to Mer's bedroom.

My sister's in her own bed for the first time in months, sleeping on her back, arms either side, face perfectly still, duvet tucked neatly under her armpits.

It's both creepy and endearing, like a hospitalised vampire.

I resist checking for blood-drained victims under her bed and instead leave a full-page tabloid article next to her so she'll see Noah's big romantic gesture as soon as she wakes up.

*Take that, Mercy Valentine.*

I pop my head into Hope's room, but then I remember that she was planning to leave at the crack of dawn to shop for school supplies with the mysterious Roz.

So I clomp down the stairs in my teetering audition heels, yawning widely. I did *try* to wait for Noah at the end of his show, but there were so many paps and fans surging towards the stage I ended up sneaking back home to learn my lines for today's audition instead.

They're not really *difficult* . . . as long as you know how to behave like a normal human being. Which – given last night – apparently I do not.

'No!' I murmur as I quickly scan online for stars I could buy and name after Noah. 'Stop the car! This is *madness*.'

An acre of the moon? Is that romantic?

'I don't *care* that we're in the middle of nowhere—'

I mean, who owns the moon in the first place?

The front doorbell rings.

'I don't *care* that we're in the middle of nowhere,' I read from my script, opening the door. 'I want you to let me go. Something just doesn't feel right about—'

Genevieve nods curtly. Grandma's filming something in Devon – a small cameo role that'll no doubt win her another Oscar for narrowing her eyes – but she's still making sure I'm arriving on time and without candle grease smeared on me.

'Morning!' I try to beam confidently.

'Where are you going, darling? Anywhere nice?'

I spin round in amazement.

My mother is standing at the bottom of the stairs in pale blue trousers and a navy silk blouse, light hair pulled tightly into a low bun. Her thin face is drawn, her bare feet bony, but she's dressed and downstairs.

It's like catching sight of a mermaid, the Loch Ness monster or maybe an errant Tooth Fairy.

I glance at Genevieve to check she can see her too. She subtly nods.

'Mum!' I spin back with a fixed smile. 'How are

136

you feeling? You certainly *look –*' exhausted, drained, devoid of essential life force – 'glowingly beautiful as always!'

Her usually bright grey eyes are sliding dully round the hallway, too smoothly, like they're on rails.

'Oh,' my mother says politely, not listening. 'How very kind of you to say so, sweetheart.'

She frowns absently at the sheaf of papers I'm stuffing into my handbag.

'Scripts, darling? For me? I *distinctly* remember telling Persephone to pass on any offers for the time being. *Pinnacle* is doing so well at the box office there's really no need to—'

'Umm.' I cough. 'Actually . . . they're mine.'

Her cool gaze flickers momentarily towards Genevieve as if she's only just noticed her still standing on the doorstep. 'Yours?' Pause. 'In what way?'

'Roles. For me.' I can feel my cheeks getting hot. 'To audition for. Persephone . . . emailed them. I'm actually . . . on my way to a callback. It's a . . . big TV show. Everyone's really . . . excited.'

Mum frowns. 'But, darling, you're *far* too young.'

*What?* 'I'm sixteen, Mum. Remember? The rule is we can act after we turn sixteen. You're thinking of Hope.'

She gazes into space again.

'Mum?'

Up at the hall window.

'*Mum.*'

'Hmm?' She switches a sliver of attention back to me. 'Oh yes, darling. You're probably right. Well. You always were the beauty of the family. Are you using that expensive cream I gave you? Those high-definition cameras will capture *every* flaw.'

I blink. 'Yes, Mu—'

'Where's your sister?' she interrupts abruptly. 'I can't find her. She's not in her room. She's never in her room any more.'

'Mercy's asleep.' My stomach twists. 'And Hope's gone out shopping for a new school satchel with Dad and . . . Roz.'

My mother stares at me.

'Well.' Her face empties, and she brushes her lips gently over my cheek. It's like being kissed by a dandelion seed. 'I think I'll go back to bed now. Goodbye.'

She slowly makes her formal way up the stairs, thin back straight, chin held high. Genevieve and I watch her go.

For a second, I can see other versions of my beautiful mother flickering like a candle: tossing Hope in the air, tickling a giggling Mercy, giving Max a piggyback, stroking my hair, snorting with laughter at a dumb joke with a hand over her mouth.

Then the candle goes out, and there's just a closed door.

'Right.' Genevieve is brisk and businesslike. 'Faith, we can update your social media in the car. I'm thinking *Positive Mind, Positive Vibes, Positive Life* with a silhouette yoga photo. Hashtag *Bhujangasana*, hashtag *livingmybestlife*, hashtag *sunlightinmysoul*. Off we go.'

I stare at my grandmother's assistant, tapping impatiently at her phone.

Where is she even *getting* these photos? It's weird to think Genevieve is out there, living my fake life or trawling the internet for pictures of it.

I'm not even sure I remember what *Bhujangasana* is. Tree pose? A bridge? Eagle? Some kind of kettle? Oh, who cares?

Grabbing my phone, I text:

Off to my second audition! Soooo nervous!
Wish me luck! See you tonight for GIFT TIME!
Love you! xxx

Then, with a wave of inspiration, I text:

Po, EMERGENCY. Need IDEAS FOR NOAH
ANNIVERSARY PRESSIE. Pls send ASAP!
Cheesier the better! xxx

Then I frown and add:

I don't mean 'cheesy' I mean 'romantic'. Obvs
xxx

If there's one person who knows romance, it's
Hope.

'Right,' I say, feeling infinitely calmer with my
love life safely in my little sister's hands, 'let's get
this show on the road.'

19

Did you hear about the actor who fell
through the floorboards?

He was just going through a stage.

OK, I am *prepared*.

The script is engraved in my brain, etched on the
back of my eyeballs. In decades to come, I'll still
have random lines screeching through my head in
the middle of the night, whether I get the role or
not.

And yes – my character seems *incredibly* passive,
bordering on empty space in female form – but, if
blank is what Teddy Winthrop, casting director
extraordinaire, wants, that's what I'll give him.

I mean, it worked last time, right?

'Hi again!' The receptionist looks up and beams

at me. 'Faith! I just *knew* you'd get this job. I could feel it in my *bones*!' She leans forward. 'I'm kind of *spoooooky* like that, you know? Get it?! Hahaha!'

I really hate people saying *get it?* after a joke.

*No*, I want to scream. *Stop asking me.*

'Oh, I *totally* get it!' I laugh brightly. 'Is there anything I need to know before I go in?'

'Don't think so!' She grins. 'Pretty much a formality. Hop right in! They're waiting!'

With a deep breath, I push through the door.

There are even more people here today, sitting on one side of the room, waiting and watching. My eyes skitter round with a pulse of panic. The lady in tortoiseshell glasses, Teddy Winthrop and a younger man I don't recognise are standing near the front.

One look at Teddy's face and I know he's not the reason I'm here. He's *rigid* with fury.

'Faith Valentine!' The man I don't know steps forward. Black T-shirt, jeans, silvery hair – oh, got it – standard director's outfit. 'I'm Christian Ellis, director of the show, for my sins.' Told you. 'I'm *thrilled* you could make it.'

I glance at Teddy. His lips are a tight, thin line.

142

'Joy,' he says flatly.

'No, it's *Faith*! Haha! I watched your first audition,' the director continues with a generous smile. 'There's *so* much to work with, you know?'

'So much work to do,' Teddy agrees drily.

'We're hoping you can bring some Valentine magic here today,' Christian says and points me towards one of two chairs facing the crowd.

'Of course.' I smile sweetly and sit down, confusion escalating. 'Thank you for inviting me.'

Umm, what is going on? The *casting* director is looking at me like I slid in on my stomach and vomited on his feet. So – *why* am I here?

'We're just waiting for the other actress to show up,' Christian concludes. 'And then we can get started.'

I stare at him blankly. *What other actress?*

'I'M HERE!' The door smashes open and makes a large dent in the wall. 'I'm here, I'm here! Oh *ship it*. Did I do that? So there was this dude on the train and he had his legs out wide, and I'm like *dude, stop manspreading on me,* and he's like *what are you talking about,* and I'm like *what are you protecting, the blue diamond off* Titanic? And he's like *what did*

*you just say to me, you jumped-up little—*' Laugh. 'Anyway, long story short, I got thrown off the train at the next stop by the conductor. Hence – late.'

Door Girl holds her hands out and bows, *ta-da!*

Then she looks up at me from under her bleached crop-fringe, green cat-eyes shining.

'Oh,' she says flatly. 'It's you. *Shocker.*'

'Everyone!' the director says excitedly. 'Meet Scarlett Bell, a *huge* new talent, nominated for Most Promising Newcomer at this year's Olivier awards. We're pretty excited to have her confirmed in the role of Frankie.'

'I didn't win,' she tells the room loudly. 'Which is good because nobody knows who I am yet and that's *way* more fun.'

She snaps her fingers at a guy in the back row.

'*Oy.* Wake up, mate. It wasn't the Most Promising New Coma award. That's nowhere *near* as influential.'

Then she breaks into peeling laughter at her own bad joke, uncomfortably loud and a little bit snorty.

My brain is spinning on one tiptoe in a single spotlight.

'Frankie? You're playing . . . Frankie?'

'Yup.' She grins at me with pink cheeks. Her

mouth is incredibly wide and slightly sharp and evil in the corners, like the Joker in *Batman*. 'Frankie. The Frankster. Franko. Frankenstein the franking machine. That's me.'

*But—* 'So that means I'm auditioning for . . .'

'Whatever you want, mate.' Scarlett flops herself on the chair opposite mine and leans back with her arms over her head. 'A pineapple? A fisherman? New member of the latest boy band? Take your pick.'

I stare at her.

'I'm *joking*,' she sighs. 'Cat on a pink bicycle. Where did you find Famous Girl? Wait, I think I know.' She starts humming. 'Aren't you the fish in a shoal? No – *wait*. You're the song in a heart. Oooh, haven't you read Descartes?'

My face is suddenly on fire. *Thanks, Noah.*

'Faith –' Director Christian smiles amiably – 'you're auditioning for the role of Agatha. I thought that was clear in the details we sent over.'

And . . . I've just spent twenty-four hours learning somebody else's lines.

*No no no no no no—*

'No problem!' I smile as serenely as possible. 'I

can absolutely play Agatha! Just let me find my . . .'
*Sanity, contents of my stomach, will to live.* 'Lipgloss.
I'm going to need shiny lips to . . . really harness
the character.'

With a swoop of panic, I dive into my handbag
and try to quickly scan my script. My hands are
shaking so badly I can't even turn the pages.

Scarlett stares at my trembling fingers for a few
seconds, then at my face. Her expression softens.

'On-page is OK, right?' she calls out much more
gently. 'Mr Ellis, can Faith have her script out? I
mean, she's been thrown a left hook here. Let her
read her lines.'

'Course she can!' Christian chuckles. 'No worries!
I'm not a *monster* like Teddy-boy over here.'

Teddy-boy – easily in his seventies – glowers.

'Yes,' he says flatly. 'Expecting actresses to know
a handful of lines in order to obtain prestigious
acting jobs in which they will recite said lines is
clearly outrageous. What a brute I am.'

Giving Scarlett a grateful grimace, I pull my script
out.

I do *kind* of know Agatha's lines, but I've no idea
what sort of character she is. I also can't help being

surprised that the livewire sitting next to me is going to play wishy-washy Frankie.

Scarlett just seems too . . . *there.*

'Come on, then!' As if she can hear me, she claps her hands. Huge lights click on and the camera starts running. 'I've got more shouting at offensive strangers to do and my remaining sixty years are running out.'

She winks at me and clears her throat.

And it's like magic: her freckled face abruptly shifts, becoming something else entirely. Her mouth is suddenly sweeter and more delicate; her almond eyes lose their cheeky sparkle and become luminous, pure, innocent.

'*Pretend you're driving,*' she whispers as I stare at her, totally mesmerised. How did she just do that?

I blink. 'Huh?'

'*Pretend. You're. Driving.*' A tiny eyebrow quirk. 'In this scene, you're driving a car, remember?'

'Oh! Yes! Umm.' Awkwardly, I put my right hand out in a fist and wiggle my left hand at my thigh. I look like I'm holding on to a really tiny cow. 'Here we . . . go.'

Scarlett glances down, then somehow Frankie glances back up with a quivering mouth.

'We've left Fred behind.'

And, for the first time, I actually feel the impact of that line. *We've left the boyfriend she loves in the middle of nowhere, screaming for help, and we've just . . . gone.*

'Yes,' I say, checking my script. 'We didn't have a choice!'

'There's *always* a choice.' There's strength in her jawline, and suddenly Frankie isn't weak – she's defiant, resilient. 'We made a choice to save ourselves.'

'To save *yourself*,' I say, but in comparison I sound flat so – in a wave of inspiration – I reach over and grab my co-star by the T-shirt, shaking her. 'NOT ME. JUST YOU.'

'*You're still driving,*' she whispers. '*Steering wheel. Gearstick. Accelerator. Eyes on the road, please.*'

'Oh!' I let go of her T-shirt, embarrassed. 'Sorry.'

'We made a choice to save ourselves,' she prompts as I take back control of our imaginary vehicle.

'*To save yourself. Not me. JUST YOU.*'

'I . . . don't understand.'

And it looks like she really doesn't. Frankie appears so genuinely bewildered that I actually want to stop the scene, hold out my script and go, *Look. Look, it's all in here. Line nine. I don't really get it, either.*

'It's *too* late for ME,' I say stiffly, scanning line ten. 'It was too late for me six weeks ago.'

Hang on. *What?*

'Are you . . . are you saying . . .' Frankie's expression becomes horrified, a muscle in her cheek twitches and she shivers with the tiniest ripple of repulsion. 'No. I don't believe you.'

*You're the only character alive.*

Teddy literally *told* me that at the last casting; how did I not notice that Frankie was being driven away by a zombie?

'Why did you help me?' Frankie's eyes fill with real water: *how?* Then she flashes with anger. 'Why didn't you just let me stay with Fred? What are you going to do to me? How does this end?'

My mouth opens.

'ANDDDDD . . . CUTTTTT!!'

I blink. How *does* it end?

'Good, good,' Scarlett says – herself again –

jumping up. 'Nice to meet you, Valentine. I'm gonna go get some pizza – I'm freaking starving. Call me when the next Agatha comes in, yeah, Mr Ellis? My bum hurts – those chairs are the *worst*. Laters!'

And she's gone.

## 20

*I did it.*

I stare at the hole in the wall made by Scarlett's entrance, my whole body slowly relaxing.

At last, I'm ready to pick up the Valentine baton, run forward and live up to the family name. To follow in the footsteps of my mother, of my grandmother, of my great-grandmother. It might even be *fun*: wearing costumes, hanging out with co-stars, learning lines, getting to play—

'See what I mean?' Teddy explodes. '*Now* are you listening, Chris? This is my *job*. It's been my job for *fifty years*. I know what I'm *talking about*.'

'Ted. Keep your voice down.'

'I will not! I am employed to cast this show, and then you *override* my decisions, *undermine* my authority and *call my professionalism into question*—'

'This is not the time or the place—'

151

'And all for a little free publicity! To get the show in the papers . . . You knew this attention-seeking, talentless *family heirloom* would get it for you!'

*Attention-seeking, talentless family heirloom?*

Wait a minute, are they talking about *me*?

Surely not. I mean, I'm standing *right here*.

'But you can see it too, yes? I don't care how pretty she is or who her parents are or how powerful her grandmother is or the fact that she's stepping out with Noddy Whatshisface. We absolutely cannot cast her!'

'*Theodore*.' The woman in tortoiseshell is loud and sharp. '*Enough*.'

I look down at my hands. I *am* still here, right?

Teddy Winthrop seems to abruptly come to his senses, suddenly registering that I'm totally equipped with every one of my auditory functions.

'I'm sorry you had to hear that,' he says as if waiting for me to leave the room was not an option. 'I'm sure you're a very *nice* girl.' He says *nice* as if it's poisonous. 'But this is the real world, Faith. I want to make a good show. A *great* show. Not a . . . nepotistic pat on the back for the Valentine family.'

'I was a publicity stunt?' I step forward. 'You gave

me a second shot and *leaked* my name just so that the papers would write about the show?'

'No!' Christian Ellis cries emphatically. 'No! Not at all! Well, yes. Yes, I did. But I *did* also genuinely hope you would be . . . you know.'

'Capable of playing a dead person?'

'Exactly!' He nods. 'Except . . .'

'I'm not.'

'. . . No. Shame,' he adds with a small shrug. 'I thought we could get something workable, but . . . I don't think it's there.'

Something inside me crumbles. So I take a deep breath and arrange my features into their prettiest, sweetest expression. I am calm, I am graceful, I am together.

Composure is easy. All you have to do is take your internal screaming and bury it so deep that nobody even knows it's there. With enough practice, anyone can do it. I've been honing the art for *years*.

'I completely understand,' I smile, firmly shaking Director Ellis's hand. 'Thank you for your candour. I very much enjoyed meeting you anyway.'

Then I turn to Teddy Winthrop. 'I appreciate your honesty.' *Dimple.*

To the woman in glasses: 'Thank you for giving me a chance.' *Dimple*. 'Perhaps you'll consider me again when I've developed my craft further.' *Dimple dimple dimple.*

And *exit*.

'Mmm,' Teddy mutters as I glide quietly towards the door. 'I feel rather bad now.'

'Well,' snaps tortoiseshell lady, 'maybe you *should*.'

My fingers touch the door handle and I hang on tightly for a few seconds while my throat tightens and my chest hurts and my smile threatens to break like a piece of string pulled too tight. *No. No. No. No.*

'Have a great day, everyone!' I call over my shoulder. 'Weather looks like it's going to be extraordinary!' Blindly, I let myself out.

*No.*

Then I close the door behind me and shut my eyes for a few seconds while the room spins and my heart jitters and thumps and panic strobes across my brain. *NO NO NO NO NO NO. NONONONONONONO—*

When I finally open them again, I see a scrap of paper on the floor, so I pick it up crossly – what

154

kind of person *litters* a reception? – glance at it briefly and stick it in my handbag. My phone vibrates as I pull it out.

**MISSED CALL: Noah**

**MISSED CALL: Noah**

**MISSED CALL: Noah**

**MISSED CALL: Noah**

**MISSED CALL: Noah**

He's such a sweetheart, but I'm not ready to talk about what just happened. Not quite yet. Maybe not quite ever.

Quickly, I text back:

Audition ongoing. Speak later xx

'*Sooooo!*' The receptionist beams at me. 'Bet you blew them away! I *knew* you'd be perfect.' She whispers shyly. 'They let me read the scripts sometimes, you know. That's what I'm doing this stupid receptionist's job for. It's my way into the industry!'

I smile even though I can't feel my mouth. 'Good luck!' My face feels like solid plastic. 'Here's hoping! See you later!'

All out of fake exclamation marks, I hold my crossed fingers high in the air and swish out of the building, back into the waiting silver limousine, where I sit, poised, elegant and contained.

Because *Valentines Always Act With Class.*

Even. If. They. Can't. Act. At. All.

21

Why do we tell actors to 'break a leg'?

So they end up in a cast.

'*Da-da-da-DA-DA!* Close-up on Faith Valentine! Trumpets!'

'Red carpet! Rose petals! Lights!'

'Open the envelope!'

'*Aaaannnd here she is,* ladies and not-so-gentlemen, the great middle Valentine sister, all-time icon of British cinema! Faith! Tell us, who is your inspiration, where is that *dress* from, how *do* you walk in those heels? Impart your secrets, lovely lady! We're not worthy to bask in your goddess-like glow!'

A genuine Oscar is shoved into my hands.

'The first of many! Wait, hang on, we need to

polish it – it's been in the downstairs loo for, like, a decade.'

'Eww, there's bog roll stuck to it. Someone's getting *fired*.'

I blink at the golden award. Then at my siblings standing on the front steps of our house. They've laid out a pink fluffy bath mat over the doormat. Damp potpourri is being thrown at my head by Mercy, Hope is waving a tattered old envelope in the air, and Max is holding the hall lamp out so it shines directly into my face.

'Speechless! Like all true superstars! And now she thanks her parents, her grandmother, the industry, her sisters, but most of all her handsome and charming *brother*, without whom none of this would be possible!'

Max jumps to the side and bows at himself.

'Why thank you, ridiculously good-looking Max! Yes, it has been my honour to gently guide this lovable monkey through her runny-nosed pre-adolescent years and to see her blossom into the lanky, obsessively athletic weirdo we see before us.'

Mercy throws more potpourri.

'And the winner is . . .' Hope ostentatiously opens

a gas bill and pretends to study it. 'Rihanna! Wait . . . wrong one. Whoops, awkward. Faith Valentine!'

A giggle pops out of my nose.

'How did it go?' Po rips the gas bill in half. 'Tell us *everything*! We're on tender hooks!'

'Tenterhooks,' Max grins. 'They're not hooks that are feeling super affectionate.'

I bite my lip.

'I think maybe it's . . .' I glance round at their optimistic faces. 'Ahh . . . too soon to know for sure yet . . .' – *we absolutely cannot cast her* – '. . . I guess we'll just wait for an email from Persephone!'

I'm never checking my inbox ever again.

'Oh, *please*,' Mer says, patting my arm unexpectedly. 'Come on, Eff. They'd be insane not to plaster your perfect face all over every bus in London.'

Amazed, I stare at my big sister. 'Say what now?'

Then I look at her hand on my forearm. Is Mercy . . . voluntarily *touching* me? Is there something hidden in her hand? A tiny electric-shock buzzer?

'I can be nice!' she snaps, folding her arms. 'Geez, Faith, can you let me be nice for once?'

I smile and kiss her cheek. 'Only if you don't make a habit of it. It's a bit creepy.'

159

'Whatever.' She scowls.

Triumphantly, Max pulls me through into the kitchen. 'We made you a cake to celebrate! And by *made* I mean ordered and by *cake* I mean doughnuts. Also, a picnic! And by *picnic* I mean . . . TA-DA!'

On the table is the most haphazard collection of food I've ever seen. Poorly constructed, soggy tuna-and-tomato sandwiches, piled in precarious stacks. Cheesy puffs spilling out of bowls. What appears to be a plate of boiled eggs with scraps of shell still hanging on. Neon fizzy drinks, already part-drunk, and a plate of tiny sausages on – I look more closely – white dental picks.

In the middle is a huge roast-dinner platter covered in glazed doughnuts. Each has a letter on it, drawn in icing.

# CONGRATLATIONSEFFIE

'"U" got dropped on the floor,' Po explains, licking her fingers. 'And then eaten. Five-second rule and so on.'

There's a huge lump in my throat. Who would I even be without these guys?

'Crikey.' I smile, sitting down and selecting a dental-pick sausage. 'And to get a professional caterer in too. Was it the same lot that do Brad Pitt's birthday parties?'

'He wishes!' Max crows. 'They have to eat and then pick their teeth with *entirely different* cutlery.'

Laughing, we gather round the table.

Max stuffs his face with a whole egg, Po and Mercy start arguing over the least mashed-up sandwich and it's almost like it always used to be. The shouting, the giggling, the insults, the ease and the comfort. Almost.

'Eff!' Hope says through a mouthful. 'My idea for Noah's anniversary gift! It's *that good* it will be *unparalysed* in the whole history of romantic gestures.'

'Unparalleled,' Max corrects.

'What?'

'You mean *unparalleled*, Po.'

'Stop presumpting.' My sister glowers at him indignantly. 'How do you know what I mean when I haven't told you what it is yet?'

I laugh just as my phone starts vibrating.

**INCOMING CALL: Noah**

'Put a pin in that, Hope,' I grin. 'Although I'll take whatever you've got, obviously.' Then I pick up the phone and chomp on a cheese puff. *Noddy Whatshisface LOL.* Something tells me my boyfriend wouldn't find that funny. 'Hey! How's it going? We're just having the world's worst picnic.'

'Oy!' Max complains, eating another egg and idly swiping on his iPad. 'Rude.'

There's a loud crackle.

'. . . Not . . . I . . . Last . . . What . . . *crackle* . . . Can . . .'

'Noah, I can't hear you,' I smile. 'We're in the kitchen. Terrible reception, as per. Hang on.' Quickly, I leap up and tuck myself neatly behind the fridge again. *Ew.* Is that a festering courgette? How does so much food get back here when we don't even *cook*?

'. . . Don't . . . *crackle*. Cannot . . . I . . .'

'Noah?' I frown. He sounds like he's inside a bottle of shaken-up cola. 'Are you in the studio? Wait a minute, I need to—'

'. . . You . . . *crackle* . . .'

'Effie.'

I hold a finger up. 'One second, Max.' Then I

stick it in my ear. 'Noah? Is everything all right? Can you hear what I'm—'

'. . . totally . . . from . . . *crackle* . . . of . . .'

'Effie.'

'*Wait, Max.* Noah's trying to tell me something—'

'*Crackle* . . . explain.'

'*FAITH VALENTINE!*' Max bellows behind me. '*PUT THAT FLAMING PHONE DOWN RIGHT NOW.*'

Shocked, I hang up. My siblings are staring at me with wide eyes. Max's iPad is glowing on the kitchen table in front of them.

'What? What's happening?' My intestines wind themselves into a tight ball. It's the audition, isn't it? The story's got out already, and now the whole world knows that I'm an embarrassment to my family— '*What is it?*'

'Sit down, Effie,' Max says gently, pulling a chair out. 'Take a very deep breath because this is going to hurt, sis.'

*What is – how is – who is—*

Be composed, Faith. Be collected.

'I'm not sitting down,' I say in an eerily calm

voice. 'I'm fine right here, thank you. Please show me what's on that screen.'

The iPad is slowly spun towards me.

And for a second it makes no sense: the photo, the headline, the caption. For a moment, it's yet another joke I don't really understand. A poorly executed gag written on a Post-it note, stuck on a wall and signed off with a kiss.

Then . . . I get it.

## POP-STAR LOVE RAT CHEATS
## WITH MYSTERY BLONDE

In the last hour, photographs have surfaced of chart-topping Noah Anthony heartily canoodling with an unknown blonde. Naughty Noah, who is in a committed relationship with celeb stunner Faith Valentine, was spotted kissing the supposed fan at his after-show party. Is this the end for Fainoah?

'Faith,' Mercy says quietly, eyes dark. 'I'm so sorry.'

I look back down.

Anthony denies everything, claiming: 'It's not what it looks like!' But look at the evidence (left)! Sources were unable to identify the mystery blonde, but onlookers confirmed that two-timing Noah was 'utterly absorbed'.

This doesn't make sense. Noah loves me; I know he does. This is just another misinterpretation, another fake story. Maybe it's photoshopped. Or a weird angle, and it was just a friendly peck. Maybe this is an *old* photo, taken years ago, from before Noah and I even met. But – I squint more closely at the fuzzy image – it's definitely Noah, and his head is clearly shaved.

Which means this photo was taken in the last two days.

And they are very *clearly* kissing.

'Straight after that amazing romantic song he sang for you!' Po has jumped up from the table, eyes wet and fists clenched. 'He's *so* not getting my romantic gesture now! What a . . . what a . . . what an absolute bed-wetting *poo-nugget*!'

My phone is ringing again.

**INCOMING CALL: Noah**

I cancel the call.

**INCOMING CALL: Noah**

I cancel the call again. Then I walk into the hallway, sit down on the bottom step of the stairs, take my huge audition heels off and start deliberately putting my neon trainers on.

'Faith!' Max furiously pulls a trainer out of my hand and throws it into the corridor. 'Stop it! What's *wrong* with you? You can't just keep . . . *running.*'

Just watch me.

'Umm,' Mercy says, glancing out of the hallway window. Her cheeks are flushed. 'Eff. You might want to run fast.'

I look up tiredly. 'Why?'

'The paps are already here.'

## 22

I'm not fast enough.

Within seconds, I'm by the back door with one trainer on, the other in my hand – I'll hop across the garden – but as I pull it open there are flashes, shouts, questions. I reel back, closing the door again.

'*How.*' Turning, I stare at my siblings who are standing in a worried, clustered knot behind me. 'I don't understand. How are they *on the grounds*? It's . . . *illegal.*'

'Somebody must have buzzed them through the gates.' Max frowns. 'We've foolishly invited them in. Like vampires or delivery men.'

*Mum?* Is she so out of her mind she thought fifteen members of the national press were welcome on our doorstep?

'FAITH!' someone yells through the letterbox.

'FAITH VALENTINE! ARE YOU OK? YOU MUST BE DEVASTATED!'

My heart is hammering.

**INCOMING CALL: Noah**

I cancel the call again.

'But I don't know what to – I don't think I can—' My cheeks are starting to burn and my throat tightens. 'Can somebody please *make them go away?*'

'Absolutely.' Max puffs up to twice his normal size. 'I will *absolutely* tell them where to go. Get to your bedroom, Eff, and I'll deal.'

My brother rolls up his sleeves as if he's going to fix the situation with a few well-placed headlocks.

'And I'm going to *rip them apart!*' Po squeaks next to him, jabbing her fists out like a boxer. 'I'm going to, I'm going to – I'm going to *poke* their little brains out of their ears with . . . *chopsticks*, and then I'm going to put those brains on a barbecue, and then I'm going to take the roasted pieces and cover them in sauce and I am going to *eat them!*'

We all stare at her, momentarily distracted.

'Blimey, Hope,' Max says. 'Bit of an overreaction. They're only doing their job.'

She considers it. 'Or I'll yell GO AWAY, YOU MOULDY CHICKEN NUGGETS as loudly as I can?'

'Slightly better.'

**INCOMING CALL: Noah**

Cancel.

Panic rising, I take a few steps up the stairs. I'm desperate to reach my bedroom, my safe space, where I can lie in the dark and work out how I actually—

'*Or*,' Mercy says slowly, 'you could go out there.'

I pause. 'What?'

'You could go out there and talk to them.' Her black eyes are flashing. 'Have a say in what's being written. Put your own story forward. Stop letting everyone else speak for you. You don't have to be the victim, you know.'

My big sister is watching me carefully.

'*Oooh*,' Max says, rolling his sleeves back down again. 'Yeah. Scrap my idea, that's *way* better. I'd do that.'

'But.' I take a few cautious steps back down the stairs. 'I don't know what my story is. I don't even know what *the* story is. I really need to speak to Noah first.'

**INCOMING CALL: Noah**

'And let him give you a lame excuse?' Mercy's teeth are tightly gritted. 'Some *it's not what it looks like, you have to believe me, it was a mistake, I love you, baby, please can't we just forget this ever happened* bull? Why? What's the point? He's said his piece, Eff. He's talked to the papers. Now it's *your* turn.'

I cancel the call again. Frowning, I take another tentative step down the stairs. 'But . . . what do I do?'

'Yell!' Hope yelps in excitement. 'Scream! Throw things!'

'Cry,' Max offers. 'Be all super-sad and weepy. That'll make him feel *awful*.'

'Be sleepy, like you're so unbothered you fell asleep!'

'Resolved but dignified! Ready to forgive, but only after a huge amount of begging!'

'But also be brave!'

'And feisty!'

'Disdrawed!'

'Resilient!'

For the love of— 'CAN YOU TWO PLEASE STOP YELLING STAGE INSTRUCTIONS AT ME! IT IS *NOT* HELPING!' I turn numbly to my big sister. She's still silent, but it's her strength and advice I need. 'Mer, help me. What do I say to them?'

Mercy frowns. 'That's the whole point, Eff. Anything you want.'

There's no time to think. Max briefly opens the front door to announce that I will be out to 'set the story straight' in ten minutes, then I'm dragged into Hope's bedroom. I'm quickly given what she's calling *The Ultimate Heartbreak Makeover*. Nobody can decide whether I should be flawless – *you have no impact on me!* – or dishevelled – *I am destroyed by this news* – or glamorous – *I am finally set free!* – or pink-eyed and swollen-nosed – *what have you done to me?* or glowing – *I have already moved on!*

'It's so difficult to know,' Hope says in frustration,

dragging her huge make-up cast-offs box out, 'what shade of lipstick says *my long-term boyfriend is kissing other girls while I'm at home in bed.*'

Max shakes his head at her.

'What?' Her eyes widen. 'What did I say?'

By the time I'm led back downstairs, I am both radiant and bedraggled, smudged and well rested, highlighted and matt, knotted and glossy: all set off with deliberate mascara stains and lurid red lips.

'Right,' Max says, rubbing his hands. 'Remember, he's a rat, you're a goddess, he doesn't deserve you, you're too good for this rubbish, lucky escape, close call and all that jazz.'

'We love you!' Po flicks some water in my face and smudges my eyeliner a bit more. 'So, so much! Good luck!'

Mercy studies my face and squeezes my arm. The door opens.

'FAITH!' Cameras flash. 'FAITH VALENTINE! HOW DO YOU FEEL?'

'WHAT ARE YOUR THOUGHTS ON BEING BETRAYED? DID YOU SUSPECT HE WAS CHEATING?'

'HOW DID YOU FIND OUT? DID NOAH TELL YOU?'

'WILL YOU TAKE HIM BACK?'

'WHO'S THE GIRL? IS IT AVERY AGAIN?'

'IS THIS THE FINAL STRAW FOR YOUR ON-OFF RELATIONSHIP?'

I open my mouth.

*BEEEEEEEEEEEEEEEPPPPPPPPPPPPPPPPP.*

Everyone turns round. An enormous silver limousine is hurtling up the driveway. It stops with a crunch, a door swings open violently and my grandmother charges across the gravel path with her walking stick thwacking the ground like a pirate's leg.

Everyone steps back.

'Away!' She waves her stick in the air. 'Away, carrion! What kind of circus do you think we're running? We are *Valentines*. You're not on one of your tacky romantic archipelagos now!'

Confused silence. Then someone rallies.

'Dame Sylvia!' A Dictaphone is bravely thrust in her face. 'Dame Sylvia! How do you feel about your granddaughter being cheated on? Did you always think Noah Anthony was a good-for-nothing?'

'No comment,' Grandma snaps.

'What about the connection between this and recent rumours of infidelity by your son-in-law, Michael?'

'No comment.'

'How does Juliet feel about the same thing happening to her daughter?'

I flinch. In all the chaos, it hadn't even occurred to me yet that somebody might tie the two events together.

*Valentines Can't Hold On To Their Men.*

Grandma bridles. 'Are you *suggesting*,' she snaps, drawing herself up to her full height, 'that women are *responsible* for the inadequacies of the male of the species?'

That shuts them all up.

'NOW *OUT*!' she booms in her gigantic-theatre voice, slamming her stick a centimetre from the journalists' toes. 'Go on, *shoo*.' Another slam. 'Or I will make sure you spend the rest of your career writing about kittens in trees, local fetes and ninetieth birthday parties.'

Within seconds, the front steps are totally clear. We watch as the paparazzi vans make U-turns and drive away.

'Grandma, I—'

'What did I say about opening the door? My darling, you look absolutely frightful. Hope, go inside and make your sister a cup of tea.'

## 23

'Absolutely unacceptable . . . living like barbarians . . . cheese on the floor . . . your mother is not . . . father frolicking around . . . appalling . . . running wild . . . not in all my days . . .'

I keep slipping in and out of consciousness.

My eyes are open, my back is straight, but I keep bobbing to the surface and then sliding under again.

'Yes, Grandma.'

'. . . Not what I . . . Don't you dare think . . . no way your fault . . . tacky behaviour . . . blame yourself . . .'

'Yes, Grandma.'

'. . . modern culture . . . attitude . . . no integrity . . .'

Blinking, I stand up.

'Sorry, Grandma, I appreciate the visit, but I think I need to go and lie down.'

Slowly, I start walking up the stairs.

**INCOMING CALL: Noah**

'Yes.' My voice sounds hollow.

'Baby?' Noah breathes out heavily. 'Eff, oh thank *goodness*. You have to listen – it's all been blown out of proportion – you know what it's like – you *know* it gets all mixed up. You're the love of my life – I would never hurt you. We can work through this together if you just let me—'

'Did you do it?'

A fraction of a pause. 'The thing is, Eff, I don't know how to really . . . It was so out of the blue and—'

'Did you do it, Noah?'

'It looks a lot worse than it was, I swear. It was like a minute and I didn't even speak to her and—'

'Noah, did you kiss another girl or not?'

Silence.

'Yes. I did. Effie, I am so sorry.'

'Who?'

'I don't know. Just some girl. It doesn't matter *who*, it just matters that I love you, that I choose *you*, you're the one I want and you have to listen to what I'm—'

'Thank you for calling, appreciate the information. Do have a nice day.'

I hang up and keep walking.

*Ping.*

My exclusive interview with Faith Valentine is conducted in her bedroom in the Richmond family mansion, an empty white space she describes as 'her haven'. Being considered for the lead role in *Fright Fortnight* is lovely, she says distantly. 'Acting is a path I've been eager to tread since I was a child. To be so many people, to live so many lives, to tell so many stories . . . there is a kind of magic in it.'

Faith Valentine is flawless, composed and – of course – startlingly beautiful. But there is also a flatness to her, a kind of absence: an overly polished quality that is strangely off-putting. She speaks as if poorly reciting scripted lines. Her eyes are blank. The only time she becomes animated is when talking about her pop-starlet boyfriend, Noah Anthony. 'We're very close,' she declares passionately. 'To have love that strong is a true blessing. We're rock solid.'

And, in a girl of just sixteen, it is difficult not to find this both disturbing and sad. Is she, I wonder, the kind of girl we want a nation of teenagers looking up to? Is her popularity among young people not a worrying sign of the times we live in?

With her star inexplicably rising, only time will tell.


So that's nice.

I open my bedroom door. There's a pile of fashion magazines lying on the bed next to a folded-up blanket, and a mug of slowly congealing tomato soup on my bedside table.

Blinking, I look down. A thick purple mist is covering the floor and it's slowly creeping over my feet until I can't see them any more.

'No.'

The mist rises until my legs have disappeared.

'*No.*'

It's covering my stomach, my waist, my hands.

'NO.'

Now my arms, my chest, creeping up my neck, and I'm just a face and I can't breathe and I can't see and I'm disappearing and I'm not here I'm not here I'm not here—

'NO NO NO NO *NO*.'

With a loud scream, I turn towards my mirror. My face is unfamiliar, a collection of distorted features I don't even recognise.

'*NO!*'

With a lurch, I pick up a chair and run forward, hurling it against the glass again and again and again. It doesn't smash, but it cracks, cracks, cracks until all I can see is my reflection divided into thousands of shards.

*Smash.*

One piece is kind, one nice, one beautiful.

*Smash.*

One is a nightmare, a diva, a horror.

*Smash.*

There's the victim and the icon, the bore and the goddess, the fake and the sweetheart. *Smash smash smash smash*— Until all I can see is a million girls trapped in the mirror: all the people they have to be, all the people they have to please, all the lives they have to live, all the lives they're not living.

*Smash.*

And I don't know what's real any more. I don't know which of these pieces I am.

Knock, knock, who's there?

*Smash.*

I HAVE NO IDEA.

Breathing hard, I put the chair down and walk into my bathroom. I pick up my electric razor, plug it in and slowly run it down the middle of my head, round the front, on both sides. I keep going until I'm completely bald.

I grab the white scrap of card out of my bag and pick up my phone.

'Hi. This is Faith Valentine.'

'Oh, hello. I was wondering when you'd call.'

# HEART. BROKEN

Faith Valentine is speechless with despair (pictured left) after Noah Anthony's infidelity (see here). Caught red-handed on their first anniversary, the pop-star philanderer was nowhere to be seen.

## IT'S NOT OVER, SAYS NOAH ANTHONY
'I'm not giving up,' blasts pop star Noah Anthony in an **EXCLUSIVE REVEAL**. 'Faith is the love of my life. I'll get her back.' His new single 'Faith in Me' remains Number One in the charts, and he claims that without Faith he would be 'nothing'.

Several girls have been cited as the 'mystery blonde', including Avery Evans, a backing dancer Noah has been photographed with on multiple occasions.

You see, Kevin?! This is what happens when hot girls date millionaire idiots and not nice, normal guys, like me.

It's my turn to show Effie I'm The One! Watch this space, T-sters!

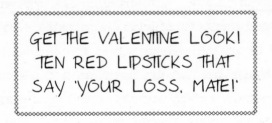

GET THE VALENTINE LOOK!
TEN RED LIPSTICKS THAT
SAY 'YOUR LOSS, MATE!'

25

What's the easiest way to get straight As?

Use a ruler.

I'm not one for grand gestures, but—

'Screw it,' I say, clambering out of my window like every teenager in every American film ever. Then I blink.

The Valentine mansion has been home my entire life. I know every nook, every oak-panelled passageway, every marble mantelpiece. But, as I stand on the fire escape, I realise I've never seen it from this angle before. The damp inside the gutter; the moss on the roof tiles; a pair of ripped black tights hanging out of Mercy's bedroom window, flapping aimlessly in the wind.

Tugging my lime-green hood up, I perch carefully

on the top rung, watching the driveway and waiting. Finally, the electric gates make a loud clanging sound and a battered orange Mini races across the gravel, squashes a flower bed of pink geraniums and knocks over a statue of Aphrodite rising out of her seashell.

I exhale in sharp relief.

'Oops!' Scarlett Bell calls out of the window. 'Smashed her boob! My bad! Your gate code is way too easy to guess, by the way!'

Swallowing, I climb down the fire escape and push the love goddess back up again. Then I stare at Scarlett's car. It's patchy and covered in bright travel stickers – *Paris, Venice, Mexico, Australia* – like a battered piece of luggage.

It also has L-plates.

'Umm,' I say stiffly, pushing aside a pile of chocolate wrappers from the passenger seat and climbing in. 'Are you supposed to be . . . driving . . . without a . . . supervising adult?'

I don't want to sound judgmental, but that statue was thirty thousand pounds' worth of love goddess.

'Nah, it's fine.' Scarlett's eating a packet of crisps:

everything in a six-metre radius stinks of cheese and onion. 'You've got a valid licence, right?'

I stare at her in alarm. 'No.'

'You don't?' Her eyes widen. 'You're kidding me. Aren't you, like, in your forties?'

She's joking. Is she joking? 'I'm . . . sixteen.'

'*Really*. Wow. Guess we'd better go *super* fast if we wanna avoid the cops, then.' Scarlett grins, hits the accelerator, races back down the driveway and takes a left so sharply that she's thrown into her car door.

Then she glances at my expression and laughs.

'I am *joking*, Valentine.' Another handful of crisps: *crunch crunch crunch*. 'I passed last month. The L-plates just give me a little extra space on the road. But your *face*, man.'

I sit in emotional silence as we speed through Richmond. Where do I even start?

*So, my boyfriend of a year cheated on me and I'm being chased by the paparazzi and the papers are dissecting me like a frog and I can't act and my future has imploded and I just smashed up my bedroom and I think I might be going insane and I called you because I had literally nobody else to call.*

*Oh, and you're a total stranger. How you doing?*

'Scarlett,' I say finally, pulling my hood down and stroking my bare head. I feel strangely exposed and vulnerable, like a baby squirrel. 'Did you leave your business card on the floor of reception for me on purpose?'

She glances at me. 'Of course I did,' she grins. 'Those things cost a freaking fortune.'

'Why?'

Scarlett thinks about it for a few seconds, then tilts her head back and pours the rest of the crisps into her mouth. She blows steadily into the packet until it's ready to burst.

Waving it – *this is you* – she smacks it hard against the steering wheel – *BANG!* – and I jump.

I stare at her and at the empty, exploded packet. Then – with a huge sigh – I smile and rest my bald head back on the seat as my whole body collapses in relief.

I don't need to explain anything. Scarlett already knows.


By the time the rusty Mini stops again, it's dark. We're parked in front of a block of flats: rectangular grey cement, grubby windows, laundry hanging off balconies.

We sit in easy silence for a few more minutes, quietly watching the world spin.

Hope used to have a gerbil when she was little. We all found it hysterical: how it would run, run, run, run, run on its little squeaky wheel, until it lost its footing and then went round and round before being ejected in a dizzy heap on the floor.

That's kind of how I feel right now: unbalanced, legs still whirring. Trying to work out where I've landed.

My phone *pings*:

I'm so sorry, Eff. It was just a kiss. Please talk to me. :( Nxx

In an instant, my stomach tightens, my throat closes. I stare at Noah's sad-emoji face. Should I call him? I should call him. It was just a kiss, he's sorry and—

My phone *pings* again.

Hi, Faith. You've posted nothing online for twenty-four hours. For maximum follower

satisfaction and algorithm success, it is ideal to post three a day so I have attached these options for you (in this difficult time).
Genevieve.

There's a photo of me wearing a crop top, sucked-in stomach, staring distantly across an ocean (one of my many embarrassing photoshoots). Underneath it says: *With the new day comes new strength and new thoughts – Eleanor Roosevelt #strengthfromwithin.*

Then another: me, smiling affectionately and holding a small, squashy-faced dog in my arms. *Calm mind brings inner strength and self-confidence – the Dalai Lama #positivevibes.*

The third: me on the red carpet, hands on my hips. *Mastering others is strength. Mastering yourself is true power – Lao Tzu #channelyourenergy.*

Umm.

It's been about six hours since the news broke. I haven't even had time to work out how *I* feel yet, let alone how Eleanor Roosevelt might react in a similar situation. Genevieve might as well write *FAITH IS HEARTBROKEN BUT NOT PATHETIC OR HAVING A MELTDOWN*

190

*SHE'S DOING JUST FINE ALSO CHECK OUT HER ABS AND HOW GOOD SHE IS WITH ANIMALS WHAT A CATCH!*

None of which accurately reflects the fact that every time I think about Noah it feels like I'm having my insides raked through with a garden fork. And hearing from him then feels like having them scooped out with a spade.

But rules are rules so—

'What are you doing?' Scarlett frowns and leans across the passenger seat. 'Ugh. What a terrible photo. Why are you staring at the ocean like that?'

'I—'

'And that one's worse. Is that even your dog?'

My cheeks are suddenly hot. 'We borrowed it to make me look . . . sensitive. I'm allergic to them. It gave me hives.'

'Hah. Do you even know who Lao Tzu was?'

My whole face is on fire. 'No.'

'He's the ancient Chinese philosopher who founded Taoism.' She laughs. 'Newsflash, but I strongly suspect the universe will survive without your selfies and misappropriated wisdom. Also, if quoting the Dalai Lama in swirly writing isn't a desperate cry for help, I don't know what is.'

My nose twitches. That's what I thought too, but—

'You don't understand,' I explain as Scarlett starts ringing her eyes with black eyeliner in the rear-view mirror. 'I'm a *Valentine* – everyone is watching to see what I do next . . . I've got millions of followers . . . I have to maintain a positive self-image . . . be a role model . . . show strength in adversity and dignity and . . . and . . .'

Scarlett's staring at me with her eyeliner poised. I've never felt more fake in my entire life. Not even when the make-up artist was spray-painting abs on to my stomach.

'And you always do exactly what you're told to, do you?'

Silence.

'Yes,' I say finally.

'Righty-ho.' Scarlett grins and swings open the car door. 'Let's start there, shall we?'

As a rickety old lift carries us up to nearly the top floor of the block of flats, I can hear loud noise.

Screaming. Shouts. Laughter. Thudding bass. *People.* My heart starts to beat faster and faster, panic steadily rising.

The lift doors squeak slowly open.

Bewildered, I stare at a girl vomiting heartily over the balcony while someone else holds her hair; a boy is sitting on the floor, crying; another is being piggybacked – screeching – down the corridor by a girl with a pink Mohican.

Stiffly, I step backwards into the lift.

*Run.*

'Well,' I say with a polite smile, 'it's been *so* nice to meet you properly, Scarlett. Thank you for coming to collect me – what a pleasure this has been. I've just realised I have an important social engagement on the other side of town that I really must attend.'

I reach out and jab the lift button, hard.

*Jab.*

*Jab.*

*Jab-jab-jab-jab-jab-jab—*

'Stop that,' Scarlett says firmly, pulling me out of the lift again. 'You'll break it and then everyone's going to have to use the stairs.'

I look at the floor. 'Sorry.'

'Wow.' She examines my face. 'You're a proper swan, aren't you? On the surface you're all serenity, but under the water your legs are busy going –' she makes frantic paddling motions with her hands – '*flip flip flip flip FLIP.*'

My mouth falls open in surprise.

'It's just a little get-together,' she says, steering me gently through the front door of a tiny flat. 'No big deal. You've been to parties before, right?'

Blinking, I stare at the chaos.

The flat is dark and hazy, lit only by fairy lights strung across the walls. At least three types of music are blasting, confetti cannons are popping, bottles and plates are scattered everywhere, nearly fifty people are laughing, screaming, shouting, dancing. It's jam-packed, sweaty, hot, pounding.

This isn't a *party*. Parties have a red carpet and guest lists, designer outfits, chandeliers, waiters, vol-au-vents, weird levels of eye contact and inappropriate questions. I automatically begin smoothing myself down, blanking myself out, getting my lines ready. With a smile, I bite the inside of my cheek and—

'Get rid of that fake dimple,' Scarlett says easily. 'You're going to give yourself a mouth ulcer.'

Amazed, I stop smiling.

'OY!' she screams over the music. 'EVERYONE! THIS IS EFF! SHE'S NEW! SAY HELLO!'

'Hey!'

'All right!'

'Nice one!'

The party continues.

'See?' Scarlett grabs a bright pink drink and hands it cheerfully to me. 'Nobody cares here, Valentine. Nobody. Gives. One. Iota. About. Who. You. Are. Or. What. You. Do.' She grins. 'Nice, isn't it?'

## 26

Be. Cool.

*But also warm, Eff; don't tip into Ice Queen territory.*

'I—'

'Loo,' Scarlett announces. 'Must pee.' Without further ado, she disappears.

Swallowing, I edge forward until I'm standing at the doorway of a tiny living room: dark, packed and heaving with sweaty, grinding, shouting strangers. Lights are flashing, music I don't recognise is blasting and there's no rhythm, just a poorly coordinated mass of bobbing, jumping, swaying, gyrating.

'You dance?'

I turn rigidly to a boy with red hair who's pumping his arms enthusiastically like one of those birds on a nature documentary. 'I'm sorry?'

'I said *YOU DANCE*?'

'Yes!' I nod and glance back at the impromptu

dance floor. 'Ballet! I find it very peaceful and grounding. It's a form of exercise I've enjoyed since I was—'

I pause my official answer and look round the room at the loose-limbed, joy-filled crowd.

'No,' I admit, flushing. 'Not really.'

'So dance with me!' The boy grabs my hand and starts swinging it around while he chops invisible bats out of the air with the other. We bop awkwardly for a few minutes while I search for a way to make this weirdly intimate interaction a little less uncomfortable.

'UMM!' I yell over the music, leaning towards him. 'WHAT DID THE DANCING BANK ROBBER SAY?'

'*WHO?*' The boy has his eyes shut now.

'THE ROBBER.'

'HUH?'

'EVERYBODY GET DOWN!'

'WHAT?'

'IT'S A . . .' My cheeks are hot. *Massive joke fail.* 'Never mind! Very nice to meet you! Thank you for the dance! I'm going to find some refreshments! Goodbye!'

The boy nods and beams, eyes still closed.

Stiff as a spoon, I attempt to make my way through the living room towards a kitchen area, tucked behind a bookshelf. 'Excuse me,' I say sweetly, tapping on oblivious shoulders. 'Excuse me, please. I'm sorry, I'm sorry, excuse me, do you mind if I just . . .'

Then I stop with a jolt.

A boy with floppy black hair is sitting on the edge of the sofa, bent over a guitar. He's playing earnestly, even though the other music's far too loud for anyone to hear a single note.

I take a step towards him. '*Noah?*'

The boy looks up and of course it's not: wrong guitar, wrong stance, wrong clothes, wrong party, wrong hair, wrong smile, wrong boy.

But his smile slays me.

*Noah.*

And suddenly that grainy after-show photo is not just a picture any more – it's happening in front of me. The shape of the lips I know so well; the taste of coffee on his breath. Did Noah know her already? Had he been watching the blonde girl through the whole after-show? Had she been watching him?

When she smiled at my boyfriend, did he smile back? How long was I forgotten?

Because there's no such thing as *just a kiss*. If there was, I'd be able to walk across this room right now, put my hands on either side of this stranger's face, pull him towards me and kiss him too.

The cute guitarist waves and nods at the sofa – *come sit with me* – and I take a few steps back, stomach twisting.

*I can't, I can't, I—*

'Watch it!' a girl scowls as I step straight into her, sending prawn crackers flying across the room. 'Oh *nice* one, Famous. That was the last packet.'

I blink and she strops off to a cupboard.

Still reeling, I get on my hands and knees and start picking up crackers, putting them neatly back in the bowl. The floor's a mess, so I gather up some crisps and pop them in there too. Dip has been dropped, so I grab a paper napkin off the table and start wiping that up, then I have a go at a bit of spilt cola in the middle of the—

'Umm. I leave you alone for, like, six minutes and you're on the floor doing what exactly?'

199

I look up at Scarlett. 'Cleaning.'

'Yeah, I can see that.' She folds her arms. 'I clearly meant *why*.'

I pause with the balled-up napkin in my hand.

'I made a mess,' I say slowly. 'So I cleaned it up. Then there was . . . a bit more mess, so I . . . cleaned that up too.' My cheeks are getting hot. 'Honestly, a few seconds now will stop it from getting trampled into the carpet for the poor host to deal with in the morning. It just makes sense.'

'So . . . it's not even *your* mess.' Scarlett rolls her eyes. 'You are not responsible for everything, Faith Valentine.'

'I know that but—'

'You clearly don't. Stop finding ways to avoid having actual fun.'

I flinch. 'Just a few more . . .'

'Up. Now.'

'I'll just—'

'*Now.*' Frowning, Scarlett picks up a bottle of barbecue sauce and squeezes it hard on to the floor next to me. 'So what? You gonna clean my mess up too?'

I stare at the brown blob.

'What about this one?' She squirts bright yellow mustard next to it. 'This one?' Mayonnaise. 'What about *this* one?' Bright red ketchup. 'Hmm? Gonna scrub, scrub, scrub all night because I feel like being a pain in the butt?'

Confusion lurches in me.

*Why?* Why would anyone do this? It's inconsiderate, it's thoughtless, it's senseless, it's—

A big gob of ketchup gets flicked at my head.

I stand up.

'What are you *doing*?'

'I.' Scarlett flicks at me again. 'Am. Showing. You.' Mayonnaise. 'That consequences.' Ketchup. 'Are for tomorrow.'

I wipe sticky, lukewarm condiments off my face and look down: my hoodie is a cross between a hot dog and a Jackson Pollock.

'Life,' Scarlett beams, 'is for *today*.'

Something is starting to happen in my chest, a tug and a sudden loosening.

I stare at her. '*Consequences are for tomorrow?*' I say slowly, wiping my cheeks. '*Life is for today?* I've never heard a cheesier quote in my entire life. Forget Instagram, wanna embroider that on a pillow?'

Scarlett opens her mouth.

'How about a fridge magnet?' I pick up the bottle of ketchup and flick sauce at her. 'Or a tea towel?' Mustard. 'What about a bumper sticker or a phone case?' Mayo. 'It would look *really* good in swirly writing, maybe with pink butterflies circling it, flowers, maybe a—'

We're both laughing now.

'Oh, shut it, Valentine,' Scarlett snorts, punching my shoulder. 'I'm feeling the burn.'

I punch her back. 'That'll be the mustard.'

And whatever it was that was wound tight inside me completely unravels and starts to float away.

'Yo, Letty!' A very tall guy walks past and high-fives her. 'Thanks for the party! Same Friday next month?'

'Abso-freaking-lutely,' she grins.

I abruptly stop laughing.

'*Wait.*' The entire flat is in chaos. Glasses and plates are on the floor – chipped or smashed – food is being trodden into the carpets, chairs are broken, sofas jumped on, lights flickering, neighbours furiously knocking. 'Scarlett, this is *your* flat?'

I look at the floor, soaked in various condiments. Guilt rushes through me.

'Oh.' Scarlett shrugs nonchalantly. 'Yeah. I mean, if I'm going to embroider a cushion with a life motto, I'd better be able to live it, right?'

'Or sit on it,' I say without thinking.

'Touché, Faith Valentine,' she laughs brightly, linking her arm through mine. 'Now let's go get messy.'

## 27

'Where have *you* been?'

It's 4am by the time I finally climb back through my bedroom window. Normally at this hour, I'd either be staring at the ceiling, clawing through another nightmare, or getting ready to go for an incredibly long dawn run.

Weirdly, I don't feel the impulse to do any of that now.

'Hmm?' I flop in exhaustion on my bed. 'What?'

Mercy is sitting cross-legged in the middle of my rug, like an indignant Aladdin. 'You've been *out.*' She looks at her watch. 'Where did you go?'

'Oh.' I rub my face tiredly. 'I just went for a quick . . . night jog.'

Mer scowls. 'Through a hot-dog stand?'

'Mmm-hmm.' In fairness, I am sticking to the

duvet with a faint *pfffft* sound. 'Tripped over a rubbish bag in the park.'

Then I close my eyes. Within seconds, I can feel my sister's warm breath on my face as she sniffs me all over like a suspicious cat.

'You *stink*,' she points out, disgusted. 'And what happened to your mirror? Did a bird fly in and smash it or something? I mean, are you . . .' Mercy pauses. 'Like. Uh.' Another pause. 'OK and stuff?'

I open one eye in amazement. *Did Mercy Valentine just ask me if I'm OK? I've been trying to teach her that question for years.*

'Yes. I'm OK.'

Interesting that it doesn't occur to my sister that I might have broken my mirror on purpose. In her mind, I am nothing but the passive victim of an errant pigeon.

Sleep sweeps over me in waves, so I tiredly pull my filthy hoodie off and fling it across the room. There's a flash of guilt – *pick it up, Faith! Fold it nicely! That's no way to treat your belongings!* – before I firmly roll towards the wall.

*Consequences are for tomorrow.*
*Life is for today.*

I mean, it's already *tomorrow*, but there's no need to be so literal.

'Did you just throw your—' My sister sucks in her breath. 'Holy guac, Eff. What have you done to your *head*?'

I shrug into my pillow. 'Felt like a new look.'

'Right.' A sharp, shocked laugh. 'Sure. *A new look*. I can't help noticing that it's very similar to the haircut your loser, cheating ex-boyfriend has. Do you have *any* thoughts of your own, Faith?'

Suddenly I'm not that tired. I sit up in bed and stare hard at my sister. Firstly, Noah is *not* my ex – it's been one day. I have no idea what to do about the situation yet. Secondly, does she really think I'm pitiful enough to shave my hair off for a *boy*?

'Excuse me?'

'You're copying him, right? To win him back.' She scowls. 'It's kind of pathetic, Faith. No offence.'

As if *no offence* nullifies everything rude that goes before it, instead of highlighting it.

Something inside me snaps.

'Get out, Mercy.'

'But—'

'*Get out of my bedroom.*'

My sister is staring at me as another crackling wave of anger whips through my body. Eyeliner all over my white pillows, hairs all over my carpet, stinky sweat seeping into my duvet, snoring, cold feet on my legs at 4am, whimpering in her sleep, every single speck of my privacy completely invaded on a nightly basis.

It's like having a really ungrateful stray dog living with me and *I don't even like dogs*.

'Eff,' Mercy says, holding her hands out in surprise. 'Maybe I'm wrong. I didn't *necessarily* mean that—'

'OUT!' I shout, jumping up. 'GET. OUT!'

With a burst of energy, I grab my sister under each armpit and start dragging her bodily towards the door. It's surprisingly easy. Who knew all that weightlifting and downward dogging would come in handy for something other than Instagram?

'Whoa. Faith.' Mercy's so shocked she's gone into rag-doll mode and is just letting herself be pulled across the floorboards. 'Come on, dude. This is mad. *All* I meant was—'

I chuck my sister into the hallway so hard she lands on her bottom with an *oof*.

'GO. AWAY.'

'But—' Blink. Blink. 'Where am I going to sleep?'

'YOU HAVE YOUR OWN BEDROOM, MERCY. OR YOU CAN SLEEP IN THE HALLWAY. UNDER THE STAIRS. HANGING UPSIDE DOWN FROM THE RAFTERS LIKE A BAT. I LITERALLY DON'T CARE – JUST GIVE ME SOME SPACE!'

I slam the door between us and lock it.

*Click.*

Then I curl up in my empty, silent bed and fall deeply asleep.

## 28

## HAVE A LITTLE FAITH!

Don't look so sad, Faith! (Pictured left, with bold new haircut.) Competition is hotting up for the most eligible bachelorette in town. Dylan Harris - star of *Wolfgang* and an old friend of the family - told us EXCLUSIVELY that he has always had a 'special connection' with Faith and it 'might finally be their time'. Cheating ex, Noah Anthony, declares that he 'won't give her up without a fight'.

Who will win? Find out here first!

*BEEP.*

*Beep-beep-beep-beep-beep-beep—*

'SHOWER, VALENTINE!' Scarlett yells as I poke my head out of my bedroom window in confusion the next morning. 'THEN COME DOWN! WE'RE GOING FOR A DRIVE!'

She beeps again for no apparent reason.

*BEEP.*

This time, the battered orange Mini has somehow ended up parked halfway across our patio, back wheels ripping up the lawn. I look at my watch: it's not even 10am yet, which means I've had less than six hours of sleep. For me, that's actually pretty good.

'*WHERE?*' I shout back.

'DOES IT MATTER?' she bellows.

I realise that, for the first time in many months, I don't actually have anything to do or anybody to see today. So I jump in the shower and wash all the sticky remnants of last night's party off.

Then I climb carefully back down the fire escape. Sure, I could use the stairs, but I don't want to run into Mercy. She might push me down them.

'Here,' Scarlett says, chomping on a cereal bar as I push yet another wave of snack detritus off the passenger seat and climb into her car. 'Nutrition.'

She hands me a cup of what is basically melted strawberry ice cream with a straw.

'Thanks,' I say, taking it anyway.

'Hold on to your horses,' she instructs me chirpily. 'Or ponies. Unicorns. Whatever animals you rich people use as transport.'

Scarlett Bell turns upbeat music on at full blast. And we screech out of the driveway, taking a sharp left and zooming across the outskirts of London until the grey melts and everything becomes green and rolling and vivid. I can feel my spirits lifting again.

As we sing and bop our heads – as I slurp on my milkshake and the warm sunshine bakes our cheeks – I start to feel . . . a little bit *different*.

Light, giddy, directionless.

'You know,' I say as the scenery turns into something out of a Merchant Ivory film. *Slurp*. 'I didn't take you for a country bumpkin.'

'Oh, I'm not.' Scarlett shakes her head. 'Londonite to the core. But I like to drive past a tree every now and then. Reminds me of how much I deeply adore concrete. Chop 'em all down, I say.'

I laugh – *slurp* – and the poor little car starts to struggle up a steep hill.

My phone *pings*:

First morning in a year without my wake-up
text. I miss you. :( N

I abruptly put my milkshake down.

'Who is it?' Scarlett glances across as the Mini
starts to race with relief down the other side of the
hill. 'You look like somebody just jammed a knitting
needle up your nostril and twisted it clockwise.'

'Noah,' I say, looking down as my phone *pings*
again.

'Ah.'

My heart is broken. I can't do any of this
without you. Please talk to me. :'( N

We're at full sob-face emoji now and my stomach
twists.

'I'm going to have to call him,' I say quietly,
turning the jaunty music low until it's almost
inaudible. 'Sorry.'

Then I hover over Noah's number in my phone
for a few seconds, knowing exactly how this
conversation is going to go. *He can't believe he did
it, he's a mess, it was an accident, can we please meet*

*to talk about it?* To which I'll end up replying: *I miss you too, I understand, everyone makes mistakes, of course we can, see you in an hour.*

Bingo. Back together, relationship on track again. Which is good, right? So why does tapping the call button feel so hard I need two hands and some kind of sky-crane?

'You don't *have to* do anything,' Scarlett says as I snatch up my milkshake so I can chew aggressively on the straw. 'You know that, right?'

'Sure,' I nod, still chewing. 'But I need to—'

'*Need to* is the same as *have to*, Eff.'

'I know that.' I continue to stare at Noah's name on my phone. 'It's just . . . I can't handle the thought of him sitting there on his own, feeling sad and lonely, reaching out to me for help, and me . . .'

'Not being at his beck and call?'

'No, it's not like that.' I bend the top of the straw over. 'Being the . . . cause of his unhappiness.'

Scarlett snorts. 'You realise he caused his *own* misery, right? Because, unless you got that blonde girl and physically Sellotaped her to his lips while he was unconscious, you're not responsible for this mess, either.'

213

I flinch slightly. 'No, but—'

'How do *you* feel, Eff?' We're driving through woods now and filtered sunlight is flickering across our faces. 'Screw what Noah wants for a hot minute. What do *you* want?'

For a brief moment, I close my eyes – trying to picture the future with all the different emotions battling inside me.

It's a big, noisy muddle.

'I don't know,' I admit. 'Time to work it all out?'

'Then *ask for it.*'

What – I could just . . . do that? I chew on my straw for a few more minutes, then send:

I miss you too, but I just need a bit of time and space to sort my head out, please. Thank you. Fx

One second later, my phone rings:

**INCOMING CALL: Noah**

My stomach lurches. I cancel it; it starts again immediately—

214

**INCOMING CALL: Noah**

*Cancel.* Again—

**INCOMING CALL: Noah**

*Cancel.* And again—

**INCOMING CALL: Noah**

I answer the call.

'Hello?' My throat is tight. Clearly, we're having this conversation whether I'm ready to or not. 'Noah, I—'

The car screeches to a halt; my phone disappears. 'What—?'

'You've asked once,' Scarlett says as she switches my mobile off and sits on it. 'You shouldn't have to ask twice.'

She turns the music up full blast.

'Now sit back, Valentine, and enjoy going absolutely nowhere.'

29

Why did the tree go to the dentist?

To get a root canal.

Scarlett arrives again the next day. And the day after that.

Every morning, I hop into her orange Mini and am offered junk food, then we turn the music up as high as it will go and race away together: driving, eating, singing, talking, laughing.

By the time she zooms up the driveway on the fourth day, smashes into a five-tiered plant pot and beeps seven times, I can't believe I ever found her intimidating.

For the first time in as long as I can remember, it feels like I've actually escaped my life. And it is *glorious*.

*Beep. Beep. Beepbeepbeepbeep—*

'I'M COMING!' I yell cheerfully, sticking my head out and waving at her. 'KEEP YOUR KNICKERS—'

'Oooh!' There's an excitable voice behind me. 'Are we climbing out of windows now, Eff? *So* cinematic! You know, I don't have a fire escape, but I think I could *totally* get out on the ledge and hop across if I work on my jumping skills.'

I pause in horror, one foot on my windowsill.

Hope's standing in the doorway – optimism lighting up her heart-shaped face – and I'm suddenly cold all over. I cannot be responsible for my little sister trying to hop across a third-storey roof in an attempt to be exactly like me.

Consequences might be for tomorrow, but mine cannot be Po splatted on the driveway.

'I'm not climbing out!' I laugh, quickly pulling back in. 'That's *very* dangerous, Hope. *Promise* me you'll never, ever climb out of your window, OK? I was just . . . checking. To. See. If . . . it's raining.'

Rain is pelting the window like bullets. I'm literally the worst actress on the planet.

217

'It is.' Po nods guilelessly. 'That's what all the water is!'

Then she plops on to the bed and stares round my room with her usual expression of awe. 'I haven't seen you in *days*, Eff,' she says breathlessly, 'and I've got *so* much to tell you. Ben's been teaching me how to play Scrabble! Except he lets me make up words because he says it's my specialility.'

I laugh. 'Good for Ben.'

'Do you want to see him? I know he's *dying* to spend some time with you.'

For the love of—

'I'm a bit busy, Po. Can you keep him entertained for me while I'm out?'

'Yes.' She nods gravely. 'I am highly entertaining. That's what Ben says anyway. Also, Effie, please, please, *please* can I touch your head? It's *all* over the papers and I'm your sister and I haven't even touched it yet! *Please?*'

With a small smile, I take my cream beanie off.

The paps caught a photo of my bald head two days ago and it's now being discussed in depth across the national media. Nobody can decide if

I'm heartbroken, or if I've had a nervous breakdown, or I'm making a feminist statement, or I'm trying to get attention, or I'm just trialling a brave new military look.

Either way, everyone has an opinion. Plus, strangers have started randomly touching my head without asking first.

'Oh my goodness!' Po squeaks, running her hands over my scalp like it's a magic crystal ball. 'So cool! The mags are saying you're even *more beautiful* without your hair and I agree – you've totally started a trend!'

'Thanks, baby.' I kiss her cheek. 'Also, I can run, like, fifteen per cent faster now. Less air resistance.'

My sister's eyes widen. '*Really?*' She pulls on her curly ponytail and grabs a pair of scissors from my desk. 'So do I—'

'*No.*' I take the scissors out of her hands and yank my beanie firmly back on. 'Hope, leave your lovely hair alone.'

'OK,' she sighs dramatically as I grab my bag and head for the door. 'Celery.'

I pause. 'I'm sorry?'

'*Celery.*' My sister rolls her eyes and says patiently, 'It's what people say when they're resigned to

219

something really unfortunate, because nobody really likes celery, but we all have to eat it anyway.'

A bubble of laughter pops in my throat.

'You mean *c'est la vie*, sweetheart. It's French for *that's life*. But keep using *celery* – I love it nearly as much as I love you. Have fun entertaining Ben today, OK?'

Blowing her a kiss, I run down the stairs in a way that can be easily copied without causing my sister bodily harm.

My phone *pings*.

Hey. What do I have to do? Tell me. :( :(
Nxx

With a sharp twist of the stomach, I reply:

I need a bit more time. Sorry. Fxx

I'm hurting too – of course I am – but I still don't know quite how I feel or what I want to say to him.

My phone buzzes again.

Please don't go out with Dylan Harris. :(

You know what? Maybe I do.

Please don't kiss other girls. Oh, whoops. Too late.

Crossly, I jam my phone firmly into my pocket.
*Life is for today.*

'Heya, Letty!' I call out, swinging open the front door. 'So which way do you want to head this time? I was thinking we could hit the motorway, drive north and—'

My stomach lurches: a different car is coming up the driveway. Silver. Big.

What day is it? Tell me it's not Wednesday. It's totally Wednesday, isn't it?

*No, no, no, no, no—*

'Quick!' Slamming the front door behind me, I run through the pelting rain as fast as I can and jump into Scarlett's passenger seat. 'Go! Go! Drive! Drive!'

'Wow,' she grins, reaching for the gearstick. 'I feel like your getaway driver. Do we get to split the cash you've just nicked?'

*What is taking so long?*

'DRIVE!' I yell as she fiddles with the ignition ('this old banger never starts first time round, hang on, there's a knack to it, just gotta—'). 'SCARLETT, DRIVE AWAY RIGHT NOW! GO! GO! GO!'

It's too late. Genevieve has stepped out of the limo and is standing calmly behind the Mini so we can't go anywhere. The rain is hammering down and she's soaking wet, motionless and unblinking – like something out of a horror movie.

'RUN HER OVER!' I yell. 'No. Don't do that. Just—'

'Faith?' Genevieve calls out through the rain. 'I'll need you to come with me.'

## 30

What do you call bears without ears?

B.

Even a bear joke can't save me now.

'Hi, Genevieve,' I say guardedly as the limo glides away with me inside it, yet again. 'So . . . how are you?' As if I didn't just yell *RUN HER OVER* at the top of my voice.

'Fine, thanks.' My grandmother's assistant is in full old-lady attire: corduroy pencil skirt, frilly blouse, patterned shawl with tasselled fringe wrapped round her shoulders. It all looks brand new. Where is she even *buying* this stuff?

'Good.' I glance over my shoulder. 'Good.'

Scarlett is driving behind us, munching on a

packet of biscuits. She waves chirpily – apparently steering with her knees – and holds a thumb and little finger up to her face: *call me*.

Nodding, I grimace and turn back. So much for my freedom. My glorious holiday from reality is very much over now apparently.

'So, umm.' I swallow. 'Where's Grandma? Is she . . . OK?'

'Your grandmother won't be able to give you a lesson today, Faith. She's been called away to discuss charitable events for next year.'

I relax with a wave of intense relief back into the seat. Then I sit up sharply again. *Ouch.*

'What the—' I pull a gold necklace with a sharp, pointed pendant away from my lower spine and stare at it in bemusement.

'Gifts,' Genevieve says in a monotone. 'Your agency forwarded them. They've been inundated with offers of romance over the last few days. Obviously, I've already weaned out the no-hopers.'

I look in the vast tote bag the necklace fell out of. Inside is a creepy Steiff teddy bear, a platinum watch, a box of pastel-coloured macaroons, an amethyst bracelet, a bottle of perfume costing hundreds (they've left the price on) and a bunch of chocolates, flowers, etc. etc.

'The no-hopers?' I repeat in a faint voice.

'Unsuitable candidates. Unattractive guys with no profile. The ones who send biscuits with gluten in them despite the risk of bloating, you know? Dame Sylvia has approved the shortlist.'

The gold scrapbook gets opened to a new page. On the right are photos – shiny, handsome boys – and on the left their age, background, career, interest they've shown.

I stare in horror.

One guy told the *Sun* I'm 'blisteringly hot'; another has publicly announced he's 'gagging for his chance'. I'm so grossed out I can't read any further.

'But –' I look up, confusion mounting – 'Noah's still my boyfriend, Genevieve. Whatever happens, I'm not ready to—'

'The world can't see you as a walkover, Faith. If you don't make it look like you've moved on, your reputation will forever be: Faith Valentine – Emotional, Discarded and Weak.'

I open my mouth. 'Except I *haven't* moved o—'

'On which topic, I notice you haven't posted anything yourself online for nearly FIVE DAYS now.' She holds up her mobile. 'You cannot disappear. Silence speaks louder than words and people read between the lines – *especially* if there's nothing there to read. Thank your lucky stars you've got me.'

Genevieve presses SEND and my phone *pings*.

A photoshopped picture of me pops up: at sunrise, lying on our swing-chair in the garden in a white lace jumpsuit, my arm stretched behind my head. I remember this shoot – Max said I looked like a Victorian invalid after a very large Sunday lunch.

I look up. 'But—'

'I'm going with: *If you can't handle me at my worst, then you sure as hell don't deserve me at my best.* Positive yet sassy. Empowered. Respectful of the pain you're in.'

My nose suddenly twitches. If Scarlett thought a Dalai Lama quote was the last step before a full-blown public meltdown, reciting Marilyn Monroe must be the final death rattle.

'But—'

'This isn't a negotiation, Faith.' Genevieve narrows

226

her eyes. 'Your grandmother made her wishes extremely clear. It's my job to ensure you follow them.'

'Yes,' I say, looking down. 'OK.'

Without further ado, I post the photo and quote across all platforms. Seconds later—

You are an INSPERATION! Xxx

Head up, girl! You can do SO much better!!!!!

OMG where is that chair from I love it

There's always someone with an eye on the soft furnishings.

'I printed you a copy of the Boy List,' Genevieve continues, holding out a piece of paper. 'See what you think in your own time.'

Short pause.

'As long as that time is by tomorrow morning,' she adds, tapping on her phone again. 'We've got to keep the momentum going or the media will just make up their own version of events.'

I stare at the list, feeling abruptly sick. Ed, Elijah,

Timothy, Jim, Toby, Jeremy, Dylan, Robert – it's like being at a pick 'n' mix, except instead of sweets I've been handed a weird mixture of potential boyfriends, all gummy and stuck together.

And I didn't choose *any* of them.

The limousine stops.

'Umm.' I blink through the dark window at a pretty London square: formal trees and ornate townhouses with stone steps leading up to them. 'I don't want to be rude or anything –' *RUN HER OVER* – 'but if there's no class with Grandma . . . what am I doing here?'

I'd assumed I was in the back of the car for a comprehensive wrist-slapping, but it looks like we've arrived somewhere specific. This better not be some random boy's house.

'As you know –' Genevieve smooths her corduroy skirt with a *vtttt* sound – 'your grandmother has *many* contacts in the film industry. Close personal friendships, developed over decades, that have resulted in discretion of the highest order.'

Oh. *Ohhhhh.* I'm starting to see where this might be going.

'It has been fed back to her that you may need

. . . extra assistance. A small amount of encouragement beyond that which she currently has time to provide.'

I close my eyes briefly. In fairness, I'm lucky I wasn't dragged out of the last audition by my hair.

'She knows I suck at acting, huh?'

Genevieve beams, and, for the first time in the full year I've known her, she actually looks her age.

'Oh, Faith.' She nods smugly. 'She knows you suck *big-time*.'

## 31

I know where we are now.

For a brief second, I consider resisting – jumping out of the car and legging it across Soho – but why bother? If anybody needs professional help, it's me.

'The four-day acting workshop started yesterday,' Genevieve explains as the chauffeur opens the limo door. 'But your grandmother says it doesn't matter if you arrive a day late. Everyone obviously knows who you are already.'

I flinch. 'Lovely. Thank you.'

Anxiously, I say a polite goodbye, climb out and make my way to yet another reception desk. It's quiet, but through closed doors you can hear shouting, screaming, laughing, crying. Anywhere else that would be a cause for concern.

'Hello, Faith,' the receptionist says as I open my

mouth. 'Seven B. Third floor, second to the right. Go in quietly, please. Class has begun.'

As I climb the stairs, I'm starting to itch all over. By the time I reach the classroom, my throat has closed, my forehead is damp, my legs are shaky and my eyes are burning.

Could I be *allergic* to the arts? Maybe it's like an extreme version of hay fever – I'm so repelled by anything creative that simply being in this building is causing my entire body to break down.

Gently, I push open the door. Outstretched on the floor are eight people roughly my age – flat on their backs, eyes closed, arms by their sides. For a second, it looks like the end of a Shakespearean tragedy, until I realise they're all humming quietly.

'*Mmmmmmmmmmmmmmmm.*'

'Come in!' The teacher beckons me over with a whisper-shout. He's almost entirely silver: salt-and-pepper hair and beard, grey jumper, charcoal trousers, like a thespian wizard. 'Find a space! No talking!'

I blink at the room. *What* space?

Taking my trainers off, I tiptoe in socks through the outstretched humans. 'Excuse me,' I whisper.

'Sorry. Sorry, just going to put my foot— God, sorry, was that your finger?'

The teacher frowns, so I quickly lie down in the corner in a bent L-shape, close my eyes and start to obediently *mmmmmmmmmmmmm.*

'Ooooooooooooooooooooo,' the teacher announces loudly.

'*Ooooooooooooooooooooooooooooo,*' says the class.

'Eeeeeeeeeeeeeeeeeeeeeeeeeeeeeeeeeeeeeeeeee.'

'*Eeeeeeeeeeeeeeeeeeeeeeee.*'

'Aaaaaahhhhhhhhhhhhhhhhhhhhhhhhhhhhhhhh.'

'*Aaaaaahhhhhhhhhhhhhhhh.*'

'Go with the flow. Feel the sound change as it moves to different parts of your body. Each sound produces a new vibration – explore how you feel in each state.'

'*Mmmmmmmmmmm – oooooooooooo – eeeeeeeee—*'

Opening my eyes, I make an executive decision to sit out this nonsense and wait until the actual acting class starts. I already do yoga: there's only so much hippy rubbish one person can take.

'Right!' There's a loud clap. 'Up! Walk round the room! Make eye contact! You're walking down a road! The sun is out!'

232

Bouncing to my feet, I obediently start walking in random semicircles. My classmates lock eyes with me one by one and blink, startled – *What the hell is Faith Valentine doing here?* – so I blush and stare at the floor.

'It's raining! Thunder! Lightning!'

My peers immediately start running, holding imaginary coats over their heads, peering up at the skies, flinching at fictional rumbles. I copy them, even though all I can hear is a clunking generator outside.

'You're going somewhere you don't want to be! You're wasting time! You're trying to be late!'

Everyone slows down, so I do the same.

'It's boiling hot!'

They all start peeling off jumpers, fanning themselves, wiping their brows. I do too.

'You have eyes made of black marbles!'

Squinting, fumbling, bumping into things.

'Now make a circle!'

I quickly loop my arms over my head, crouch down and try to make myself as circular as possible. Somebody snorts and I glance up – everyone else is standing in a loose circle round the teacher, staring at me.

233

*For the love of—*

Feeling humiliated, I stand up and join them.

'Now!' The teacher surveys us carefully. 'Grab a chair! When I say GO, I want you to tell your chair you want a cup of coffee. And . . . GO!'

Yup. I've definitely missed something.

'I want a cup of coffee,' a blonde girl with IVY on her nametag tells her chair.

'I *want* a cup of *coffee*,' ZACH demands.

'*I want a cup of coffee!*' A tall brunette – ZOE – is furious. '*Give me a cup of coffee!*'

Blinking, I glance at the teacher.

'Is there a problem?' He wanders over with a broad, friendly smile. 'Would you prefer to ask the chair for tea instead?'

'No, no. Coffee's . . . fine. It's just . . .' How do I put this politely? 'I think, sir, I . . . might be in the wrong class.'

I'm finding it hard to believe that Dame Sylvia Valentine – or my mother, for that matter – has *ever* asked a chair for a hot beverage. This is like an underground Starbucks training programme.

'Acting for Film and TV.' The teacher nods easily. 'What is it that's bothering you exactly?'

I glance round the room.

'I WANT A CUP OF COFFEE!'

'I want a cup of . . . coffee?'

'WHERE IS MY FLAMING CUP OF COFFEE?' Zoe has lost it. 'WHERE IS IT? WHERE? GIVE IT TO ME!'

'Umm.' I swallow. 'It just feels a bit . . . silly.'

The teacher laughs. 'Of course it does,' he agrees. 'And that's *exactly* why we're doing it.'

## 32

*I want a cup of coffee.*

For the next hour, I bellow, scream, whisper and plead to no avail. I just don't sound like a real person. I'm too flat, too loud, too squeaky, too breathy, too deep, too high. The sentence speeds up, slows down, surges, lifts, breaks. The six words keep shifting and wriggling until they don't mean anything at all.

By lunchtime, I'm so frustrated I just want to rip the chair's legs off. It's *my* voice; why can't I control it?

'Right!' The drama teacher – his name is Mr Hamilton – claps his hands. 'Good! Take a break, everyone.' He grins. 'There's a drinks machine at the end of the corridor.'

I look up blearily. I'd actually forgotten there was anyone else in the room. I'm starting to understand why Mum was always so absent-minded during filming.

Nervously, I turn to face my classmates. All eight immediately head towards the sofas and sit there: whispering, eating crisps, covertly staring at me and pretending not to. For actors-in-training, a lot of them are surprisingly bad at it.

Awkwardly, I pull out my phone. *Ping*. Google alert.

> 'Faith Valentine is my dream girl!' says Dylan
> H—

'Hey, newbie.' Ivy waves at me, then gestures *shhhh* at the rest of the group. 'Why don't you come and sit with us?' She elbows a guy in orange jeans. 'Move over, dingbat.'

'It's Diego,' he mumbles, pointing at his chest. 'I am *wearing* a *nametag*.' But he shuffles over so there's a tiny space.

Embarrassed, I put my phone back in my pocket, smile and take the half-seat, perching stiffly on the edge of the sofa like a Harrods mannequin.

Silence.

237

I mean, of course *silence*: I was clearly the topic of conversation before I sat down, and my awkwardness would have ruined it even if I wasn't.

'Uh,' soft-spoken Mia starts. 'How—'

'*Soooooooooo*—' Theo in glasses and a crumpled denim shirt leans towards me. 'You *are* you-know-who, right? Zach thinks it *can't* be you, but then Jem said it *definitely* was, and I'm, like, divided.'

'She's not *quite* hot enough,' blond Zach explains. 'I mean –' he turns to me – 'not being rude – you're obviously hot and stuff – but your boobs are tiny.'

I smile: *not being rude*—

'Oh, mate, you are so deluded. You couldn't score this girl in a million years, regardless of who she is.' Curly-haired Jemima shakes her head. 'And it *is* her. No question. *Look.*'

There's a short silence while she passes her phone round. Everyone looks at the screen.

Then at me.

Then at the screen again.

Then at me.

'*Soooooo* –' Zoe suddenly scooches over so she can examine my face more closely – 'seriously, what the heck are you doing in this am-dram class? It's like watching Angelina Jolie play the dog in a school panto.'

'*WHO!*' Rafe – in brown vintage suede – suddenly explodes. 'WHO IS SHE? I DO NOT RECOGNISE THIS GIRL.'

'You don't recognise *Faith Valentine*?'

'WHO?'

'Faith *Valentine*. Rafe, mate, if you wanna be an actor, you're going to have to put down the *New Yorker* once in a while and pick up a tabloid. It's straight-up *weird* you don't recognise her. You don't live at the bottom of the ocean.'

They all turn to stare at me again with wide eyes. My entire face is on fire.

'Ah.' I swallow and pull off my beanie. 'You can call me Effie.'

'I *knew it*!' Jemima jumps up and punches the air. '*Yesssss*. In your *face*, Zachary. You blew that one. She's newly single and you have totally screwed up your shot.'

'Darn.' Zach scratches his head and frowns at my chest. 'Sorry. Photoshop and Wonderbras and stuff. It's very confusing.'

'This is *sooo* cool,' Zoe says, still examining my face.

239

'I've been following the Valentines for *years*. How's Mercy? How's your mum? And how's *Max*?' She turns to the group with a sigh. 'Her brother is an actual god. Picture *her* but *taller* and *older* and *a boy*.'

'And an idiot,' I add without thinking.

They all laugh.

'Is this research for some undercover role?' Mia frowns. 'Are you filming a movie about an acting class . . .' She glances around and lowers her voice. 'Are we being *filmed right now*?'

Zach smooths back his hair.

There's a long, uncomfortable silence while they all stare at me, waiting for my words of wisdom and experience.

Smile: *on*. Dimple: *go*.

'Well,' I say, opening my hands in a modest gesture, 'I guess I'm here for the same reason as you guys. When you really love acting, there are no limits to learning the craft. There is no point at which the actor should stop exploring. Playing. Investigating. After all, are we not eternal students of this beautiful thing we call *life*?'

I want to puke down the front of my Moschino sweatshirt. Grandma would be so proud.

'Sure.' Zoe nods, clearly disappointed. 'Absolutely. Yeah, like, *totally* get that. Cool. Deep and stuff.'

Another silence.

'I mean, I'm here because I want to find an agent and get a big movie role and score really hot women for the rest of my life,' Zach says, frowning. 'Until I'm ancient and grey-haired and yet I *still* manage to score them, for reasons known only to their therapists.'

'I'm here because I got a voucher,' Jemima offers.

'I'm here because I need a proper audition tape for RADA,' Diego adds. 'So far all I've done is sit in the café in *Corrie*.'

'Me too!' Ivy laughs. 'Students' Union in *Hollyoaks*.'

'*Eastenders* for me.' Theo shrugs. 'T-shirt market stall.'

'My parents thought this would be a good way to make me feel more comfortable in front of strangers,' Mia admits softly.

'I'm a very *gifted* actor.' Rafe crosses his arms and scowls. 'I'm waiting for *somebody relevant* to notice.'

Everyone laughs, but I don't think they were supposed to.

'Great!' I smile and – for some unknown reason

– clap a few times. 'Well, I'm *sure* it will totally happen for all of you! Good luck!'

They really hate me now, don't they? Yeah, I hate me too.

'Right!' Mr Hamilton walks into the class. 'For our next exercise, I want you to partner up and repeat the word *rabbit* to each other. That's it. Just the word *rabbit*. Find a way to create a dialogue.'

Within seconds, everyone else has paired up.

*So weird* that nobody picked me. Why doesn't anyone want to work with the snotty rich girl who just clapped at their dreams like a patronising seal? I stare at the floor.

'Rabbit,' Mr Hamilton says to me. 'Rabbit?'

'Rabbit.' I nod in reply, with no idea how to say it at all.

## 33

What kind of flower grows on your face?

Tulips.

Somebody has done their research.

As I open the front door of the Valentine mansion a few hours later, there are *yellow roses* everywhere – in huge vases crowding the entrance hall, bouquets on the antique cabinets, scattered all the way up the stairs to my room. I cannot move for yellow roses.

Shame my favourite flower is actually the angel's trumpet: a beautiful, cream, bell-shaped flower so poisonous it can suffocate, paralyse and ultimately kill you.

Apparently, that was an 'unsuitable answer' for *Vanity Fair*.

'What—'

'Every hour,' Mercy says, walking out of the kitchen in a black jumpsuit paired with matt-black lipstick. She looks like she's been eating coal very carefully. 'A bunch of twelve has been turning up every single hour, on the hour, all day. That's a rose every ten minutes, in case the maths escapes you.'

'Five,' I say quietly, staring at the hallway. 'Every five minutes, Mercy. In case telling the time escapes you.'

'Whatever. Mum zombied downstairs and thought they were for her. She was going to chuck them all in the bin. You're lucky I was here or you wouldn't be getting any of this rubbish.'

'Cheers for being such a hero.'

We both stand in silence for a few minutes. Yesterday's fight appears to be temporarily paused. We're united by the fact that the entire house smells like it should be put in a bowl and left on top of a toilet cistern.

'*Yellow roses*,' my sister snipes. 'What an *original ex-boyfriend* you have, Eff. Noah literally doesn't know you at all.'

244

'Boyfriend,' I correct, picking up a flower and staring at it. It's quite pretty, I guess. If you're into killing things you like, then watching them slowly shrivel in a foreign environment. 'We haven't broken up. I'm just giving myself a bit of space to work things out.'

But my heart has started beating suspiciously fast.

*These are from Noah?*

God, he must be *really* hurting to make such a grand gesture. Should I call him? I should call him. I don't want to – I still need more time – but, if I don't, isn't that . . . cruel? Churlish? Ungrateful?

And what if I don't and he—

Hang on.

> I'm not a photographer but I can picture you and me together.
> Dinner?
> Dylan Harris
> (TV star, currently on Netflix) xx

Confused, I pick up another little paper tag.

245

> Is it hot in here or is it just
> us? Call me.
> Dylan Harris
> (TV star, currently on Netflix) xx

And another:

> My parents told me to follow
> my dreams. You're one of them!
> Dylan Harris
> (TV star, currently on Netflix)

On the reverse side of each tag:

> These flowers are from Budding
> Romance! Your One-stop Shop
> for Love and Apology Needs! x

I laugh so loudly, Mercy jumps.

'What the—'

'It's not Noah.' Relieved, I go and sit on the

bottom stair so I can giggle a bit harder. 'It's some random dude from Genevieve's Boy List. Look.'

My sister reads the tags.

'Wow. W-o-w.' Then Mer starts laughing too – a rapid gunfire noise – and plumps down next to me. 'Who the hell does Tesco Value Casanova even think he is?'

'*Dylan Harris*, Mercy.' I roll my eyes. '*TV star, currently on Netflix*, obviously. What a dumb question.'

We start giggling together.

'Although apparently he's an old family friend of ours.' I frown and pick up another tag. 'That's what the papers say anyway.'

Roses for my English rose.
Let's go out a bunch!
Dylan Harris
(TV star, currently on Netflix)

'Not close enough to know we're only half English.' Mer snorts and wipes her eyes. 'Though I *do* vaguely recognise his name.'

'Me too,' I admit. 'And face. But I'm more of an Amazon Prime kind of girl.'

This time our laughter slows into silence and *bang*: our fight resurfaces, waiting to be picked up again.

'Eff, your mirror—'

'It's nothing.' I stand up quickly. 'I accidentally kicked it during an intense warm-up. You know how I am. Exercise, exercise, exercise. Tone, tone, tone.'

'Yeah.' Mer frowns. 'Freakoid.'

I don't want to fight today: I don't have the energy. I don't want Mercy to know that I smashed my mirror on purpose. Also, I haven't exercised since it happened, and I'm worried the two might be in some way linked.

'Where is everyone?' I say suddenly, looking round. The house is weirdly quiet.

'Mum's hibernating.' Mercy shrugs. 'Ben's taken Hope out rollerblading or something. And Max has disappeared again. A hundred quid says the idiot's got a secret romance going on.'

'Ew.' A wave of sympathy. 'Poor girl.'

'Yeah, rollerblading is the worst.'

Mercy gives me a sideways smile and I prod my

big sister gently with my foot, then get my phone out:

MAX, WHO IS IT??????? ME AND MER ARE ON TO YOU! SPILL!!!!!!

*Ping.*

WHO IS WHAT and BTW what did you do this time, you fire-starter? Max xx

I frown and glance at the kitchen.

Huh? What are you talking about?

CHECK TWITTER! x

With a sinking stomach, I click on the app.

*1,604 notifications.*

Blinking, I scroll quickly down.

OUCH *@Scarlettbell OH NO YOU DIDN'T!*

*@Scarlettbell How insensitive are you? Know what poor Faith's going through RN? Have some decency!*
*@Scarlettbell Haha! So true. Get her! #BasicB*
*@Scarlettbell BUUUUURRRRRRRN!*

*Scarlett?* I scroll even faster. Then I go cold:

*If you can't handle @FaithValentine at her worst, you sure as hell don't deserve her WHEN SHE'S STEALING PERSONALITY FROM #MarilynMonroe. #dull #yawn*

'What?' Mercy says curiously, leaning over to see my screen. 'Is Max denying it? Why've you got your scary marble face on?'

'Umm.' I blink numbly. There's a photo of Scarlett in a panda onesie and a blue tick: it's definitely her.

My eyes have started stinging.

'Eff?'

'I think I'm just going to . . .' Run? Bedroom? Run? Bedroom? Run? Bedroom. 'Umm. Go for a quick lie-down. It's . . . the pollen from the roses. Hay fever. I think I'm allergic.'

250

'Faith, roses don't have any—'

'Oh, shut it, Mercy.'

I drag myself up the stairs until I'm safe on the dark landing. Then I stand very still and pinch the bridge of my nose.

*Stealing a personality. Dull. Yawn.*

All those days spent with Scarlett – all the things I *told* her – and she was quietly saving them up to use against me? *I trusted her.* I opened up to her. I *liked* her and I made myself vulnerable and I'm so stupid stupid stupid stupid *stupid*.

*Consequences are for tomorrow*, and here they are now, spread all over social media.

Eyes wet, I open my bedroom door.

'Greetings!' Scarlett grins from my bed. Her short hair is spiky and her cat-eyes are smudged. 'Fire escapes work two ways, you know. Might wanna lock your window in case Dylan Harris climbs up to watch you sleep and tries to make you immortal and stuff.'

I wipe my eyes. '*What?*'

'Oh!' She waves her phone in the air and laughs loudly. 'I got bored waiting for you. Come on then, Valentine. Let's see you give as good as you get.'

34

Not being rude but—

This is *exactly* why Valentines are discouraged from fraternising outside our gene pool. We've got quite enough unhinged behaviour going on inside our family without additional input, thank you very much.

'Hi there.' I perch stiffly on the bed next to Scarlett. 'I'm not entirely sure I understand, but—'

'Get a move on,' she chirps, tapping away on her phone with both thumbs. 'Or I'm gonna rip you a new one while you're busy being all swan-like. Oops. Too late.'

I look down.

@FaithValentine *Great minds discuss ideas; average minds discuss events; small minds POST PHOTOS OF WHAT THEY HAD FOR BREAKFAST – #Basic #EleanorRoosevelt*

Scarlett sniggers as the notifications take off again. 'Your turn.'

For the love of— Genevieve is going to be furious with me. She *adores* her smoothie-bowl shots.

'Look,' I say desperately because Scarlett is enthusiastically typing again. *Fix this. Fix this right now.* 'You have to stop, Letty. *Please.* This might be funny to you, but an awful lot of time and money has gone into making sure my online presence is—'

*Ping.*

*@FaithValentine Life is what happens to you while you're busy FILTERING PHOTOS OF YOURSELF WITH VALENCIA – #Vain #JohnLennon*

I stare at her. 'I'm not *vain.*'

'I know that, but your six million followers don't. Anyway, it doesn't *matter* what strangers think about you. So hit me.'

*Don't tempt me.* 'But I—'

*Ping.*

*@FaithValentine If you want to live a happy life, tie it to YOUR SOCIAL-MEDIA ACCOUNTS, not to people or things – #Shallow #AlbertEinstein*

'Right,' I snap. 'Fine.'

I start tapping on my phone.

*I think maybe @Scarlettbell needs to—*

'*Maybe?*' Scarlett rolls her eyes. 'You *think*? Step it up, Valentine.'

Frowning, I delete the post. Then I write:

*We are all born ignorant, but one must work hard to remain stupid. You must be exhausted, @Scarlettbell. #thick #BenjaminFranklin*

Scarlett laughs delightedly. 'Better! Go again.'

*Being @Scarlettbell on Twitter is like running a cemetery; you've got a lot of people under you and nobody's listening. #6kfollowers #BillClinton*

We start giggling.

*Keep calm and SELFIE on @FaithValentine. #Selfobsessed #Churchill*

*You're nobody till somebody loves you so*
*@Scarlettbell is just . . . #Who*
*#FrankSinatra*

*Our greatest glory is not in never falling, but in*
*POSTING EVERY FALL TO INSTAGRAM.*
*@FaithValentine #attention #Confucius*

*A thing of beauty is a joy forever. BAD LUCK*
*@Scarlettbell #sad #Keats*

We're rolling around in fits of giggles now.

*@Scarlettbell This too shall pass WIND*
*CONSTANTLY. #Stink #Anon*

Our notifications are going mad, retweets and comments flooding our phones.

*Yessss! WAR!*

*Joke's on them, these do not seem accurate*
*quotes in any way. #Dumbgirls #fail*

'Y'know,' Scarlett comments as she taps away. 'Curating your life for the consumption of others is turning everyone into their own PR these days. And it's Freaking *Terrifying*. Also—'

*@faithvalentine smells like a badger's butt.*
*#Descartes*

I start hiccuping.

'I'm gonna be in *such* trouble.' *Hic*. 'Genevieve's going to take me –' *hic* – 'out in a boat at night and –' *hic* – 'drop me in the ocean with Grandma's Oscars roped to my toes.' *Hic*. 'On which note—'

Slightly delirious with giggles, I impulsively take a selfie, making a face like a rabid badger – mascara eyes smudged with laughing too hard – and update my profile picture.

'Who's vain now?'

'How the hell did you get your face to make that shape?' Scarlett is so hysterical she's started coughing. 'That shouldn't be possible for a human. Also –' *cough* – 'tell your nan Golden Globes are heavier.' *Cough*. She looks down. 'Oh *hello*. We are no longer alone.'

256

*@Scarlettbell I AM COMING FOR YOU WATCH*
*YOUR BACK YOU JUMPED-UP LITTLE NOBODY*
*#wannabe #leavemysisteralone #MercyValentine*

My hiccups abruptly stop.

*Blimey, Mercy.* Only my sister could threaten physical violence and then hashtag herself.

'Oh, Letty.' Scarlett is staring at me with wide green eyes. 'Umm, Mer's in the kitchen downstairs. I'll go and explain that—'

'Are you kidding?' A hand has gone over her heart. 'That's the most beautiful thing I've ever seen. To jump in like that for you? No questions asked? I'm an only child and I'm choking with envy right now.'

A sudden wave of pride. 'Mercy *is* pretty brutal.'

'Ferocious. Possibly a sociopath.' Scarlett smiles and leans back on my pillow. 'She has a point too. I *am* a nobody. I mean, the industry knows who I am – critically acclaimed awards coming out of my nostrils – but your sister is right. I'm a *wannabe* because I'm not doing what I *actually* want to do.'

'Which is?'

A slightly embarrassed grimace. 'Musical theatre.'

'No.' I blink in surprise. '*Really?* Like dancing, singing, wearing cat-ears and so on?'

'Oh yeah. The whole jazz-hands shebang. That's where my true secret heart lies.' She taps her chest. 'This one is made out of marzipan.'

I laugh. 'So why—'

'Have I taken a role in a television show about zombies? I'm a broke working actress, Eff. I live in a trashed studio flat in Brixton. I take whatever I can get. You know, I really feel like a pizza.'

Umm, random.

'I . . . know what you mean.' I nod slowly, trying to roll with the metaphor. 'Like . . . there's a base of cheese and tomato, but then other people cover you in toppings – pepperoni, mushrooms, olives – and nobody even *asked* what you wanted, you know? Like—' I start to warm up to the theme. 'Maybe you're a crabmeat pizza. Maybe you're strawberries and goat's cheese. Maybe you're caramel apple and coconut or squid ink! But how are you ever going to find out if people keep *adding the toppings for you?*'

Silence.

'Yeah.' Scarlett frowns. 'I meant let's order pizza.

You might want to talk to a professional about that, dude.'

My face goes cold and hot simultaneously.

For the love of—

'Oh!' I nod. 'Yes. Umm. Pizza sounds . . . good.'

'Hmm . . .' Scarlett grabs a pencil off my bedside table and chews on the end of it with her pointy little teeth. 'That could be an actual business, you know. Caramel apple and coconut pizza? I'd eat that. You need to go and see a bank manager or something.'

I take the pencil off her and smack her with it. 'Dumbo.'

'Muppet.'

'Unhinged psycho.'

'Emotionally constipated robot.'

We start giggling again.

'Right.' Scarlett tosses her phone to the bottom of the bed, grabs a twenty out of her jeans pocket and lobs it into my lap. 'Internet terrorised, followers scandalised, Einstein destroyed. Order me a blue cheese with extra pineapple, yeah?'

259

# CATFIGHT OVER FRIGHT

There's growing concern for the mental health of FAITH VALENTINE – who hasn't been seen in public since ex-boyfriend NOAH ANTHONY cheated on her and is now caught fighting with up-and-coming actress Scarlett Bell.

The erratic sixteen-year-old, who shaved her head in response to Noah's affair (left), ripped into the lesser-known actress on Twitter after Scarlett nabbed Faith's debut role in *Fright Fortnight*.

'Faith's angry,' insiders claim. 'She's feeling disrespected by being replaced so quickly. She's insulted and pretty fragile right now. Faith is fuming.'

This out-of-character Twitter tirade from Faith referred to Scarlett as 'thick', 'a nobody' and 'sad', as well as mocking her follower-count and uploading a threatening profile picture. 'We're seeing a side of Faith we don't recognise,' a worried close friend confided. 'We hope she takes Noah back. Faith's usually such a nice girl.'

## 35

Have you heard about what happened on Twitter?

I'm sorry, I don't follow.

I've been cut off.

Never mind being dropped in the ocean, by 7am the next morning, I have been thrown out of the internet like it's an exclusive nightclub and I'm wearing trainers. I can no longer access a single social-media site. My passwords have all been changed, the tweets have gone, the badger profile photo has been swapped for a flawless headshot and a series of earnest apologies have been posted:

*I would like to say sorry for any offence I may
have caused lovely @Scarlettbell yesterday. I am
deeply ashamed of my outburst. 1/3*

*I have no excuses other than that I am very tired
and a bout of flu had left my judgement impaired.
Scarlett is a highly talented actress, I respect her
immensely and wish her well for the future. 2/3*

*I appreciate the support from my followers and
fans at this difficult time. Faith xxx
#LoveLightLaughter ♥ ♥ ♥ ♥  3/3*

There are also several new photos on my Instagram.
The latest is a heart drawn in white sand, covered
in pink shells and lapped at the edges by turquoise
water. Underneath it: *The love is real, never let your
inner light dim. Donut let the haters hate
#LoveLightLaughter ♥.*

A lot of people are finding the typo very funny.
Genevieve is not.

'*Don't,*' she's muttering under her breath as I
climb into the limo to head for my second acting
class. She taps furiously on her phone: *bang bang*

*bang bang.* 'I meant *don't.* That's not even how you spell doughnut in England.'

Startled, I take my seat. My grandmother's assistant is in ripped jeans and a T-shirt, hair in a scruffy ponytail, no make-up, furious expression. All professional reserve and tasselled old lady styling is gone.

'Genevieve . . .'

'You do realise the damage you've done?' she snaps, tapping away. 'I keep so much out of the media – your mother's breakdown, your parents' imminent divorce, Roz's existence, Hope's unchaperoned excursion to LA, Max's indiscretions, Mercy . . .'

She stops there: the word *Mercy* encompasses a lot.

'And here you are *bullying* an unknown actress *ONLINE.* Do you know how that makes the Valentine family look? Your grandmother is *livid.* She's requested to have the whole of Twitter deleted!'

My nose twitches and I abruptly dip my head down.

Oh, *Grandma.*

'I'm sorry, Genevieve,' I say, looking back up with

a twist of guilt. 'I didn't mean to make extra work for you, I just—'

'Oh, that's fine,' she snaps, blowing a strand of blonde hair out of her face. 'I'll keep spending every evening drawing flowers on cappuccinos and taking photos of my neighbour's pug. It's not like I want a *life* or anything.'

Scowling, she keeps tapping away.

I stare at her in amazement. OK, hang on – that dog isn't even hers? Does she actually do yoga? Has she got a quote file, or does she know them already?

*Is everything fake?*

'I—'

'Have you picked a boy yet?' She looks up sharply. 'There are *ten* eligible young bachelors on that list and all we need you to do is choose *one*. It's not that hard, Faith. The majority of girls would really quite like to have a famous replacement boyfriend lined up for them.'

Fresh anger zips through me. 'I don't want a—'

'In the meantime, I've released a press statement and donated money in your name to a number of youth charities. I will contact Scarlett's people to arrange a friendly, candid photoshoot. I suggest a health-food café with good lighting.'

Scarlett texted me first thing:

MATE, are they legit insane? They can all see I started it! xxx

No worries. It was kind of worth it :) xxx

'But I—'

'Until that happens,' Genevieve continues, ignoring my attempt to get a word in edgeways, 'keep yourself to yourself. We cannot add *any* more fuel to this fire.'

She puts on a pair of rimless glasses that I guarantee she doesn't need.

'Right,' I say, quietly simmering. 'Sorry.'

'And put these on.' Genevieve pulls out a huge pair of mirrored sunglasses and hands them over. 'And this.' She produces a white, box-fresh baseball cap. 'Also these.' A baggy white jumper and long white skirt. 'Try to walk hunched over if you can. Ashamed of yourself. Horrified by your own behaviour – you know.'

In silence, I tug it all on as the car draws up to the acting school.

*Smack.* A hand hits the window near my head.

'FAITH! FAITH VALENTINE!!! WHY DID YOU PUBLICLY ATTACK A WORKING-CLASS ACTRESS?'

'ARE YOUR OUTBURSTS WHAT DROVE NOAH AWAY?'

'HAVE YOU LOST YOUR MARBLES?'

Fuming now, I turn to Genevieve. 'The paps are *here?*'

'I called them,' she nods as a dozen people with cameras and Dictaphones swarm round the car. 'We were trying to hide it before your little online charade, but now it's a suitably *humbling* class to attend.'

'Sure.' My stomach twists as the cameras flash and I yank my cap even further down. 'So. What do you want me to say?'

I step out of the car.

'Nothing,' Genevieve snaps behind me. 'Just keep your mouth shut.'

*Three. Bags. Full.*

# 36

Shall I tell you a joke about butter?

Better not, it might spread.

Silence I can do.

Unfortunately, by the time I've squeezed through the yelling paps – sunglasses on, baseball cap tugged firmly down – the class is in full sway. Jemima's crouched in the corner, pretending to lick her leg; Zach is roaring; Ivy is bouncing across the room on her haunches and Mia is sliding on her stomach, making *sssssssss* noises.

My phone *pings*.

A selfie of me uploads to my Instagram: I'm lying on the floor, smiling, surrounded by paper butterflies.

*Love and compassion are necessities, not
luxuries – the Dalai Lama #learningcurve
#I'msorry*

I shudder. Genevieve needs to be paid overtime.

'Come in, Faith!' Mr Hamilton calls. 'Put the mobile device away and pick an animal! And sunglasses and cap off, please! You're not in Hollywood now!'

Embarrassed, I remove them and blink.

Diego is soaring round the room with his arms held out rigid: every now and then he swoops on Theo, who squeaks and tries to climb under a chair. Rafe and Zoe are charging at each other.

Swallowing, I try to work out what animal I am. Shame *mouse* is already taken.

'Ah,' I say. 'I think I'll be—'

'Keep it to yourself, please! Interact with your classmates without telling anyone what you are! Let your *actions speak for themselves*!'

So I roll up in a tight ball and put my hands over my head. Then I wait for the noise to stop.

'Great!' At last, there's a loud clap. 'Take a break,

everyone! After this, we'll be using Spolin's theory to explore living in the moment of the scene!'

Stiffly, I unroll from my ball and stand up. Good luck, Mr Hamilton. My grandmother's been trying and failing to teach me that for a solid year.

My classmates have headed straight to the sofa corner, where they're keenly discussing this morning's exercise. ('What was up with your eagle, Diego?' 'I was a *kestrel*.')

Awkwardly, I pull my cap on, fix my sunglasses and go and sit with them, hunching down as small as possible in my seat. *Keep yourself to yourself, Faith.*

My phone *pings* again. Surreptitiously, I glance at it: it's me in a blue ballgown, spinning in circles.

*Have no fear of perfection – you'll never reach it*
*– Salvador Dali #Mistakes #Movingon*

Ironic, really, that before Photoshop my waist was eight centimetres thicker, my biceps more defined and that dress was actually yellow. I shove the phone back in my pocket.

'Who is this Spoon dude anyway?' Jemima's asking.

'Viola *Spolin* was a very famous theatre academic and acting coach,' Rafe says with a small eye-roll. 'I personally lean more towards *method* acting as demonstrated by Lee Strasberg.'

'Is he the guy that invented jeans?'

'No.'

'What about Chekhov?' Zach is looking at the itinerary for the rest of the week. 'Is that the same thing? Meisner? Adler? Uta Hagen? Who are these people?'

There's a collective silence.

'Well,' Rafe intones, 'why don't we ask the *famous* girl? She must know *everything* about the world of acting.'

They all turn to me with expectant faces.

*Don't say anything.*

'Umm.' I hunch down further as my phone *pings* again. 'Chekhov is more about a physical body connection. Meisner encourages actors to respond directly to the environment. Adler emphasises imagination over emotional recall, Hagen tells students to insert their own experiences into a scene while Spolin focuses on improv.'

270

Then I tug my baseball cap over my face. I've spent a long, tedious year learning that stuff; it seemed churlish not to answer the question.

*Sorry, Genevieve.*

'Why are you even *here*!' Zoe throws her hands up. 'You *already* know it all! If I was you, I wouldn't be wasting my time with us lot. I'd be at A-list parties, eating caviar, making out with really beautiful—'

'BECAUSE SHE CAN'T ACT!' Rafe roars. 'Have you not been *watching*? She is *terrible*. She's the worst in the class! Fame means nothing if you don't have the talent to do anything *with* it!'

I think I've found Mercy's dream boy.

'*Actually, Rafe,*' Zoe says witheringly, 'the Valentines are bona-fide acting *royalty*. We're lucky to share *air* with one of them.'

And I've just found Grandma's dream girl.

My classmates turn to stare once more, and suddenly I'm so sick and so tired of always always always *keeping my mouth shut*.

Something inside me pops.

'He's right,' I say, taking my stupid sunglasses off and tossing them on the floor. 'I can't act.'

A warm tingle rushes through me: *whoosh*.

271

'I'm sure you—'

'Nope.' Another *whoosh*. 'I. Can't. Act. At all. If you want the truth, I'm in this class because I am *so bad* at acting, my family are terrified that I will single-handedly destroy their precious reputation.'

OMG, that felt *so good*.

The class blinks and it's like the floodgates have opened and I can't stop, don't *want* to stop . . .

'What's a cow's favourite party game?' I take my baseball cap off and rub my bald head. '*Mooo-sical chairs*. What do you call a fake noodle? *An impasta*. Want to hear a joke about construction? *I'm still working on it*. What did the cheese say to itself in the mirror? *Hallou-mi*. What's green and has two wheels? *Grass, I lied about the wheels*.'

Bewildered silence.

*Whoosh*.

'Yeah,' I say, grinning wildly.

*Whoosh*.

'Can't tell jokes, either. No timing. Not funny. I don't like dogs, and what kind of *monster* doesn't like dogs? I wear the same pair of running leggings for, like, eight days in a row and frankly they smell and it's gross. And look.'

272

I pull out my phone and it obligingly *pings* with a new post on my feed.

A picture of slender brown feet wearing silk ballet shoes.

'That's not even me.' I show them all. 'An extremely irritated blonde is sitting in the back of a limo stuck in traffic somewhere, updating *my* social media. I don't even have access to my accounts any more. Everything you read about me is fake. Always has been.'

Silence.

But I'm suddenly warm all over – and so freaking relieved I could cry. Scarlett was right. *I don't have to care what they think, I don't have to care what they think, I don't have to care what they—*

'Erm.' Zoe coughs. 'I photoshop my nose smaller in *every single photo* I post online, wear loads of make-up and hashtag "no make-up". You're not that special, Faith Valentine.'

'I once pretended to go to Glastonbury,' Ivy chips in. 'Got all dressed up, took photos of me dancing at the back of a field. Never been. Hate crowds.'

'Ooh!' Theo claps his hands. 'I faked a girlfriend to make my ex jealous! My flatmate took a photo

273

of me on the sofa with my eyes shut and I posted it with: *Hate it when bae watches me sleep #newlove.*'

'I buy expensive clothes I can't afford, tuck the tags in, take photos in them, hashtag "ad" and "influencer", then send them back.' Jemima flushes.

'I fake hobbies,' Diego admits loudly. 'A lot.'

'My boyfriend and I hate each other,' Mia whispers. 'We spend all day screaming and I cry and I cry and then, when he's stomped off home, I post a picture of us, curled up on the sofa together, and put hearts all round it.'

'I pay for followers,' Zach admits, grinning. 'I'm followed by, like, sixteen thousand robots in Russia.'

We all instinctively turn to look at Rafe.

'Pathetic,' he says, wrinkling his nose. 'What kind of world are we living in? I eschew social media.' He pauses, then looks at the floor. 'But my dachshund's account is pretty awesome. Do you want to see it?'

Everyone is now howling with laughter. Bent double, snorting, making ugly *ack-ack-ack* noises. Every time one of us makes eye contact, it starts all over again. We're all so busy editing a perfect version of ourselves, we don't notice everyone else is faking it too.

'Right!' Mr Hamilton returns. 'Make a circle!'

In one united motion, the entire class drops to the floor and puts their hands over their heads. Then we all collapse in hysterics.

'Very funny,' I laugh as warmth and brightness flood through me until I'm shining everywhere. '*Now* I get it.'

And I don't feel famous any more.

I feel seen.

37

*Know why you never see elephants hiding up trees?*

*They're really good at it.*

The rest of the class is *fun*.

Obviously, I'm still rubbish – we're supposed to use imaginary keys to get through a make-believe door and have a pretend reaction to something totally non-existent on the other side of it – and I can neither see the keys nor the door, let alone the monster.

But Jemima kicks my door open, Zoe drags the beast through and Diego punches it in the face while I pretend to scream hysterically with my hands on either side of my face. And I'm too busy laughing with my classmates – and exchanging phone numbers – to care that I'm still the world's worst actress.

By the time I arrive home, I feel . . . happy. *Light.* As if I'm being slowly untied and let go.

Buzzing, I text Scarlett:

Class was amazing! Wanna come over? I'm hyper but too exhausted to go out xx

She texts back:

Got table-reads for FF, need to work on script. :( But yassss, girl, I knew you could do it! Acting just takes practice! Proud of ya xxxx

Still texting, I open the front door with a smile. *I'm proud of me too.*

Sure, good luck with th—

Something whacks me in the face.

'*YYYAAAAAAAAAAAAGGGHHHH!*' I scream crazily. 'DO NOT TOUCH ME I'M TRAINED IN SELF-DEFENCE I WILL DESTROY Y— *oh.*'

It's a heart-shaped helium balloon.

Blinking, I stare in surprise at the hallway. There are dozens of pink hearts floating vertically from weighted bases, strings dangling like a terrifying forest. It's like a horror-film remake of *Up*.

'What the—'

They've all got tags attached.

> You make my heart float!!!
> Drink??
> Dylan Harris
> (TV star, currently on Netflix)

I'm not going to bother reading the rest. You get the picture.

Gritting my teeth, I grab the heartstrings together and rip all the tags off. Then I drag the bouncing, squeaking bunch upstairs. They keep bopping me in the face and getting twisted round the elaborate bannisters, and I'm getting crosser with every step.

What is this dude's *problem*?

If a *girl* behaved like this, she'd be labelled a desperate loser unable to take a hint, but because it's a guy I'm supposed to swoon and consider myself thoroughly wooed? *Yeah, right.*

Grumbling, I knock on Hope's bedroom door – no answer, she's obviously out with Ben again – so I let myself in and release the pink balloons to hit the ceiling. There are already yellow roses filling every available space. Looks like my little sister and I had the same idea: might as well put all of *this* somewhere it'll be appreciated.

I'm aggressively whacking the dust out of Po's red velvet curtains when my phone rings.

'Uh-huh,' I answer, whacking again.

'*Excuse* me?'

'I said –' *whack* – 'uh-huh.'

'I *heard* what you said,' my grandmother trills indignantly. 'That is *not* an acceptable phone greeting, Faith. It's not even a word. It's not even *two* words.'

'I've got two words for you,' I say, and put the phone down.

A *whoosh* of warmth again.

OK, this is starting to get addictive.

My phone rings.

'We were inexplicably cut off mid-sentence,' my

279

grandmother continues blithely. 'And we don't have time for pleasantries. I need you in central London in an hour.'

*Whack.* 'Why?'

'I'm *sorry*?'

'I said *why*?' *Whack. Whack.* 'Because I'm kind of busy right now.' *Whack. Whack. Whack.*

There's a shocked silence.

'Faith Valentine! If I wanted a *laissez-faire* attitude, I would ring your brother. You have made the proverbial pig's ear of your reputation with the national media, so it's time for me to guide you directly.'

I scowl and let go of the curtains. Of course it is.

'Right,' I sigh resignedly, heading out of Hope's bedroom and back towards my own. 'What's the plan?'

I feel like one of Dylan's gross pink balloons – tied to words I don't mean, tethered by something heavy, battering against the ceiling.

'Sketch, Mayfair. The table is booked for seven pm.'

I survey my wardrobe. 'Dress code?'

'Glamorous but respectable. Pretty but not

280

attention-seeking. Simple but striking. You mustn't look heartbroken or triumphant. You're not a *victim*, nor are you an *aggressor*. Try the pale blue Chanel.'

I yank the hangers about, then pull out a very dull tailored shift dress.

'You don't even like Sketch,' I snap, stripping out of Genevieve's 'meek and mild in public' outfit into my brand-new 'demurely feminine' costume. 'You complain about it all the time.'

'Darling, if I wanted milk chocolate on my foie gras and strawberries on my cod, I'd get a five-year-old to make my dinner. But I'm not the one meeting you there so I care very little.'

'You're not?' I go very still. 'What do you mean?'

'What would meeting your grandmother for dinner achieve? Ridiculous notion. No, I'm sending you on a first date.'

A gigantic wave of fury flashes through me, prickly and hot.

'You're NOT.'

'*YES, I AM.*' Grandma is projecting in her large-theatre voice.

'You can't just do that!'

'I can and I have. You didn't choose so I picked

*281*

for you. I don't expect you to fall in love, obviously, just enjoy a mutually beneficial arrangement you both stand to gain from. The candidate wants newspaper coverage. You need to be seen as valuable, wanted and strong. Moving forward, irrepressible. It will work.'

Another burning tidal wave of anger. This isn't *find and replace* on a Word document. You can't just highlight *Noah* and type another boy's name in. This is my *heart*.

'So no more of this silly behaviour, please. Be the kind, thoughtful, sweet Faith we all know and love and it'll go beautifully, darling.' My grandmother is back to using her small-theatre voice. 'It might even be fun.'

I hurl the shift dress to the floor and kick it savagely.

'Who is it?'

'A television star, I believe.' I can hear Grandma checking the list. 'Goes by the name *Dylan Harris*.'

38

And . . . I'm done.

'Faith Valentine? Welcome to Sketch. Your table is . . .'

'DYLAN? DYLAN HARRIS? ARE YOU HERE, DILLLLLLLLLLLY? GET READY FOR THE DATE OF YOUR LIFE, BABY!'

Because the whoosh of anger that got me here just keeps on burning, hotter and brighter.

'WHERE IS HE?' Heads turn as I swagger through the beautiful restaurant, yelling at the top of my voice. 'WHERE'S MY FUTURE HUSBAND? YOU'VE WON THE GIRL LOTTERY, HONEY-BUNNY!'

For this evening of hot romance, I selected some massive, skanky tracksuit bottoms from the depths of Max's laundry basket, an enormous khaki hoodie

283

from Dad's room, a pair of mismatched neon socks and the pink sliders Mum uses in the garden.

Pretty. Simple. Not *tooooooooo* glamorous.

'Oh *hello*,' I say, grabbing a bread roll from another table's basket. 'I do *luuuurve* free carbs.'

Then I sit down opposite Dylan and grin.

Even without the photo, it would have been easy to work out which one he was. Handsome, bronzed, bright white teeth, gelled black hair, green eyes, and trying inordinately hard to resist slipping under the table.

'All right there, Dilpot?' I stuff the roll in my mouth and spray crumbs as I continue. 'Good call, picking a seat near the loo. Big breakfast, if you know what I mean.' I pat my stomach. 'Fingers crossed they've got *lots* of air freshener, and I'd say *if you know what I mean* again, but *I think you do*.'

I wink and his eyes open even wider.

The voice inside me is screaming, *Be beautiful! Be elegant! Be feminine! Be nice!* But for once I'm not listening.

'. . . Faith?'

'You betcha it is.' I scratch my left boob. 'Oh, I *like* your fake tan, Dylster. It's *so* cool that you're allowed to pick a colour not normally found in nature, you know?'

Dylan opens his mouth. 'It's actually a real—'

'Skin cancer.' I shake my head. 'Be wise, man.'

Then I lean back and cradle my naked head in my hands while I look him up and down, up and down, up and down again. He is incredibly hot, in fairness. If you like your boys shiny like a piece of glazed ham, which I do not.

'Cheers for the flowers,' I say, sticking a finger up my nose, rummaging a bit and then flicking an invisible bogey across the room. 'And the heart balloons. Bit needy, but hey – you won! I'm here! My heart is yours!'

'Well, competition was fierce so—'

'Please don't interrupt me when I'm talking. So tell me *alllllll* about yourself, Dilcakes. Who are you? What do you do? Your life history. Brief synopsis, please. I don't have all day.'

He gapes for a few seconds.

'Well . . . as I think I mentioned, I'm currently

on Netflix. It's a show called *Wolfgang* and I've got the starring role, so I'm a normal guy at school, but during the full moon I turn into a—'

'Piano-playing hamster?'

'*No-ooo*. A werewolf.'

'Wow. Left swerve.'

'Yeah. And—'

I click my fingers at the poor waiter. 'Bring us two plates of the cod. I'm *freaking starving*.'

Dylan clears his throat. 'I don't actually eat—'

'Oh, you'll love it, sweetheart. Trust me.' Leaning back, I put my foot on the table and roll up my tracksuit leg. 'What do you think of my calves? Nice, huh? They're so hairy it's like walking round with two poodles in my trousers.'

The couple at the table next to us start giggling.

For a split second, I feel guilty, then I remember that this total stranger told the national media that we had a 'connection' and that he thought it was 'finally his turn' and 'it's our time'.

*Whoosh.*

'So,' Dylan says, 'I was going to—'

'*Shhhhhhh.*' I hold a finger tenderly up to his lips and take a deep breath. 'Hold that thought. I *really* need to concentrate.' I roll my eyes dramatically. 'Not yet. Not yet. Not—'

A huge belch rips out of me.

'Goodness.' I smile at him triumphantly, waving my hands about. 'That sounded like my brand-new Ferrari. Have you got one? I bet you don't.'

Dylan opens his mouth.

'Close your mouth, babe. You look like the fish we just ordered.'

The table next to us snorts again.

'You're not . . . quite what I was expecting.' Dylan glances at the surrounding restaurant – everyone is watching – and flinches. I don't think this is quite the *publicity* he was looking for. 'We've met before – I'm sure you remember. At your mum's premiere, a few weeks ago. At the Tate Modern. You looked . . . a bit different.'

Is *this* why we're 'old family friends'? He met me *once*?

It wasn't even a good party: it largely involved me dragging a self-destructive Mercy off a DJ table, having a huge catfight with her and then realising much later that Hope had gatecrashed, heard it all and run away to a different country.

287

Yet he thinks *he's* my lasting memory of that evening?

'Don't remember you.' I shrug, picking my nose again. 'Pretty boys all blur into one.'

'Thanks!' He looks inexplicably thrilled. 'I talked to your little sister for a while. Hit on me pretty hard, but she's not my type. Bit intense, if you ask me.'

Says the guy who sent me *a rose every five minutes*.

Also, I'm absolutely certain that my sweet, romantic, hopeful little Po didn't hit on this total . . . OK, who am I kidding, she totally did.

'I've seen her ask out an Alsatian,' I say shortly. 'Incredibly poor eyesight and judgement.'

'Here you go, madam, sir.' Two tiny plates of white fish covered in strawberries are placed on the table between us. 'I do hope you enjoy your meal.'

I quickly smile at the waiter. I'll tip him heavily later.

Time to start wrapping this up. A little more effort, and I can go home, curl up in my pyjamas, eat a cheese toastie, ring Scarlett and fall asleep. Target achieved – Dylan annihilated – Boy List ruined. Genevieve and Grandma will never send me anywhere with any of them ever again.

Official Worst First Date Ever: *nailed it*.

'Umm,' I say as the star of *Wolfgang* picks up a fork. 'Hang on, yours is bigger. Swap?' I swap the meals over and examine them again. 'Nope, changed my mind. I'd like mine back. Except with your sauce. And some extra strawberries.'

With a huge grin, I take a dessert spoon and start transferring most of his plate on to mine. You know, Grandma was right: this *is* fun.

'*What?*' I say as Dylan stares at me. A bit of fish-spit shoots out of my mouth. '*What'sh wrong?*' Swallow. 'This date is going *really* well, isn't it, Dilly-baby? I think you might *totally* be The One. I'm feeling a *real connection*. Like it's finally *your turn*. It's really *our time*, isn't it?'

There's a long silence.

And – just like that – I completely run out of steam.

'You know,' Dylan says eventually, leaning back, 'my agent said asking you out would be great for my reputation. She thought that dating an actual *Valentine* would give my career a boost.'

I dig into my fish: yes, we all know why he's here, thanks for clarifying.

'I wasn't that keen,' he continues. 'I mean, you're gorgeous, but you've always seemed . . . I dunno . . . boring? Cold? I date fitties all the time – nothing gets the ladies like a wolf off the telly – but it's . . . a bit blah, you know? They're all the same.'

I gulp down my mouthful, hard.

'But you're not like other girls.' A blindingly white smile is spreading across his face. 'I mean, this is . . . *refreshing*. This is *challenging*. You're clearly not into me and I'm . . . *loving* it.'

Appalled, I blink three times.

'So, yeah.' Dylan Harris nods, as if he's just made a decision. 'I would *love* to see you again, Faith Valentine. Thanks for asking.'

You have got to be freaking *kidding* me.

## 39

## ROMANCE BLOSSOMS
## FOR VALENTINE

**Gorgeous Faith Valentine was spotted last night with TV star Dylan Harris, confirming rumours that they are the hottest new couple in Celebsville. Secretly growing closer ever since Faith's break-up with love rat Noah Anthony, they made their first public appearance at Sketch. 'She seemed really comfortable,' an onlooker said. 'Dylan's loved up,' agrees a mutual friend. 'He thinks Faith might be The One!'**

*Noooooooooooooooooooooooooooooooooooooo, says the T-zone. Missed my window again!*

**MISSED CALL:** Noah

**MISSED CALL:** Noah

**MISSED CALL:** Noah

**MISSED CALL:** Noah

Heya! We forgot to exchange numbers! Don't worry, I got it off your agent! I'll call you. Dilpot xxx

**MISSED CALL:** Unknown number

Party tonight – want to come with?
D xxx

PS Dress code is formal so no tracksuits and maybe shave! LOL xxx

**MISSED CALL:** Unknown number

**MISSED CALL:** Noah

**Eff, WHAT'S GOING ON? Is this why you need 'space'? So you can date other people?! Nx**

And somehow *I'm* the 'crazy' one? Quickly, I type:

**Noah, it was a set-up. Promise. I am not dating anyone else. F xx**

I'd love to tell Dylan where to go, but sadly I overslept and I'm late again for my acting workshop. Plus, he would probably see it as a declaration of my eternal devotion.

Quickly, I change his number to **WEIRDO: DO NOT ANSWER.** Then I run down the stairs.

'All right, sis!' Max appears in the hallway, shaking a can of whipped cream. ''S'up? How was your big rebound date? I've already had to run that slimeball off once when he tried it on with Po. Just let me know when it's time to do it again.'

He flexes a bicep; I grab my bag. As much as I love my brother, I'm not discussing my non-romantic escapades with someone spraying half a can of cream directly into his mouth.

'Max.' I look at the kitchen and blink. 'Did you . . . *clean?*'

'Hmm?' He sprays whipped cream again and swallows. '*Noooo*. Are you mad? I've only just got home. Mum's been roaming the house at night again like a skinny Santa. Looks like she finally picked up a J-cloth, hurrah!'

*Oh, Mum* – must check in on how she's doing after class. I pick my keys up. 'How was *your* night?'

'Grand.' He grins at me, a blob of cream on the end of his nose. 'All I'm going to say, Eff, is that I'm finally getting the level of adoration I deserve. It's *allllll* about me.'

Seriously, somebody tell this new girl to *run*.

'Speaking of attention,' my brother continues as I open the front door. The chauffeur is already waiting for me outside, but no Genevieve, thank goodness. 'Another not-so-little gift arrived for you, Heartbreaker. Hang on.'

Max disappears into the living room, then reappears holding the biggest, fluffiest, most hideous pink teddy bear I've ever seen in my entire life. It's the size of a small cow and is holding a heart saying *YOU'RE MINE*.

*I am flaming not, Dylan.*

'Wanna know what the card says?' Max asks, waving a gross fluffy paw at me. 'Dizzer's really gone for it. A rhyme and everything.'

'No,' I say shortly. And I slam the door behind me.

The class is in full flow by the time I arrive.

'I'VE GOT A MACHINE GUN!' Diego is roaring at Zoe from the corner of the room. *'I'm going to use it! Don't try and stop me, don't try and—'*

At least I *hope* the class has started. Either that or somebody needs to check that poor Diego's OK, and maybe take the firearm off him.

It's been an intense week.

'Morning,' Mia whispers with a mischievous look as I slip quietly into the spare seat next to her. 'How was your date with Dylan Harris? I read it in the papers this morning. He's *so* cute. Are you madly in love or is that lies too?'

'Complete fabrication,' I whisper back with a wry smile.

'I have no idea what to believe any more.' Mia mimes her head exploding. 'Anyway.' She points at

Diego, still screaming at poor Zoe. 'We're finally *filming*, Effie! Actual scenes! For actual showreels!'

Ivy leans forward, pink with excitement. 'Improv first, then this afternoon it's scripted drama.'

I shudder slightly. *Improvisation.*

Of all the types of drama I'm bad at – which is all of them – making up your own lines is the worst.

'What have they done so far?' Fear is starting to tighten my throat. 'Do we get scenarios?'

'This is the first one,' Theo whispers back. 'Diego's supposed to be a sixteenth-century monk, but he's gone all Liam Neeson on us. Zoe's trying to roll with it.'

'I don't think that's a machine gun, *Father*,' she's saying desperately. 'Mainly because they haven't been invented yet.'

My classmates and I grin at each other.

'I've got "Waiting at a Bus Stop",' Ivy confides. 'Bit disappointed, to be honest. I literally did that about forty-five minutes ago IRL.'

'I'm a flight attendant,' Mia tells me, bouncing in her chair. 'Rafe is a pilot who's passed out mid-flight and I've got to wake him up before we crash! I mean, *drama*.'

'So unfair,' Rafe moans darkly. 'My talents are not being accurately showcased if I'm asleep for the whole scene.'

'Something tells me he won't be,' Ivy sniggers.

We all smile again.

Mr Hamilton frowns at us – *shhhhhh* – so we huddle closer.

Theo shows me a piece of paper that says *You have been caught stealing in a shop.* 'Jem's the security guard who's hunted me for years.'

'Yup,' she grins. 'A pack of gum and you're going *down*.'

'AAAAAAAAGHHH!' Diego yells from the corner of the room, pulling out what we can only assume is a sixteenth-century hand grenade and abruptly ending the scene. '*KABOOOM!*'

'Oh, for goodness' sake—' Zoe snaps, throwing her hands in the air. 'Dee, I appreciate the commitment, but we had, like, three-quarters of our time left and I only said two lines.'

'I was led by gut instinct,' he says defensively.

'I'll lead you by your gut instinct,' Zoe growls back.

Still grumbling at each other, my classmates make

their way back to the group. Swallowing nervously, I look round the remaining cast.

I guess that means I'm with—

'Zachary and Faith!' Mr Hamilton calls brightly, checking his list. 'You guys are up next! Let's see if we can last the allocated ten minutes, shall we? Or it'll be back to warm-up ball games!'

The camera light blinks on; I freeze.

Three years ago, I went to see Mum play Hermione in Shakespeare's *Winter's Tale*. There's an incredibly powerful scene where everyone thinks she's a statue, but she comes back to life. It suddenly feels like the opposite is happening to me: as if I've been trapped inside a stiff, cold body, unable to move.

So much for acting exercises and warm-ups and encouragement. I've been demoted from wood to *marble*.

'Hey!' Zach says cheerfully, prodding my arm. 'Eff, I thought we could play this as a *romance*? You know, a few longing glances, maybe hand-holding. We could perhaps . . . make out? I mean, if you're game. I'm game. Anything for the art, y'know?'

'Nice try,' Jemima sniggers. 'Didn't see *that* coming, Z.'

out it feels like grey cement is

\_h my veins. I can't move, I can't

t *move.*

\_an do this!' Mia squeezes my arm. The rest

\_y classmates smile at me affectionately. 'Don't

\_e nervous, Eff! This is your birthright, remember? You're a *Valentine!*'

'Here.' Zach hands me a piece of paper. 'Our scene.'

I stare down at it: *You are sitting in a hospital emergency waiting room.*

Made of stone, I stand up slowly.

'And –' Mr Hamilton beams at us – 'camera's rolling!'

## 40

I shuffle into position.

'Oh my days,' Zachary huffs with an elaborate sigh, sitting on a prop-chair. 'There is *nothing worse* than Sitting in a Hospital Waiting Room. Am I right, baby?' He takes my hand and kisses my cheek. 'How shall we spend all this extra time? *Hmmmm?*'

My classmates giggle.

I stare at him. This is nothing like a hospital waiting room. There are no peeling posters about bowel conditions or the importance of checking your boobs for lumps. There isn't a weird, tangy, metallic smell in the air. Everything's not painted mint-green. My chair isn't hard and sticky, and there aren't people slumped around us with anxiety and tiredness etched on their faces.

Nobody's whispering, nobody's crying, nobody's whimpering in pain, crumpled on the floor.

'How do you think she is?' Zach squeezes my hand and looks at the clock on the wall. 'I hope she's OK. She's been in there for *hours*.'

I glance up too.

It hasn't been hours.

It feels like it's been days, weeks, years, and stars have imploded and civilisations have died and the oceans have dried up and rainforests have emptied and we're still here, still staring at the door.

'Do you think we should go and get some coffee?' Zach touches my knee. 'I could do with something to keep me awake.'

I look at his hand.

I don't need something to keep me awake. It'll be sleep I can't find.

Sweating in the middle of the night, looping my arm over Mercy, setting my alarm for 6am so the night is shorter.

'Faith?'

Wandering the hallway in the dark on my own.

'Faith?'

Pain rips through me.

'Hello, Faith? Are you still there?'

Across me, like somebody's slowly paring back

my skin. Flaying me, stripping me, peeling me like an orange an orange an orange an orange *an orange.*

'Umm, Eff—'

'GET AWAY FROM ME! GET YOUR HAND OFF ME! DO NOT *TOUCH* ME!'

'S-Sorry, I didn't—'

'NO!' I jump up, shaking all over. 'STAY AWAY. I DON'T WANT YOU TO SAY SORRY. I WANT YOU TO *ROT IN HELL.*'

Make it stop. Make it stop. *Make it stop.*

'Faith, I—'

With both hands, I grab Zach's jumper, haul him out of his chair and drag him bodily across the room.

'*I HATE YOU!*' I scream, slamming him against the wall.

'Uh.' Blink. 'I don't know what you—'

*Slam.*

'YOU WERE ON YOUR PHONE.'

*Slam.*

'YOU WERE ON YOUR PHONE, YOU SELFISH IDIOT. I WANT TO HURT YOU. I WANT TO KILL YOU. I WANT TO BREAK YOU INTO TINY PIECES THE WAY YOU BROKE US.'

My face is wet: tears, spit, snot.

*Slam.*

'Ow, Faith.'

'YOU LEFT ME WITH ALL THIS MESS. I'M SUPPOSED TO BE THE ONE WHO HOLDS IT TOGETHER AND CLEANS IT UP AND I CAN'T, I DON'T KNOW HOW TO, I'M NOT *STRONG ENOUGH.*'

'*Faith!*'

'SO I DON'T *CARE* IF YOU'RE SORRY. I DON'T *CARE* IF YOU HAVE SLEEPLESS NIGHTS. BECAUSE YOU'RE A STRANGER AND YOU GET TO LEAVE THIS ROOM AND NONE OF US *EVER WILL.*'

'*Cut*, Faith. *Scene over.*'

I'm crying openly, blind and trembling.

'And I'm *tired*,' I whisper. 'I'm so *tired* of pretending. I can't be an actress because I am *acting all the time.*'

'*FAITH!*' Mr Hamilton shouts. 'Let go of Zachary before you hurt him!'

Sobbing, I open my hands and stare at them.

Purple.

Purple, purple everywhere.

*I've gone insane.*

'Umm.' Zach rubs his shoulders. 'Faith, you OK? I mean, kudos for the investment, but I think you may have dislocated something.' He turns towards Mr Hamilton. 'Also, I could totally have escaped, but the hot girl's surprisingly strong. Just saying.'

I keep staring at my hands.

*This is it. What happened to Mum is happening to me. It's rising like a mist and swallowing me whole.*

Numbly, I turn to face my classmates. They're staring at me in shock, their bodies tense, faces drained, eyes round and blank.

'Oh, sir,' Zoe whispers, hand over her mouth. 'You gave her *that* scene?'

And I don't know how to—

I will not—

They've seen something I can't take back.

'I'm sorry,' I say, wiping my face and grabbing my bag. 'I'm so, so sorry. I've got to . . . go.'

41

What's red and goes up and down?

A tomato in a lift.

How does NASA organise a party?

They planet.

What's a balloon's least favourite kind of music?

Pop.

How does a farmer mend his overalls?

With cabbage patches.

Why does Humpty Dumpty love autumn?

He always has a great fall.


Want to hear a roof joke?

The first one's on the h—


'. . . let her go. Are you kidding? She is *not* in the right headspace to be out in public! Can you *imagine*? It would be *humiliating*.'

'She can make her own decisions!'

'Not to mention that it would be all over the papers. Do we want our reputation ruined? *The Valentines: officially bonkers*? And what about the *hair*?'

'I like it! The hair is cute!'

'It's not cute – it makes her look even more *insane*.'

'She's vulnerable – it's hitting her all at once. She's just not ready.'

'Yeah.' A sharp laugh. 'And she's the only one in this family who matters. She's the *only* one with emotions. Don't forget that.'

So much for creeping home to cry alone.

No wonder Hope ran away a few weeks ago. You can't *move* in this family without running into a brutal conversation about one of us. Maybe we should start wearing bells or something.

My hot anger is building again. It's like I've found a huge well of it inside me and now I don't know how to turn the tap off.

'And what about her little *outburst* the other day?' Mercy continues furiously. 'Do we want something like that happening in—'

'STOP!' I shout, pushing through the door. 'CAN YOU—'

*Thwap.* A heart balloon hits me in the face again. I punch it back, hard.

'—*STOP.*' The balloon skitters away on its little pink string. 'I am *NOT BONKERS* –' I might be bonkers – 'or VULNERABLE –' I am extremely vulnerable – 'or in the wrong headspace to go out in public –' I am *absolutely* in the wrong headspace to go out in public – 'and I won't HUMILIATE you –' I probably will – 'and my hair was a—'

Another balloon *thwaps* me in the face.

*Punch.*

'WILL SOMEBODY GET THESE FLAMING BALLOONS AWAY FROM ME!'

'Sorry!' Hope springs up hurriedly, grabbing the bobbing bunch and dragging them away. 'Sorry, Eff! I found them in my room! I don't know who they're from, but *hundreds* of yellow roses came the day before too. Somebody must have a *devastating* crush on me! Probably a really hot boy from school. I obviously made *quite* the impression.'

She beams – totally giddy – and I glance at Mercy in surprise. Did *she* put the roses in Hope's room?

Our big sister shrugs.

'Look,' I say in a much lower voice. 'You don't need to keep me locked inside the house like a—'

'Umm,' Max interrupts. 'No offence, but you just literally punched two heart balloons straight in the face, Eff.'

'Also,' Mer frowns, 'you're holding a stack of Post-its covered in crazy scribbles.'

I flush and stick them in my pocket.

'Oh, come on,' I say. 'If you can't punch a heart now and then without being—'

'We weren't actually talking about you, Eff.' Max

pats my raised shoulder. 'We're talking about Mum. She's supposed to be hosting some massive charity auction tonight—'

'But we can't let her out of the house in her present state,' Mercy interjects.

'I think she looks pretty,' Hope says protectively. 'Like something Maggie sticks in the garden to scare away pigeons.'

'Mum?' I blink, my heart sinking. 'But . . . why were you talking about her hair?'

'Go and see for yourself.'

Confused, I head into the corridor and gently tap on my mother's door for a solid minute before it finally opens.

*Knock, knock, who's there?*

'Oh, hello, darling.' Mum looks straight through me. 'How very kind of you to visit. But you can't stay, I'm afraid. I'm on my way out, as you can see.' My mother glides back into her stale, dark, airless bedroom. 'Although I can't seem to find my wedding ring. What on earth is your father going to say?'

*Very little, I'd expect, given that he has a new girlfriend, he doesn't live here any more and you're in the middle of a messy divorce.*

'Erm, Mum.' I step into the rancid room. 'Where are you going?'

'A party, darling.' An elegant flick of her thin hand. 'All my old friends will be there. They're very eager to see me, as I'm sure you can imagine.'

I stare at my mother's pale, bony back.

She's wearing a long green satin gown – once glorious, now far too big for her – and her feet are bare and unwashed. Her normally gleaming blonde hair is dull and knotted, with thick ashy roots, and woven through it are myriads of tiny jewels. Diamonds, emeralds, sapphires, amethysts; necklaces, brooches, earrings. She's glimmering in the low light like the nest of an enthusiastic magpie.

In her mind, Juliet Valentine is permanently playing Ophelia.

She was *so* not ready to leave rehab.

'Oh, Mum.' I step forward quietly. 'What have you done to your hair?'

'Such beautiful hair. All those curls.'

'Mum.'

'It was the first thing I saw, you know.'

'*Mum.*'

'But, you see, I *have* to go, darling.' She takes a

310

beautiful gold-and-cream card off the top of her dresser and hands it to me. 'Look. They said it's *For Charity.*'

I swallow, hard. My siblings were right. Mum absolutely cannot be allowed to leave the house. Not just because she'll be all over every front page by tomorrow morning – bedraggled and twinkling and grubby and vacant – but because it would break whatever inside her is still left unbroken.

And it's my job to make sure that doesn't happen.

'Actually,' I say abruptly, kissing her cheek, 'the agency has just rung me! Turns out they've moved tonight's auction back a couple of weeks. Big problem with the caterers. Some kind of fridge malfunction, no cold drinks, vol-au-vents ruined, total disaster!'

Mum sits delicately on her bed. 'Oh.'

'They *absolutely* want you to host it, as soon as everything's up and running again. Everyone's really missed you, you know that.'

My mother nods vaguely. 'OK, darling. If you think it's for the best.' She blinks, refocuses, looks straight at me. A gentle hand goes to my cheek and she smiles a soft, bright, weirdly present smile.

'Thank you, Faith. You always *were* the sweetest of my baby girls.'

My throat abruptly closes.

Gently, I remove the jewels from my mother's hair, place them in a glass box by the bed and then pull the silk sheets over her. 'Get some sleep,' I whisper, kissing her forehead. 'There'll be plenty of time for parties when you're better.'

Mum nods and closes her eyes. I open the curtains and windows a touch; spritz a little perfume into the air and load my arms with untouched plates of food and cups of cold tea. Then I return to where my siblings are waiting.

'You know,' I say, handing them the plates and cups, 'you *can* go in there yourselves. She's not going to bite you. Sadness isn't contagious.'

'It flaming is,' Mercy says, peering inside a mug.

'So what's the plan?' Max is following me down the corridor like a lanky puppy. 'Because the tickets for this swankathon were silly expensive, Eff. I'm talking thousands of pounds. And nobody is going to host for free with less than an hour's notice. Do we need to caffeine her up and wheel her in?'

I head towards my bedroom. I have never felt more like a Valentine: as maddening and messed up and malfunctioning as we are.

'No,' I say calmly. 'Because I'm going to do it.'

## 42

I have been training for this my whole life.

Couture dress, designer heels, limited-edition clutch, bespoke perfume, primer, foundation, highlighter, bronzer, blusher, contour, eyeshadow, eyeliner, eyelashes, eyebrows. Years of perfecting my grooming routine so I can tweak and pluck and spray with the diligent, switched-off focus of a poorly paid worker on a meat factory line.

Except . . . I'm also the chicken.

With a few minutes left before John the limo driver arrives, I grab what looks like a sleeping Pomeranian off my bedroom floor and stick it firmly on my head. The wig is expensive, lace-front, made out of real hair. I kiss it gratefully. *Thanks for being such a slob, Mer.*

Then I stand in front of my cracked mirror.

My dress is floor-length, handmade and worth

thousands: layers of sheer white with wide, floating sleeves and a slit down the side. The gold Prada heels make me well over six feet tall, my legs cartoon-like. The wig is glossy and soft and black, skimming my shoulders. My face looks doll-like: full lips, angular cheekbones, a small nose, enormous hazel eyes with thick, bushy eyelashes like some kind of deer.

My body is brown, slim and perfectly toned. I mean, it should be: apart from the past week, I've been exercising more than four hours a day for two years.

There is nothing I can see that Grandma would possibly change. I am perfect.

A wave of nausea whips through me.

'Hey!' Max says as I clomp down the stairs. He's holding up a camcorder. 'Smile, little sis!'

Without stopping, I stick a finger firmly up. Never mind which one. Then – glossy and flawless – I climb into the limo.

*I can do this. I can. I can do it.*

All I have to do is go onstage, be nice, smile, dimple, say thank you, read out scripted lines and

315

everyone will be happy. Mum will be given her privacy, Genevieve will have something real to post, Grandma will be proud, the paparazzi get their photos and the charity get their money.

*Faking it for the Valentines.*

'Faith! FAITH VALENTINE! HOW'S YOUR MOTHER?'

'Is it true that you'll be hosting instead of Juliet tonight? What's wrong with her this time?'

'Wasn't this supposed to be her big return?'

The limo has stopped smoothly outside the Dorchester hotel – cream and wedding-cakey, with its frilly canopies and ornate iron balconies – and paparazzi are already swarming, yelling at me through a blacked-out window.

I wait a few seconds until my hands aren't shaking. Until my real self is tucked safely away somewhere deep, like in a kidney or maybe my pancreas.

'Ready,' I whisper. 'Let's go.'

The chauffeur opens my door and I step out exactly as I've been taught to: knees firmly together, swing towards the exit, heels on the ground, legs bent gracefully, stand up slowly. Then I dimple at the media sweetly.

'Good evening.' *Flash flash flash flash.* 'I'm afraid that my mother is indisposed, due to a last-minute dental emergency. She is recovering well. Thank you for the concern.'

*Flash flash flash flash flash.*

'WHAT ABOUT DYLAN HARRIS?' *Flash.* 'Will he be joining you this evening, Faith?' *Flash flash.* 'How does Noah feel about him? Have they met yet?'

'You are *glowing*, Faith! Is it *LOVE*?'

'This evening,' I say with a gracious smile, 'is about raising money for an excellent cause, and I am naturally very excited to be focusing exclusively on that for the next ninety minutes.'

Should have worn less highlighter.

'Faith! Faith! What—'

Smiling sweetly but coldly – *This Conversation is Now Over* – I swish through the crowd, past bowing doormen, through revolving glass doors and into a reception room of marble, gilt and gold, oak walls, bouquets of roses, carved ceilings.

The rich and famous are milling about in the foyer. Sleek and glossy in tuxes and gowns, murmuring politely like wood pigeons. Heads bobbing as they spin to see who else is in the room and if there's somebody more influential or attractive they should talk to.

I have an overwhelming desire to spray ketchup all over them. Or mustard, so it burns.

'*Effie!*' One of my mother's A-list friends sweeps across the room in a long fox-fur coat and takes my hand in her claw. 'Oh, my *darling*! Aren't you getting more *beautiful* by the minute! And just *look* how long your hair has grown!'

Funny she can't tell the difference between real and fake, given the coat she's wearing.

'*So* kind of you,' I smile.

'And how –' the woman leans forward with a creepy intake of breath, as if she's trying to sniff my collarbone – 'is your *dear mother?*'

Falling apart quite nicely, thank you.

'Very well, thanks.'

'Faith!' A producer saunters over, straightening his tie. 'Aren't you a *sight* for sore eyes! Tell me, how old are you now?'

'Sixteen!' *At least three decades younger than you.*

'Oh, *rrrrrrreally*! And . . . ah . . . where's your

father these days? Still in Hollywood, cooking up his next masterpiece?'

'Dad's in London, actually.' *Take another step towards me and he will kill you with his bare hands.* 'He might turn up this evening, in fact.'

*Not likely. He hates stuff like this.*

'Well! I – er – must catch up with him soon . . .'

My phone starts ringing:

**WEIRDO: DO NOT ANSWER**

I cancel; it rings again.

**WEIRDO: DO NOT ANSWER**

'EFFIE?' An unwanted, familiar voice yells across the room. 'YOU SHOULD HAVE CALLED ME BACK! WE COULD HAVE MADE A GRAND ENTRANCE TOGETHER.'

Dylan is energetically pushing his way through the crowd, waving his phone in the air.

For the love of—

I've been here less than three minutes and I'm already exhausted. Maybe everyone *isn't* looking for somebody better to talk to. Maybe we're all just trying very hard not to talk to each other.

In desperation, I search the crowd until I spot a platinum-blonde bun in the corner. '*Do* excuse me,' I say serenely to the producer and my mother's so-called friend. 'It's been *lovely* to catch up, but I'm afraid I have to be going now.'

The fur-coat woman begins gossiping as soon as my back is turned. 'Daughter of . . . *Yes*. Icy little madam, wouldn't you say?'

'Nothing like her mother, who is completely—'

You'd think a room full of actors would understand how to stop projecting for a few precious seconds.

My hearing range cuts out just in time.

'Darling!' Dame Sylvia Valentine is holding court at the centre of an elite circle, wearing a glittering black Givenchy gown, walking stick planted like a maypole. 'Everybody, *do* meet my granddaughter Faith Valentine.'

I glance over my shoulder. Dylan mouths, *Shall I come over?*

Alarmed, I shake my head and turn back.

'Tell me, Faith,' a middle-aged lady in lace

enquires, 'how are your *auditions* going? Your grandmother tells me you're *quite* the committed pupil.'

'Although –' an older woman nods – 'I wouldn't worry too much about studying, dear. Much better to get your beauty sleep!'

'Absolutely,' an even older man agrees. 'Protect that pretty face at all costs. Dear Sylvia was always a *character* actress – superb talent, but never the best-looking girl in the room. You're more like your mother, Faith. A romantic lead through and through.'

'*Exactly*.' A man with grey teeth leans forward as if I'm a slice of cake he's considering. 'And which *financiers* are you working with, Faith? Because I have contacts to—'

I open my mouth.

'If you don't mind,' my grandmother says smoothly. 'This dear *character* actress may need to find a seat. My legs aren't what they once were. Faith, darling – shall we?'

With a small pale hand, she leads me away.

'Are you tired?' I ask in surprise as we reach a quiet corner. 'Because I can go and get you a—'

'Don't be naive, dear. Sometimes I wonder if

I've taught you anything. Now.' Dame Sylvia lowers gold-rimmed glasses and stares at me. 'I understand what you've done this evening, Faith, and I'm grateful. Your mother is my only child, and there is nowhere I'd less like her to be than here.'

A bell rings in the foyer and people start to exit through a side door. A lady in an elaborately ruffled skirt scurries over, squeezing her hands together.

'Faith! Oh, *gracious*, we need to get you—'

My grandmother looks at her. She scurries away again.

'I offered to host the event myself,' Grandma continues, subtly straightening my wig. 'But they want fresh blood. With fewer potential clots in it, I'd imagine. Please don't forget, Faith, that – no matter what happens – you are a *Valentine*.'

'Yes, Grandmother.'

'We may be powerful, but the people here can still make us and they can still break us.'

'Yes, Grandmother.'

'*Valentines Always Act With Class*.'

'Three bags full, Grandmother.'

We blink at each other.

*Oops. I said that out loud, didn't I?*

Grandma raises her eyebrows.

'Dame Sylvia Valentine?' The ruffled woman coughs behind us again. 'I'm *very* sorry, but I really *do* have to prep Faith now. If you'll please make your way to the ballroom, we've reserved a table with the best *possible* view for you.'

I lick my lips nervously and turn back to my grandmother. 'Thank you.'

She places a small hand on my shoulder and squeezes. 'What I'm trying to say, darling,' she says gently with a tiny, rare smile, 'is *good luck*. I'm sure you'll make us very proud.'

## 43

*Make us very proud.*

In a side room, I'm dusted with mattifying powder, my lipstick is reapplied and I'm wordlessly handed a script. A door swings open for a waiter who brings me a much-needed glass of sparkling water. Behind him, the ballroom glitters and buzzes, full of laughter and conversation.

A microphone screeches on the stage. I lick my lips again and gulp some water.

*Make us very proud.*

My pink lipstick is reapplied once more with a small *tut*.

'Ladies and gentlemen!' *Tap.* 'Silence, please.' *Tap.* 'Welcome to an evening dedicated to raising money for RSS. Do please give a *very* warm hand to your glamorous hostess, the beautiful actress Faith Valentine!'

A burst of applause.

My hands are so damp I can't open the door properly; a sweet-faced waitress balancing a tray of prawns holds it for me and I smile gratefully. Then, with a deep breath, I swish out on to the stage and carefully collect the microphone from its stand by the podium.

*Make us very proud.*

Bright lights momentarily blind me, the applause rises and falls into silence, and – just like that – I'm suddenly nine years old: onstage, dressed in a white sheet and my mother's hat and tennis shoes.

I swallow and blink at the audience.

Many of these faces were there that night: the famous, the beautiful and the powerful, gathered in a white marquee, toasting my parents on their wedding anniversary. Laughing as Max swung his mustard skipping rope, while Hope danced in turquoise, and Mercy stole the show in her red dress.

I haven't seen any of these people in . . . years. Almost exactly two, to be precise.

*Focus, Eff.*

'Good evening, everyone.' With a measured smile, I tap the mike. *Tap tap.* 'I am Faith Valentine.' I

325

glance at the script scrolling on the iPad that's on top of the podium. 'It is an extraordinary pleasure to be here tonight, surrounded by friends and family. By people with huge talents, huge hearts and even bigger bank accounts.'

A collective laugh from the room.

'*Whoop!*' Dylan shouts from the back. 'That's my girl!'

My eyes are starting to adjust to the stage lights. I spot my grandmother at a table near the front, hands folded together neatly, lips thin, watching me with cool grey eyes.

'I am delighted to be here,' I continue, looking back at the lights, 'to help auction some very generously donated items to raise money for—'

A quick glance down. *What in fresh living—*

'The Artists' Retreat for Support and Solace.' I clear my throat. 'Otherwise known as . . .'

'The "A" is silent,' a woman at the side of the stage hisses.

'Yes.' My nostrils flare very slightly. 'The . . . *RSS*, a brand-new charity created to provide sanctuary for those in the acting profession to recuperate from the stress of their difficult jobs.'

*This cannot be happening.*

'I think we all agree –' I look at the iPad again and hurriedly take a gulp of water from the glass discreetly balanced next to it – 'that we are working in an *exhausting* industry. We dedicate our very lives to the pursuit of *truth*. Of *art*. The *exploration* of what it is to be human. Often under difficult circumstances, at the expense of our own health.'

I look up at my grandmother. *Make us very proud.*

And suddenly I cannot do it.

Just . . . *no.*

'Because, let's be honest.' I lean forward to rest my elbows on the stand. 'Nobody needs leisure time *quite* like those who play dress-up for a living, right?' I pretend to pause thoughtfully. 'Other than maybe nurses. Doctors. Firefighters. Teachers. The police. The armed forces. Farmers. Roofers. Paramedics. Plumbers. Electricians. Taxi drivers. Cleaners. Bar staff. Waiters.'

The girl carrying the tray of prawns looks up.

And – just like that – a bolt of hot, uncontrollable anger spikes me from head to toe.

*Whoosh.*

'Let's get started, shall we?' I delete the script

327

and tap on the iPad to bring up the first lot. I am pulsing with a thick, glittering fury as I snatch up my miniature gavel. 'What are we multimillionaires flogging to raise money for ourselves, hmm?'

A photo of a tropical beach glows on the enormous screen behind me.

'Ah.' I laugh. 'A *luxury five-star holiday* for those who pretend to be nurses instead of actually being nurses. I'm starting the bidding at two pounds fifty. Anyone?'

The room has gone completely silent.

'*You*, sir.' I point at a waiter quietly cleaning up a red-wine spill on a white tablecloth and bang my wooden hammer. '*Sold.* Congratulations, you're off to the Bahamas.'

He knocks over the wine bottle.

With a big grin, I tap the iPad again and look over my shoulder. 'Oh, *lovely*, an anonymously donated green Porsche 911 3.8 Carrera, which is one of fourteen cars currently tucked away in storage and being given away for tax purposes.'

I study the crowd carefully.

'Three pounds,' I announce into the microphone. 'Three pounds for this *beautiful* piece of metal, worth more than the deposit on an actual house. Anyone? Waitress with prawns, I'm going to take that as a bid.' *Bang.* 'Sold for three pounds!'

The girl drops her tray with a smash.

'What's next?' I click the screen. 'A depressing painting of a dead blonde in a boat. A fiver?' The producer's hand has hilariously gone up. 'Nobody? No? OK, four quid? Can anyone afford four quid for an old master?'

The door to the kitchen opens.

'*You.*' I wave my hammer in the air as an old guy in a white shirt and black trousers enters with a tray of champagne glasses. 'I'm afraid that interruption counts as a bid. Congratulations, you are the proud owner of a very valuable piece of art.'

'W-What?' He sits down abruptly on a spare seat and puts his hands over his face. 'Oh, my.'

The entire room is starting to bubble. Everyone is slowly turning to examine the shadowy waiters dotted round the room – serving them, cleaning up after them – as if they've *literally never seen them before in their lives.*

'You can't do this!' An ageing actor stands up. 'That's *my* Porsche, you jumped-up little—'

The cameras are going crazy.

'Sit down, please, sir.' I beam at him as my rage powers on. 'Your mid-life crisis is much appreciated and we're well on our way to making a tenner! But let's wrap it up now. Five pence each for the remaining lots.' *Bang.* 'Dude carrying the pigs-in-blankets, you've won a diamond Tiffany necklace.' *Bang.* 'Man tidying table six, you've got a yacht.' *Bang.* 'A brand-new laptop computer to the lady with the pastries.' *Bang.* 'Girl sweeping in the corner – apologies, you've just won a slap-up dinner with this idiot.'

A giant headshot of Dylan is shining behind me.

'Faith!' He jumps up, outraged. '*You* were supposed to bid for that! You could make the grand romantic gesture to buy me just like in the movies!'

'Actually, it's now free,' I say, turning back to the young cleaner. 'I'm sorry – make sure you order the lobster.'

She looks delighted and waves at Dylan. He slumps in his chair, arms folded.

'And that's it, folks.' I gaze round the room now erupting into chaos. *Tap tap tap.* 'I *would also* like to say thank you on behalf of the whole Valentine family. It's been amazing, the way you've completely turned your backs on us over these last two years.'

I smile graciously at everyone.

'*Especially* those who ignored my mother when she so desperately needed you. She was your friend, your co-star and your mentor for thirty-five years. Your behaviour has been *quite* the education.'

For just a second, my eyes accidentally rest on my grandmother and I feel a swoop of shame. She's rigid, white and suddenly looks so very, very old.

'Did you hear about the fed-up pancake?' I ask the audience loudly. 'HE JUST FLIPPED.'

Total silence while I start laughing hysterically.

'So here's to us, me included.' I hold up my glass of sparkling water and cheer everyone so it splashes. 'We are officially a right bunch of RSSs.'

Then I drop the gavel to the floor.

*Bang.*

44

What's easy to get into, but hard to get out of?

Trouble.

I walk offstage and I don't stop.

With my head up, I keep going: out of the back door of the Dorchester and straight across London. Round Hyde Park Corner, past Buckingham Palace and Westminster Cathedral and Tesco Express and the Embassy of Lithuania; across Vauxhall Bridge and the Thames; through Stockwell, past Lidl and the O2 Academy.

Two hours of walking in the street-lamped dark. Fifteen minutes in painfully high Prada heels – the rest hobbling with a twisted ankle and blistered bare feet on the filthy pavement. And I'm not going to lie – I barely notice the pain.

I. Am. *Buzzing.*

*Buzz buzz buzzz. Buzz. Buzz. Buzzzzzzzzz buzzzzzz buzzzz.*

*Buzzzzzzzzzzzzzzzzzzzzzzzzzzzz—*

That's the sound of a doorbell being pressed, by the way, not me; I was speaking metaphorically.

'Dude, that is an unnecessarily aggressive entry request. Come on in, whoever you are. Fifty-fourth floor. The lift's broken.'

The door clicks.

I look down: my left ankle is visibly swollen and both feet are dark grey and covered in weeping white blisters. There's a small cut on my right sole that is leaving a little smear of blood with every step.

I look up the cement stairs. *Fifty-four floors.*
*Cool.*

Wincing, I start limping up. *First floor. Second . . .*
Ow.
*Third.*
Seriously: ow.
*Fourth . . .*

Leaning against the wall, I rub my sore ankle. One of my pus-filled blisters explodes against my

333

fingers. Bet Marilyn Monroe had the same problem.

Then I keep limping. *Fifth*—

'Faith?' An amused voice carries up from the floor below me. 'Where are you going, Looney Tune? And why are you leaving a trail of blood through the hallway like a snail on its period?'

I stare down. Scarlett's freckled, elfin face is poking over the stair rail and tilted in my direction, eyebrows sharply raised.

'I thought you said it was fifty-four floors?'

'Yeah, that was a joke, pal,' she laughs with a snort. 'We're in Brixton, not Dubai.'

I look up. *Ohhhh.* I'd blush in embarrassment, but the majority of my blood is tracked all over the stairwell.

Grimacing, I limp back to the fourth floor and into Scarlett's flat.

'Do you want some Prada heels?' I ask her, ripping my wig off, collapsing on the carpeted floor and handing the gold horrors to her. 'I can't fully recommend them as hiking boots.'

Scarlett holds them up to the light, then tosses them aside.

'Hmm, I'll pass, thanks. And this small pedigree

dog?' She nudges the discarded wig with a toe. 'No sale. I think it's dead.'

'Finally. It's been chewing on my head all night.'

We both chuckle.

Then Scarlett slides down her living-room wall until she's sitting quietly next to me. I've had hundreds of people staring at me tonight – outside the hotel, at the auction, while I was limping through Westminster barefoot – but this is the first time it feels like someone's actually *looking*.

'Go on, then,' my friend says, carefully wrapping a jumper round my lacerated feet. 'Before the blood poisoning sets in. Tell me everything, right from the start.'

I clear my throat, take a deep breath and allow this morning to come back to me.

'So I . . . had another meltdown. A . . . big one. I . . . umm . . . lost it in an improv class. In front of everyone. Got . . . carried away.'

'*How* carried away?'

'Picked up a boy I barely know, physically hauled him across the room, slammed him repeatedly against a wall, screamed death threats at him and started crying hysterically?'

335

Scarlett bursts into laughter. 'Sounds like *he* was the one getting carried away, Eff.' She elbows me. 'Too soon for jokes? OK, please continue. What was the exercise?'

'Just some . . . improv scene.'

Too soon. Too raw.

'Faith.' Scarlett frowns. 'You do realise *everyone* melts down in acting class? You're supposed to. It's what you're paying for. You can't shake a bottle of intense human emotions and not expect it to fizz up and explode.'

My eyes open wide. 'Really?'

'Ah, *yeah*. When I was at drama school, somebody cried, screamed or vomited every day and they were thrilled. It meant we were getting some actual *work* done.'

*Huh.* 'So I'm not . . . mad?'

'Of course you're mad. You're an actor.' Scarlett grins her sharp, Joker-smile. 'Eff, this is great! I knew you could do it! You'll be a movie star in no time. Congratulations! And what else has happened today?' she asks, pointedly staring at my battered feet.

My stomach twists sharply – sickness rises.

I open my mouth. The warm buzz of adrenaline is wearing off – along with the numbness of my feet – and what I did this evening is only now beginning to hit me.

Grandma's horrified face.

The entire industry.

The outrage.

My dramatic swan dive into career oblivion.

I don't even think they all deserved my tirade. The majority of that audience didn't even know my mother personally. They were just there because they'd been told to be.

Shame, guilt and fear lurch across my stomach.

*You'll make us very proud.*

'Nope,' I say uncomfortably, tugging my floaty, dirty-white chiffon dress round me. 'That's everything.'

'Sure?'

'Mmm-hmm.'

'So.' Scarlett frowns. 'You definitely *haven't* been giving away Porsches or diamonds or holidays or priceless paintings today? Because frankly that's a very disappointing Friday.'

I stare at her.

'It's *everywhere* online.' A bright laugh as she holds her phone out. 'Sometimes I think you forget who you *are*.'

## FAITH VALENTINE
## ROBS THE HOOD

'Oh God.' My hand goes over my mouth. 'I'm a *thief*?'

'Absolutely.' Scarlett scrolls down. 'The most famous fox in the world. Read it.'

Frowning, I study the article.

This evening, Faith Valentine – granddaughter of esteemed thespian Dame Sylvia Valentine – handed £2.8 million worth of donations over to staff at a celebrity auction at the Dorchester. 'I went in with £32 in my bank account,' said 61-year-old waiter Tim McConnell. 'I came out with a yacht. I'm not sure what else to say.'

After a standing ovation from the audience, Faith's political stance is being widely supported by prominent members of the film industry. 'It's about time,' an A-list actor tweeted. 'Spread the wealth. Faith is an inspiration. Rename it Actors' Redistribution and Support Society and I'll donate right now.'

The up-and-coming actress, who also gave away a Tiffany diamond pendant, a priceless painting, a luxury holiday and a Porsche 911, disappeared immediately after the event. Her grandmother, also in attendance, was similarly unavailable for comment.

An official spokesman for RSS said: 'THE "A" IS SILENT.'


'Maybe you should have meltdowns more frequently, Valentine.' Scarlett grins and squeezes my hand. 'Maybe we *all* should.'

I grin and squeeze back, eyes suddenly stinging as I catch an unexpected expression on her face.

My phone starts ringing.

'Scarlett?' I cancel the call without looking and frown. There's an unfamiliar sadness in her eyes, a tightness in her jawline, a wobble in her top lip. 'Tell me, right from the start. Before the blood poisoning sets in.'

She laughs and blows out slowly. 'Well . . . I've

been invited to play Éponine in the touring US version of *Les Mis*.'

My breath disappears.

'*No*.' I'm on my feet. '*No*, Letty. No way! That's . . . EVEN I KNOW THAT PART AND I KNOW NOTHING ABOUT MUSICALS! YOU DID IT!'

Who knew I could even *squeal* like this?

'We've got a place in New York!' I jump up as my phone starts ringing again. *Cancel.* 'You can stay there! And I can visit, and we can go and see Broadway shows, and you'll tour Boston and Colorado and Chicago, which has the *best* deep-pan pizza, and – and—'

She bursts into noisy tears.

'Oh, Scarlett!' I sit back down next to her, alarmed. 'Don't be nervous! America is super cool and you're going to be brilliant! You are *made* for this role!'

'I *knowww I am*!' she howls into the air. 'I've been singing "On My Own" into a shampoo bottle and swiping dirt on my face since I was three years old. It's *my* part. *Mine*.'

'So why—'

'Because I can't take it!' She hiccups and wipes

her eyes. 'I start filming *Fright Fortnight* in Iceland next week, and I'm contracted for six months. They'd *sue* me.'

My phone rings for the third time. I cancel it again.

'But can't you—' My brain spins. 'There must be a way you can—'

'No. I can't. The network took a huge risk giving such a prominent part to an unknown. I can't screw them over last minute. You know that, Eff.'

We both stare numbly into space.

I desperately want to comfort her in some way, but she's right – pulling out now would be career suicide.

My phone starts ringing yet again.


**Noah**


I watch my boyfriend's handsome face flash for a few seconds. Looks like he's read the papers too.

'Sooooo.' Scarlett wipes her face and smiles faintly. 'You gonna answer that or do I have to sit on the poor fellow again?'

I chew on my top lip guiltily.

341

'I'm going to answer. Maybe. I don't know. I asked for time, but . . .' My breathing is starting to quicken, flatten, tighten. 'I need to make a decision. I know that. He's waited long enough. I just don't . . . I'm not . . . I . . .'

Where the hell are my running shoes when I need them?

The call runs out and the blue light flashes. My friend gently takes my phone from my hands, puts it on the floor and stands up.

'Before you decide, there's something I want to show you.'

# 45

Why don't skeletons fight each other?

They don't have any guts.

Umm, *now* it's time to start cleaning?

I watch in amazement as Scarlett begins to tidy her apartment: pushing the sofa bed to the wall, grabbing both sides of the coffee table and sliding it over. She rolls up the rug and props it against the door, moves a few cushions and shuffles a big yucca plant into a corner.

With a growing sense of confusion, I watch her clear a large space in the living room. I thought Scarlett enjoyed mess? Is she . . . going to make me *wrestle* her?

Once the room is almost empty, she begins to walk round her chaotic flat, picking up small objects:

the remote control for the television, one gold Prada shoe, the wig, a cup of cold tea, a half-melted candle, a framed photograph, Stanislavski's acting book, a small cactus, a yellow plastic toy robot.

She places each on the floor, one by one.

'OK.' Slightly out of breath, she puts a saucepan down and brushes her fringe back. 'In the middle, please, Valentine.'

I stare at her, then at the shape she's made on the floor.

OK, Scarlett Bell is probably my best friend and I think the world of her, etc. etc., but this is the kind of stuff *Satan-worshipping cults* do just before they sacrifice you.

'There?' I check, standing up dubiously.

'It's a circle, Eff.' She laughs. 'Geometrically, there's only one middle. Stay there for the purposes of this exercise, please.'

Obediently, I enter the circle and sit down.

'Do I have to block the whole world out now?' I glance worriedly at the acting book. 'Because I have to tell you that my grandmother has already tried to teach me that technique multiple times and I'm really not very—'

'Oh, screw Stanislavski. Stay seated.'

Scarlett disappears into the kitchen and returns with a multipack of Mars bars, some ginger biscuits, crisps and a large bucket of jelly beans. Then she climbs up on top of a chair and starts eating them all noisily.

My stomach grumbles; a couple of really public meltdowns, no vol-au-vents and a long, bare-footed hike across London can really sharpen the appetite.

'Letty, can I please have—'

'No,' she says. 'Be quiet, please.'

Ah, I get it. She's going to deprive me of sugar until I'll say just about anything.

'So how long do I— *OW.*'

A lime jelly bean just smacked me in the face.

'Oops,' Scarlett says, shoving a biscuit into her mouth. 'Didn't mean to do that. My bad.'

With another very deliberate flick of her wrist, an orange jelly bean flies at my head and bounces off.

'Hey!' I stare at her. 'What are you doing?'

'Nothing.'

This time a mini Mars bar gets lobbed hard, whacking me on the nose.

'*Scarlett!*' I jump up. 'I'm not sure what's going on or what kind of game we're playing, but I—'

Now a ginger biscuit frisbees into my stomach.

'Oh my God –' a few crisps – 'will you please *stop* throwing things at me? I know you like lobbing food at people, but—'

'What's the problem?' Scarlett frowns and chucks another jelly bean. 'You joined in last time.'

'Yes, but—'

Making direct eye contact with me, she kicks the yucca pot plant over. Then she stamps on the plastic robot, boots the cup of tea so it splashes everywhere and flings the remote control at the wall. Savagely kicking out at everything. Grinning, she steps over the toppled houseplant.

With a terrifying, Joker-like expression, she begins to walk slowly towards me. My heart is thumping. My throat is tightening. Everything's feeling itchy and hot. Whatever kind of dumb bonding game this is, I do *not like it*.

'Letty—'

My friend prods me with a finger. 'Hmm?'

'Please stop prodding me.'

'I'm not prodding you,' she says, prodding me again.

'You are and I'm asking you to stop, please.'

'Well, newsflash.' Prod. 'This is *my* living room.' Prod. 'It's *my* finger.' Prod. 'And if I feel like prodding it in your face—' Prod. 'Then that's what I'm gonna do.'

There's a lump in my throat and I feel like I'm about to start crying. *Don't cry, don't cry, don't cry, don't cry—*

Instead, I instinctively turn to run.

'Legging it again, are ya?' Scarlett grabs my wrist and pulls me back into the centre of her circle, holding me firmly. 'Well, I'm not going to let you. So *whatcha gonna do about it, Valentine?*'

It isn't a warm *whoosh* this time. It's a cold knife.

Anger rushes through me so sharply and so cleanly that I could hold it out and slice the room in half. With a set jaw, I shake Scarlett off.

Moving away, I crouch down and start furiously snatching up all the kicked or thrown items: the teacup, the pot plant, the remote control, the broken toy robot, the wig, the candle, the gold shoe. I grab a few more things for good measure: cushions, a laptop, a handbag.

Then, shiny with rage, I move to the spare part of the room and start placing them on the floor around me.

Scarlett takes one big step towards it.

'NO!' I yell, jumping up.

She raises her eyebrows. '*Excuse* me?'

'I SAID NO!' I hold my hands out like a ninja, trembling with icy, clear fury. 'I do *not* like having things kicked or thrown at me. I do *not* like being told to shut up. I do *not* like being prodded. I do *not* like being pulled at or grabbed. I *asked* you to stop, but you didn't. So STAY OUT OF MY CIRCLE!'

Breathing hard, I pick a red jelly bean off the floor next to me and lob it into my mouth.

'MMMMMMMM!' I add, chewing defiantly. 'DELICIOUS.'

There's carpet fluff attached to it – I swallow anyway.

We stare at each other.

*Come on, then.* I lift my chin and set my jaw. *Come on. Fight me. FIGHT ME, SCARLETT. DISRESPECT ME JUST ONE MORE TIME AND SEE WHAT HAPPENS.*

With a satisfied laugh, she begins to clap slowly.

'*Exactly.*' She walks over until she's standing at the edge of my neat little ring. Her face is soft again, the Joker expression gone. 'It's not about pretending there's nothing outside the circle, Eff. It's about making your own circle and then deciding what you let *in*.'

Scarlett bends down and picks up the crushed toy robot.

'You're allowed to ask for what you want. You're allowed to say *stop* and *no*. It's called having boundaries. You keep going "crazy" because you don't *have* any, so everyone just pushes and pulls at you until you either explode or run.'

I open my mouth but nothing comes out.

'It's *your* life, Faith.' Scarlett gently pushes the little robot into my hand. 'Which means *you* get to make the rules.'

In my pocket, my phone has started ringing loudly again and I reach for it on autopilot. My head feels like it's about to explode.

'Faith?' Persephone is clipped. 'Where are you?'

'At a friend's house,' I whisper.

'The location, please. We're sending a car. You need to get home right now.'

## 46

*You're allowed to ask for what you want.*

'. . . could have done a lot of damage. Faith, you must check with me before you—'

*You're allowed to say* stop *and* no.

'. . . had a huge impact on peers and public. Everyone is rallying behind—'

*It's called having boundaries.*

'. . . given your brand an unexpected edge. You're no longer the generic beautiful girl—'

*You keep going 'crazy' because you don't* have *any.*

'. . . in PR terms you've pulled a one-eighty—'

*So everyone just pushes and pulls at you.*

'. . . offers flooding in – pick any role you want—'

*Until you either explode or run.*

'. . . the world is your oyster—'

'Do you know where that saying comes from?' I interrupt.

350

Then I put Persephone on speakerphone and prop my mobile on my knees. I stare blankly out of the taxi window into the darkness. 'It's from Shakespeare's *The Merry Wives of Windsor*. I watched it six times when Mum played Falstaff in an all-female production.'

It's the first thing I've said this whole journey.

'Well, yes!' Persephone sounds *waaaay* more enthusiastic than she normally does. 'And it's true! It's—'

'Do you know what it means?' The taxi turns a corner. 'It means you have to struggle to prise life open with a knife and even then there's only a tiny chance of finding a pearl.'

'How interesting—'

'But we stick *The World Is Your Oyster* on everything as if it means that we can have anything we want, whenever we want it. And it's not true.'

'That's very—'

The taxi pulls up outside the gates of the Valentine mansion.

'Sorry, but I've got to go,' I say, ending the call.

There are more paparazzi here than I have ever seen before in my life. Dozens and dozens huddled together in the dark. As soon as they spot the taxi, they start yelling, waving their arms, taking photos.

*Flash flash flash flash.*

I swallow, hard.

'Miss Valentine?' The taxi driver glances at me in the rear-view mirror. 'Do you want me to take you somewhere else?' *Flash flash flash.* 'Literally anywhere else?'

'It's OK, thank you.' With shaking hands, I smooth down my dress. 'I've got this.'

I reach out of the window – *flash* – and type in the security code on the gate pad, and, with a click, the gates swing open.

The paps swarm through and the taxi crawls up the driveway with them all running next to us. They're shouting, banging on the car doors, racing towards the elaborate front steps of my home.

We stop and I take a slow, deep breath. Then I open the taxi door and climb out, holding the little plastic robot tightly in one clenched fist.

*You get to make the rules.*

'FAITH! FAITH! RSS IS THREATENING TO TAKE LEGAL ACTION – DO YOU HAVE A RESPONSE?'

'HAVE YOU SPOKEN TO DAME SYLVIA?'

'WAS THIS A POLITICAL MOVE? HOW LONG DID YOU PLAN IT?'

'DID DYLAN HARRIS HELP YOU?'

Slowly, I walk barefoot through the paparazzi in my floaty, filthy evening gown until I'm standing on the top step. Then I turn to face them.

'OR,' someone yells helpfully, 'ARE YOU HAVING A FULL MENTAL BREAKDOWN, JUST LIKE YOUR MUM?'

There's silence while I search for my own words. Because this time there's no script and no pre-approved answers. This time I won't be hushed or talked over, I won't be spoken for and I won't *keep my mouth shut* any more.

My voice is mine. It's up to me to use it.

'Hello,' I say clearly. 'I am Faith Valentine.' *Flash flash flash flash.* 'I'm introducing myself because we've never met before. Yet here you are, in front of my home.'

I look across the mass of unknown faces.

'Everyone here has probably had their heart broken,' I say slowly. 'We've all cried, and laughed, and been scared or unhappy. We've all said the wrong

353

things, worn the wrong things, dated the wrong people.'

My eyes travel over the crowd.

They land briefly on the T-zone blogger from Richmond Park, standing towards the back with his phone in the air. He gives me an excited wave and I smile slightly.

'But how many of you have your most painful, treasured or humiliating moments turned into entertainment for strangers?'

Silence.

The blogger looks at the ground.

I draw myself up as tall as I can. 'Every day, for nearly a year, I have been chased, judged, criticised, questioned and exposed. You have commented on my body and graded my face. You have mocked my personality and my love life. You have called me names and taken photos of me without my permission. You have put me on a pedestal and knocked me off it again.'

A few older journalists shuffle uncomfortably and I see the blogger from the park stuff his phone into his pocket.

'I am *sixteen*, and you're treating me like a doll

you can squabble over until you break me. At which point, you'll throw me away and move on to another girl who's shiny and new.'

I think of my mother lying in her darkened bedroom. No longer shiny. No longer new.

'But—' A journalist holds his Dictaphone up. 'Faith, *surely* with the fame you've been born into, with the *privilege*, comes—'

'Payment?' I raise my eyebrows. 'For a life I didn't choose or ask for? You are deciding who I am before I've even decided myself.'

I know I'm incredibly lucky to be born into an extraordinary life of opportunities and fortune. But the world is *not* my oyster.

And right now it's *me* that's being prised open; me having the pearl ripped out and sold without my permission, over and over again. Look what we found! Do we like it? How much can we get for it? Was it worth it? Should we keep searching for a new one? Everybody, look!

Maybe the oyster wanted to stay shut. Maybe it just wanted to keep its secret treasure to itself and for everybody to *leave it the hell alone*.

'*None* of this is real.' I gesture at myself. 'Not my

social-media posts. Not my quotes. Not my interviews. Not the clothes I wear or the people I date or the places I go. You have *no idea* who Faith Valentine is.'

The door behind me opens and a large hand appears.

*Quick, quick, quick—*

'So I'm asking you, please, to—'

In one swift motion, I'm pulled into the house.

47

—*STOP.*

'Right,' Max says, carrying me into the living room and dropping me into an armchair. 'Enough of that, Little Miss Scrappy McScrappison. Don't make me get the imaginary dogs.'

Livid, I kick and then bite him.

'Ow!' my brother yelps, sitting on top of me. 'Eff, did you just *bite* me? This is new – I'm both impressed and possibly infected.'

'Get *off* me.' I punch him. 'What are you doing?!'

'This is an inter-action,' Hope explains solemnly, perching at my feet with huge eyes. 'We are inter-actioning you, Faith Valentine.'

'An intervention,' Max corrects, standing up.

'That too.' My little sister nods in agreement. 'What happens is that we *vent in* you, Eff, and then

357

you can *vent in* us.' She frowns. 'Although shouldn't it be *vent at*? *At-a-vention*. Somebody needs to sort that out.'

I stare at my brother and sister in amazement and then at Mercy standing silently by the fire, fiddling with a candlestick.

I snort in frustration. They're doing this *now*?

'You've *got* to be kidding me. I don't need an in—'

'You do.' Mercy turns to stare at my dirty feet. 'Where are your shoes? Where is your hair? Faith, this isn't you. Smashing mirrors? Twitter fights? Ranting at the media on our front doorstep? Punching, yelling, *biting*? None of this is you.'

'We *know* you're heartbroken,' Po says gently, patting my knees. 'I can't even *imagine* what it's like losing Noah, your soulmate, the person you trusted over everyone—'

I open my mouth and Mercy exhales loudly.

'Stop it!' Hope wheels round on her, furious. 'Stop it, Mer! Just because *your* heart is all shrivelled and empty and black doesn't mean that others can't be hurt!'

Our sister winces and looks abruptly at the floor.

'This is not about—' I start.

'She's right,' Max says, frowning. 'You haven't been yourself since that kiss, Eff. We *miss* you. We just want the sweet Faith we know and love back again.'

'I—'

'We are *here* for you, Eff.' Po grabs my hand. 'Whatever will make you happy again we will *do* it. Just *tell us how to fix you.*'

She squeezes my fingers and they all stare at me. Silence.

'Can I speak now?' I say, standing up. My siblings open their mouths. 'Oh. Nope. Looks like you're not quite done yet. Please, do continue. Would somebody like to sit on me again or are you happy to do that verbally?'

They shut their mouths.

My heart is starting to beat very fast. My breath catches, as if I've been running a really long way, for a really long time. Maybe I have.

'You don't get it, do you?' I snap. 'I am so *done* with being the person you need me to be. Sometimes it feels like I exist just to balance you all out. Like you took the decent roles, and I'm just a blank secondary character for you all to bounce off.'

Their eyes get a little rounder.

'Do you think I want to be the Pretty One? The Good One? The Nice One? Do you know how *boring* that is? How it makes me feel like I can't *breathe*?'

My brother opens his mouth. 'No, Max. I've listened to you, now you listen to me. You get to do whatever you like, go wherever you like, *be* whoever you like. You're the eldest, but you don't want the prestigious Valentine acting mantle. Too much hard work? Fine. Don't worry about that – reliable old Faith will pick it up.'

Max goes uncharacteristically pink and I turn to Hope.

'Sweetheart.' My stomach clenches with guilt. 'I'm sorry, but I am so far from perfect. Everything I do is not *right*. Everything I think is not *good*. I make mistakes like every normal, screwed-up teenager. But I can't *move* for fear of letting you down.'

Po blinks a few times, then sits in the armchair I just vacated.

'Gosh,' she says in a small voice.

I turn to Mercy.

'And, Mer.' The blood has drained from her face,

360

but I can't stop, I *won't* stop. 'You're allowed to be *you* because I have to be *me*. You get to be sharp and mean because *I* am kind and sweet. You get to be the Black Swan because *I* am the White Swan.'

My throat tightens.

'But I didn't *choose* this part and I never wanted it. I don't want to keep spinning in circles in the spotlight, trying as hard as I can not to fall over with the whole world watching.'

My heart is racing, my voice wobbling.

'So maybe I'm not *myself* right now. Maybe I'm not the Faith Valentine you *know and love*. Maybe I wanted to see who I could be if I *wasn't*.'

'Faith—'

'Please! I need you all to *give me some space*.'

Cheeks hot, I run upstairs and take my passport out of the safe in the landing and shove it in my handbag. Then I head to the back door.

It swings open before I reach it.

'Effie!'

'Noah?'

'Eff, I'm so glad you're here! The media are going crazy out front and I've rung like a million times, but you won't talk to me so I figured I'd have to—'

'No,' I say, walking straight past him.

'Umm.' Noah follows me. '*No* . . . what? I know I should've been to see you before now, but I am on tour, Eff, and I did text you a *lot*. It's not like you haven't been busy – I've seen the papers – trying to make me jealous with that Dylan guy and—'

'No.' I keep walking.

'I don't understand. What are you saying?'

Noah speeds up until he's standing in front of me – blocking my path – and in a rush of sadness I can suddenly see the entire year we've spent together.

All the times I went where he told me to go, wore what he told me to wear, became whomever he told me to be. All the times I nodded and smiled and dimpled on cue.

All the times he didn't listen to how I was doing, or even ask. All the times I tried to tell or show him what I needed and he ignored me, all the times we both put what he wanted above what I did.

All the times I said *yes* or *OK* or *fine* when I meant—

'No.'

'But—' Noah races after me again. 'I *love* you, Eff, you're—'

362

'You don't love me,' I say simply. 'I'm sorry, but you love Faith Valentine, and that's not the same thing.'

My boyfriend of a year frowns in confusion. Even now, he can't see the difference.

'But . . .' He pulls desperately at my sleeve. 'Is this *still* about that stupid kiss, Eff? Because I am telling you, for the millionth time, it didn't mean *anything*. Just forgive me, and I *know* we can go back to exactly how we were.'

I stare at him. He. Does. Not. Get. It.

I don't want a *mouldy sandwich* love. I don't want a relationship where it feels like *I'm disappearing and that's OK*. I want to be with someone who lets me say *no*, and Noah is not that person. Because he was happy when I didn't.

I shake him off.

'No,' I say for the final time, climbing through the bushes. It's not about the kiss – it never actually was. 'I'm sorry, Noah. But this is very much over.'

## 48

My agent picks up immediately.

Through the hole in the fence at the bottom of the garden – the secret hole Valentines have been escaping out of for nearly a century – I can see the roof of my home, partially visible over the trees.

*It's* my *life and* I *get to make the rules.*

'Hi, Persephone,' I say. 'Did you mean it when you said I could pick any role I wanted?'

The next move is my choice.

And I know exactly who I want to be.

**49**

## LEAP OF FAITH

Following weeks of speculation, Faith Valentine is officially reconfirmed as the lead in *Fright Fortnight*. The British Ice Queen, who had previously withdrawn from filming for personal reasons (see Chart of Shame), publicly admitted that she had 'made mistakes'.

'We are delighted to have Faith Valentine back,' a spokesperson announced. 'She was always our first choice.'

Scarlett Bell – the unknown actress who has been axed from the show – is said to be 'in total shock' at this last-minute switch.

*Finally*, the newspapers nail it.

Scarlett is indeed in shock for forty-eight hours straight, from the second I turn up at her flat.

'I just— I can't—' Letty keeps wandering around in bewildered circles, like a gerbil with a head injury. 'I didn't mean for you to— It doesn't— I cannot believe that you—'

I laugh and eat another piece of cold lasagne.

It's been two days since I walked out on the Valentines. There are no queen-size beds, no pure silk duvet covers, no dawn birds singing sweetly, no yoga sessions, no marble en-suites here. The threadbare sofa bed is scratchy and at one point I roll over and the whole thing folds in half with me inside it, like a burrito. The towel I'm using smells of unwashed socks; the pillow has lumps in it and I don't know what they are.

At 3am, Scarlett's upstairs neighbours start screaming.

At 5am and 6:10am, a baby joins in.

But – even in the chaos – it still feels like I made the right decision.

'Scarlett,' I laugh, stuffing more lasagne in my

mouth. 'Stop with the pacing. A wise girl knows her limits; a smart girl knows that she has none.'

My friend narrows her bright green eyes.

'Imperfection is beauty,' I nod with my mouth crammed full. 'Madness is genius, and it's better to be absolutely ridiculous than absolutely boring.'

She puts her hands on her hips.

'We are *all* of us stars.' I throw my arms out at her, wiggling my eyebrows. 'And we *deserve* to twinkl—'

A cushion is thrown at my head.

'*Stop Marilyn Monroe-ing me*,' Scarlett laughs, brandishing a takeaway box. 'I'm grateful, Eff, but not *that* grateful. Who *wouldn't* want to move to a frozen lava field in Iceland for six months?'

A hand claps over her mouth and she goes back to pacing.

'Oh my days.' Scarlett pauses. 'You're moving to *a lava field in Iceland for half a year because of me*, Eff.' Another circle. 'I'll be partying in the US and you'll be . . . I cannot believe that I— You—' She suddenly disappears from the living room and returns laden with clothes.

'Scarlett,' I smile. 'You don't need to—'

'I *know*,' she declares, thrusting the heap at me. 'Warm coat. Snow boots. Thermal vests. Jumpers. Gloves. Scarves. Sunglasses. Take it. Please. It's going to be cold out there. It's going to be lonely. It's going to be empty and dark and bleak and icy and—'

With a *mew* of distress, Scarlett jumps on the bed and wraps her freckled arms round me tightly.

'*Thank you*,' she whispers.

'Look, you may not know this,' I say, patting the top of her bleach-blonde head, 'but I am very, very rich and very, very famous. I don't need you to give me free clothes. Especially not from . . .' I look at a label. 'Primark.'

'Sale,' she adds earnestly. 'Take the suitcase too.'

'And,' I laugh, 'this is what I *want*. I've thought about it carefully and I think you underestimate just how much I'm looking forward to getting out of England. Moving my circle away for a bit. Cold, icy, empty, bleak? I'm the *Ice Queen*, Letty. My favourite colour is *grey*. Iceland has got me written *all* over it.'

Scarlett grins widely.

'You know, that's kind of true. It's your spirit

368

home, you beautiful, inhospitable goddess.' Then
she drags a huge wad of papers out from under the
sofa and lobs it at me. 'Here. This is yours too.'

My stomach twists abruptly: *the script*.

It's the only thing I've been trying not to think
about. I'm happy to leave my home, fly to another
country, get set up in the middle of nowhere. But,
when I get out there, I'll still have to . . . you know.
*Act*.

'Cool!' I smile and nod. 'This looks fun!'

'OK, the fake happy expression is wasted on me,'
Scarlett sighs. 'Pour some of this talent into the job
you just nicked off me, please.'

'Excuse me?' I laugh. '*Nicked?*'

'Generously borrowed – please don't give it back.'
Scarlett snorts and opens the chunky script. 'We've
got two days before you leave for the airport, so
we'd better start now.'


We study for the next forty-eight hours.

Together, we camp out on the sofa with a series
of pizzas and give it everything we've got. Scarlett
goes through my scenes with a highlighter, drilling
the lines until I know them, until I understand them,

until I remember what each reaction should be. She writes notes in the margins: *don't cry here*; *internalise the pain*; *flicker of alarm*; *how does she show fear?*

And, slowly, my new character starts to slot together, until Frankie starts to feel . . . almost real. Honestly, my friend teaches me more about acting in two days than my grandmother did in a full year.

A sharp twist of guilt. *Grandma.*

I turned my phone off straight after leaving home, and I haven't turned it back on again since. I used Scarlett's to call Persephone again and make my travel arrangements. But my grandmother's face at the auction is still imprinted on my brain – ghostly white and full of disappointment.

And Mum?

I can't even think about Mum right now. It's time my siblings did their share. I-I just . . . *can't.*

'Right,' Scarlett says, dragging my bulging Primark suitcase into the lift. The studio car is patiently waiting outside. 'This is it, I guess. Next time I see you, you'll be standing in Reykjavik airport, asking why I'm video-calling because you only left a few hours ago and I need to get a life.'

I laugh and step into the elevator. Tomorrow, Scarlett flies to America and all I can feel is a blur of bittersweet happiness and gratitude. She somehow saw the real me without needing to crack me in two first. She gave me the chance to open up slowly, because I wanted to, and it has changed . . . *everything.*

In a wave of love, I jump out and hug Scarlett tightly.

'Whoa,' she smiles, raising her arm as the lift doors try to shut on us. 'What is this out-of-character display of warmth? Careful, Eff, or your icy reputation will be in tatters.'

I laugh and wipe my eyes. 'Have fun in America.'

'Have fun in Iceland.'

'Hey.' I step back and blink. 'I thought you said the lift was broken?'

Scarlett flashes her sharp, wide grin as the doors begin shutting between us.

'Jokes, Valentine. It's all jokes.'

## 50

**WELCoME BACK To A VERY SPECIAL PRoNoUNCEMENT FRoM THE T-ZoNE.**

*After careful consideration, this blog is closing down.*

*Thanks for all the followship – see you at break outside the chemistry block, Kevin.*

*Love and dragons. Tim x*

*PS What actually IS a T-zone, does anyone know?*

Silence.

I step into the cold.

It's night-time in Iceland when I arrive, and the crisp air is clean and somehow bright-smelling, even without daylight. The few remaining passengers mill quietly through Reykjavik airport, passing through the glass doors and into the car park. No journalists, no cameras, no questions. Tentatively, I take my sunglasses off.

The sky seems somehow further away, faintly tinged with orange light from the city. With a small sigh, I close my eyes and tilt my head back. Deliciously fresh air rushes up my nose and down the back of my throat, so icy and clear it feels like water.

Blinking, I inhale again.

And again.

Again.

'Miss Valentine?'

A blonde woman in a puffy green parka stands in front of me, her fur-lined hood pulled round turquoise eyes. She wears an official production lanyard and holds a large laminated sign saying *Scarlett Bell – Fright Fortnight*.

I smile and take another long, deep breath. Where has all this *air* been hiding?

'I'm Berglind.' Her voice is soft, accented. 'I'll be helping you to be settling into Iceland. But you are coming with me now.'

Without another word, she takes my suitcase and starts rolling it towards a black jeep.

For a second, I don't want to move. I just want to stand here, breathing, feeling the emptiness and the stillness and the cold rushing in and out of me.

Biting my lip, I pull my phone out of my pocket, turn it on and wait for the messages, the emails, the missed phone calls, the notifications, the headlines, the *ping ping ping ping ping*.

## NO SERVICE

With a smile, I take another long, frozen breath. And I turn my phone back off again.

We drive for hours.

Away from the lights of Reykjavik into an expanse of darkness: just two yellow headlights shining on a long black road. Berglind doesn't say anything so I stare out of the window, trying to work out where we're going. With every minute, the night gets darker, the countryside emptier, the road lonelier. Finally, we pull on to a gravel track.

The jeep crunches and bounces through nothing

374

up to two tiny wooden cabins – square, painted black, barely visible.

'We stay here one night,' Berglind announces.

She gives me a key and a flashlight, points to the furthest hut, waves goodnight and that's that: assistance over. Swallowing – this country doesn't have its own genre of horror movie for nothing – I make my way through the pitch-black, open the wooden door and turn the light on.

Plywood nailed to the walls, an exposed bulb hanging from the ceiling, one grey chair, one white cup, one single bed, one pillow. One wall is a sliding glass door and through that I see a lake. Silver water edged with stick-like trees outlined in the moonlight.

I drop my suitcase. I have traded all the gold and velvet and marble and silk of the Valentines for a single bulb hanging in front of a pale grey lake.

Opening the glass door, I walk towards the water.

I can't see or hear a living thing. Even the shrubbery seems bony and dead. The solitude is a rattling, wind-blown emptiness.

I reach the lake and look up at the sky. It's so black it's almost blue. It pulls away, stretching back from the ground like a lid being lifted. A mass of

*375*

white stars are sprayed across it, the wind is fresh, the silence aches and I feel . . .

Clean. Calm. *Free.*

And slowly I begin to experience it again – that loosening, untethering.

With a burst of happiness, I lift my chin.

'WHAT DID THE BUDDHIST SAY TO THE HOT-DOG VENDOR?' I scream into the darkness, spinning in a circle. 'MAKE ME ONE WITH EVERYTHING!'

Above the lake, a flicker of lime-green twists across the sky.

*Ha.*

Knew that was a good one.

Then – laughing – I turn and make my way back to solitude.

## 51

*How do you work out which direction the sun is coming up?*

*It will dawn on you.*

'Faith?' Berglind knocks on my door softly. 'Are you dressed? It's a long drive and the storm is coming.'

Quickly, I tug on two pairs of leggings, a fleecy hoodie and Scarlett's snow boots, zip the case up and grab my tote bag.

By the time we've piled our luggage into the jeep, the sky above us has deepened to charcoal grey and thickened with clouds. We bounce down the gravel track, then start speeding along the straight black road.

The empty landscape shifts with every mile, from

flatness to mounds to hills to mountains. Volcanoes poke in jagged peaks into the gathering clouds, lined at the tips with dazzling snow. Neon-turquoise water runs next to us, streaming through lime-green grass, pooling into rivers and lakes, dripping down crags.

As the car gathers speed, I watch the land rise and fall. Sharply, as if it's breathing hard.

Fields of once-molten lava have settled into expanses of flat blackness. To our right, a furious sea appears, smashing like a fist. The sky darkens further and bright water gathers in gullies until an enormous waterfall roars and pounds the rocks – so brutal it's as if it wants to destroy everything in its way.

Something lurches in my chest. This is beautiful but it's not passive. It's not *pretty*. It is bubbling and alive. Dangerous. Powerful. Iceland is a country that stares back.

'I think maybe they see you.' Berglind nods as if she can hear what I'm thinking. 'The *hudolfólk*.'

'The—' I turn towards her. 'Sorry, who?'

'Hidden folk,' she nods. 'Elves. Imps. Fairies. They are super curious about strangers. Those rocks—' She points at two enormous crags, connected briefly at the top. 'They are trolls kissing, turned to stone by the sun.' She lowers her voice with a secretive smile. 'Trolls do not like us. They are very strong, but luckily not so smart.'

I stare until the crags are behind us.

'Do many people in Iceland believe in magic?'

'Já.' Berglind nods. 'Most of us, I think. What else is there to believe in?'

At any other time, in any other place, I might have assumed it was a joke I didn't understand and would have attempted a polite laugh. But, if there's magic anywhere, it's here.

The storm clouds build and Berglind – narrowing her eyes – speeds up even more.

Drop by drop, rain starts to hit the window. Wind begins to howl.

'Here we go,' says Berglind calmly.

And within seconds the sky cracks, shuddering as water descends in a sheet so thick that we can barely see the road. The car skids again, veering towards the grass as if it's being pushed by an invisible hand. It's so dark we have to switch the headlights on, even though it's not yet midday. Lightning flashes across the sky; the air bellows.

I glance at my driver.

Sure, I've said I'm *scared* a lot. *Scared* to go onstage, to talk to strangers, to be filmed by a camera, to say the wrong thing to the right person and the right thing to the wrong person. But I'm starting to realise I was exaggerating because *this* is fear.

I take a deep breath, hands gripped together.

'We are . . .' I exhale slowly. '*Safe*. Right?'

'Oh no,' Berglind says as the car swerves again. 'People die all the time in Iceland. Storms are very, very dangerous.'

OK, not totally the answer I was looking for.

'Maybe we should . . . stop?'

'Why?' She glances at me in surprise. 'I come from a village over there.' A quick nod. 'We live at the bottom of an active volcano. It was due to explode eighty years ago. We get ten minutes' notice before it pops. Maybe fifteen.'

My eyes widen. And I know it's a dumb question, but: 'What happens then?'

'Fire.' Berglind shrugs. 'Lava. Ash. Village gone. *Poof!* Family is steam.'

*Oh.*

The sky cracks in half again; the car judders.

380

My hands tighten. 'So . . . what do you do?'

'We live every moment knowing it could be the last we have.' Then she laughs. 'Or maybe we get a job in the film industry.'

The storm ends as abruptly as it started. The shift changes the entire landscape, as the sky clears until it's sapphire.

And finally – just after midday – Berglind drives into a packed car park. My stomach knots. Dozens of people in big coats and hats are setting up huge film cameras on tripods, lights, reflectors, metal trolleys with complicated equipment piled on them, heaps of wires, a guinea-pig-shaped clump of grey fluff on the end of a long black stick.

Never mind Meisner, Chekhov, Stanislavski, Hagen . . .

*Why did I never learn what any of this stuff is called? What do all these people do?*

'Faith!' Christian Ellis emerges from the crowd, still dressed in trademark director black.

'Hello, Mr Ellis.' I smile and stick my hand out. 'Thank you for having me back. I'm so grateful to—'

'Bring it in.' Without asking first, he wraps me in a massive hug. 'Let's get the awkward out of the way. Did you smash the first audition? No. Did you smash the second audition? Absolutely not. Had we given you multiple auditions would you have smashed any of them? *Highly* unlikely.'

He pulls back with a wry smile.

'But free headlines are free headlines so let's call it even, yeah? Stoked you're here.' My director waves at the crew. '*EVERYONE!* Faith Valentine, our brand-new star! *Not* Scarlett Bell, as per the memo.'

Everyone looks up, waves and carries on setting up.

I feel my shoulders relax. Nobody's expecting me to be *Faith Valentine* here – in fact, the point is that they need me to be someone else.

'We've got enough light left.' Christian waves a pretty brunette over. 'Can we get Frankie into make-up sharpish?'

I grab the script from my bag.

Thanks to Scarlett's rehearsals, I know most of my lines. In fact, I reckon I can handle almost anything thrown at me.

'So,' I say in my most confident voice, 'which

scene are we starting with?' I flip through the wad of paper. 'The speech at the waterfall, or the breakdown in the hut, or maybe the—'

The director laughs.

'Today, you'll be jumping out of a moving car.'

## 52

Yeah, that's not in the script I'm holding. Pretty sure I'd have noticed.

'Excuse me?'

'We've made a few tweaks,' Christian explains as the make-up artist leads me to the largest trailer. 'Taken out a bunch of words. Added in a whole lot of action. You're the sporty Ice Queen – might as well make the most of it!'

That's a joke, right? He's joking.

I totally didn't spend my last two days with Scarlett and the entire journey here learning my lines so that they could be scrapped at the last minute.

*Again?*

Stumped, I stare at my director.

'Yes!' He claps his hands. 'That's the exact expression I'm talking about! Cold, emotionless,

384

steely. Love it! Now – go get bloodied up, my frosty popsicle.'

Couldn't they have just *texted* me?

'Mmm,' I breathe as my blood boils.

Then, with narrowed eyes, I glide coolly into the trailer with my head up and my back set in a cold, straight line. This is a job I've chosen and I'm playing a role.

They need me to be athletic and strong? Done.

They want me to jump out of a moving vehicle? I'll do it.

They think I'm a frigid, distant nightmare? That's what I'll give them.

I am Faith Valentine, I'm an actress and I can be whoever they want.

The make-up artist replaces both pairs of leggings with ripped, muddy jeans, my fleecy hoodie with another much grubbier hoodie and my trainers with an almost identical pair. She sprays my face with a weird glycerine mix to make it look sweaty. With a huge amount of skill, she attaches a prosthetic top to my ear and moulds it so I look like I've been heartily snacked on.

Then she grins and gets a bottle of red liquid

out. 'This is the best bit,' she confesses happily. 'Close your eyes.'

I obediently do as I'm told and she carefully drips and smears red all over my clothes, my neck, my face, my ear, my hairline. 'OK. Done.'

I blink in the mirror. I'm drenched in blood – sticky and coated in thick red goo. Bar that first party at Scarlett's, I've never looked more like a hot dog in my entire life.

'Cool.' My nose twitches. 'Thanks.'

Then I take a deep breath, leave the trailer and walk calmly towards my director and his crew with an expression of pure steel. 'Good afternoon.' I nod, my voice flat. 'Point me towards the vehicle you'd like me to leap from, please.'

Christian stares at me for a few seconds. 'You're going to do it?'

'Of course.'

'It'll be going at seventy miles an hour.'

'Yes.'

'You're going to jump from a moving car at seventy miles an hour on to a tarmac road with no training whatsoever?'

'Yes.'

He blinks, then bursts into laughter. 'Oh, I *like* you. Tough as nails, just like your grandmother. I was messing with you, Faith. Obviously, you're far too expensive to kill on the first day. Meet your extremely talented stunt double, Dominique Weston.'

Confused, I turn round. A girl is standing behind me: tall, brown-skinned, toned. Huge hazel eyes, a little nose, full lips. We're wearing exactly the same outfit, her left ear is similarly noshed on and even the fake blood seems to be in precisely the same splash marks.

She's also completely bald.

'Hi,' she says, holding out a hand. 'Westie. And don't worry. I was financially compensated for the haircut. I'm kind of digging it, though. Do people keep trying to touch your head too?'

I laugh, then remember I'm supposed to be humourless. 'No.'

'Huh. My skull has never been so popular.'

I wait until Christian's looking the other way, then grin at her, nod and mouth: *Yes, all the time.* She chuckles and fist-bumps me.

'Westie's done her cut already.' The director walks me towards a long, cordoned-off section of road. A small white car is parked in the distance, and about a hundred metres away is a tight knot of crew and equipment. 'We just need the close-up.'

I nod, my inner swan-feet starting to thrash.

*Flip flip flip fli—*

'Yes.'

'As soon as the car reaches that marker –' he points at a chalk line – 'I want you to hit the ground, Faith. Don't worry too much about an emotional reaction. Physically slamming the tarmac should be enough for us.'

His expectations of my acting skills are literally zero.

'Yes.'

'Can you do that?'

'Yes.'

'Excellent.' Christian steps back. '*EVERYONE QUIET ON SET! Final touches!*'

A wave of hushed activity starts: cameras turning on, lights shining, final set-ups, the fluffy guinea pig on a stick being held up. I have *got* to find out what that's called.

'Finals are done!' somebody yells back.

'Lock it up!'

'Sound?'

'Sound speed!'

'Mark it!'

'Marked.'

'Camera ready?'

'Camera rolling!'

'Scene forty-two, take one.'

'ACTION!'

A clapperboard clacks and I take a deep breath.
The car begins to rev in waves. The wheels
screech. And – with an enormous roar – it accelerates
down the road. It seems to take forever to reach
me. But I can do this. I can do this.

*Just fall, Faith. Let go and fall.*

Fall fall fall fall fall fall fall *fall*—

The car hits the mark and my legs give way. I
slam to the ground. The force knocks the wind out
of me and my head whacks the tarmac. I lie – stunned
– for a few seconds as the ground spins in circles.

*I did it.*

'And CUT!' Christian steps forward. '*Again!*'

I hit the floor fifteen times.

Over and over again, until the pain and shock

389

become very real, and also possibly some of the blood.

The last CUT is yelled. I stand up stiffly. It's only when somebody wraps me in a large sheet of tinfoil and hands me a mug of tea that I realise I'm shaking.

'OK?' my director asks, walking over.

I look him coolly in the eyes. 'Yes.'

'Gotta confess, I'm impressed. Teddy will be furious.' He smiles warmly. 'Now I suggest you get as much rest as you can tonight, Faith. We've got a very early start and we need you in peak physical condition.'

What's it going to be? Bungee jumping, rock climbing, skydiving . . .

'Right. Do I need to prepare anything?'

'No.' My director grins wolfishly. 'Tomorrow, you run.'

53

What kind of shoes are made from banana skins?

Slippers.

Running I can do.

Just before dawn, I am driven to an isolated spot in the darkness. I'm given identical clothes to yesterday and briefed quickly on the story context. Then, surrounded by a reduced camera crew, I run. Sprinting through low grass, high grass, and up and down mountains; across thick mud and freezing streams; over hills and fences; round trees and horses and sheep and logs.

I run for hours, and – as the sun comes up – I feel it.

A familiar roar in my chest. The burn in my legs,

the thump of my heart, the heat in my cheeks and the rhythmic *whoosh* of my lungs. As the sky lifts from black to silver, and my feet pound through the landscape, something starts to shift in me.

Because I'm not a Valentine when I run. I'm not an ex-girlfriend or a big sister or a little sister; I'm not a daughter or a disgraced granddaughter; I'm not a heartbreaker or the heartbroken.

But I'm not *nobody*, either. I'm me. And oh, I have *missed* this.

'CUT!' Christian cries as I hurtle out of a wood so fast it feels like my feet are on fire. 'Blimey, Faith. I thought we'd have to do some heavy editing, but you've got this sprinting thing nailed, haven't you?'

I exhale and swipe at a scratch on my cheek.

'Though you've barely broken a sweat,' he sighs, gesturing at the make-up artist. 'Somebody spray her with something shiny. And can you breathe harder, please? You're supposed to be running from zombies, but it looks like they're running from you.'

A laugh escapes me. 'Got it. Let's go.'

I keep running, and the landscape splits into black, white and blue. With a frown of concentration, I sprint over a car park, up a hill and across a ridgeway,

392

one camera following at a distance, another waiting for me at the top.

I reach the peak and exhale sharply. In front of me, a snow-topped black volcano sits quietly behind a glacier lake. In the flat turquoise water are hundreds of giant electric-blue icebergs: opaque, like broken pieces of frosted sea glass. Grey seals laze on top of them – lolling around like sunbathing holidaymakers – and on the grey sand by the water's edge lie hailstones the size of golf balls, footballs, beach balls.

It's so beautiful – and so cold – my tears well up and immediately freeze – little razors of ice prickling my lashes.

I blink and the cameraman gets really close. I bet he thinks I'm acting, but I actually just forgot he was even there.

'CUT!' Christian yells, then waits until I'm back at the bottom of the hill. 'Awesome! Hop in the car and take a quick break. You've got one more run to do today.'

Wordlessly, I climb in and fall back against the seat.

My feet are numb, my clothes are soaking and

my face is thumping. And I am absolutely freaking starving. I'm trying to work out how Scarlett would have handled today. Double pepperoni and extra cheese, I reckon.

'Here.' A tuna baguette is lobbed at me and Christian climbs in the back. 'You must be hungry.'

I shove half of it in my mouth before nodding thanks.

'Good work today,' he says as the car trundles on to the main road. 'Tomorrow's less physical and we've tweaked the script again to fit you a little better, you'll be pleased to hear.'

With my mouth full, I manage a garbled: '*Shankkkz.*'

'I'm emailing it to you now so we can run through some of the changes after this shoot, then you can practise more at the hotel.'

I uneasily gulp down the baguette.

'Umm. Is there a . . . paper version I can use? I . . . prefer . . . the look . . . and . . . feel . . . of a real . . . script.'

'Sure, Faith. I'll go and get that seal over there to print it out for me.'

*What?*

394

'We're in the middle of nowhere,' Christian clarifies with vague amusement. 'It'll be easier to read onscreen anyway.'

With infinite slowness, I retrieve my phone from my bag.

With the exception of that thirty seconds at the airport, my mobile has been turned off for nearly a week. I was hoping I'd be able to extend the silence a bit longer, but it appears that my self-inflicted exile is over.

Wincing with my whole body, I switch it on.

*Ping. Ping. Ping. Ping. Ping. Ping. Ping. Ping. Ping. Ping. Ping. Ping. Ping. Ping. Ping. Ping—*

'Blimey,' Christian says. 'Is that a phone or a bike just before it hits you?'

I stare at all my missed calls.

**Noah. Hope. Hope. Hope. Max. Grandma. Genevieve. Dad. Dad. Hope. WEIRDO: DO NOT ANSWER. WEIRDO: DO NOT ANSWER. Max. Grandma. Dad. WEIRDO: DO NOT ANSWER. Noah. Genevieve. Grandma. Max. Hope. WEIRDO: DO NOT ANSWER. Persephone.**

Then at the messages:

Where did you gooooo? Please come home!
Don't leave us! Xxxxxx

Yo, sis, you still stropping? Can you bring back
food? Mum's gone on another night rampage
and trashed the place. We need you here.

Hey! Wanna hook up tonight? I can come to
you! Dilpot x

Sis, that tanned slimeball is at our front gates.
Can I punch him?

Problem solved, I just lobbed the giant teddy
at him.

Hi, Faith, this is Genevieve. The password to
your social-media accounts is
LIFELOVELAUGH666 – please update regularly.

ARE YOU OK? None of us have heard from
you since you ran out of class – we're all

really worried about you. Please let us know you're all right! Mia x

EFFIE, I JUST SAW THE PAPERS. HAVE YOU MOVED TO ICELAND WITHOUT SAYING GOODBYE? Po xxxx

PS Please bring me back one of those cool jumpers.

PPS Also one of the horses x

Effie, I have just been told you have MOVED OUT without speaking to either your mother or me about it. We need to discuss this urgently. Please call me ASAP, love Dad x

Faith, where are your updates?! Posting for you RN, Genevieve.

This is your grandmother. Contact me at your earliest convenience. Thank you.

*Ping.*

That's Mercy.

I'm not even going to think about opening my emails or Google alerts. My breath is already starting to shorten, my throat close. I'm not sure what I thought would happen – I'd firmly ask for some space and everyone would just . . . *give* it to me?

How the hell do you put boundaries in place if everybody just *ignores* them?

The car pulls into another barren car park.

'Ready?' Christian asks as I slip my phone into my bag and throw in the rest of my baguette too. 'The crew's set up, so all we need you to do is peg it down the beach as fast as you can. There's something horrible chasing you, so try to look trapped and desperate.'

I mean, I haven't done anything wrong, have I? It's not like I randomly disappeared. *I took an acting job.* Isn't this exactly what everyone's been pushing me towards my entire life?

'We'll try and get it in one take. Ideally, I'd like to shoot the rest before the next storm.'

So why do I feel like it's still not enough? Why do I feel like I've let everyone down again?

'Once that's done, Westie will take over and film running into the water.'

*When does it end?*

'Sure.' I put a hand to my throat. 'OK.'

Numbly, I get out of the car and start walking towards a black sand beach backed by looming black cliffs. The sea is grey and foaming white. The sky is slate-grey. It's as if the world has suddenly switched to black and white, but I'm left in colour.

Quietly, I wait at my mark. Breathe. A blur of *everyone quiet on set, final touches, finals are done* – breathe – *lock it up, sound, sound speed* – breathe – *mark it, marked, camera ready* – breathe – *camera rolling, scene twenty-six, take one* – breathe – *and—*

'ACTION.'

I start running, pelting across the black sand.

*I can't do this any more. I can't.*

My legs stumble. I trip, fall, push myself up again, keep running. Because Scarlett was right – that's what I do, isn't it?

I do what I'm told and, when it gets too much, I run.

*399*

When I can't say *no*, I run.

Something hurts, I run.

Someone I love is unhappy and I can't fix it, I run, I run, I run, I run, I run. But it's never fast enough, never far enough, and it never gets me anywhere. I always end up back where I started because I don't know what it is I actually *want*. So here I am—

'And . . . CUT!'

*Trapped.*

'*CUT*, FAITH!'

The foaming sea rages and I turn and run towards the smashing waves.

'FAITH VALENTINE! THIS ISN'T YOUR SCENE!'

Inhaling sharply as the icy water hits my legs.

'FAITH, WHAT ON EARTH ARE YOU DOING?'

Holding my breath and plunging into water so cold and angry it feels like I've been punched.

'FAITH, NO!!'

I close my eyes and feel a wave crash over my head. Water roars – ripping at my clothes, washing away the blood – until it feels like I've disappeared.

But I haven't, I won't, I don't want to.

*Enough.*

I kick my legs hard beneath the surface. And – with a ragged breath – I burst through the waves and struggle back to shore, staggering on to the black sand.

'Faith!' A furious Christian and crew run towards me, with towels and hot drinks and tinfoil blankets. 'Weren't you *listening* to me? That scene wasn't meant for you!'

I take a towel and wrap it round me.

'Oops.'

When what I mean is: *exactly.*

## 54

What did the ocean say to the shore?

Nothing, it just waved.

I send one message:

I will be in contact when I want to be.

To everyone. Then I put my phone on airplane mode and spend the evening trying as hard as I can to practise my new scene. There's turmoil inside me that I can't seem to shake. An anger, a fierceness – like I want to do some damage. I'm starting to understand how Mercy must feel ninety-eight per cent of the time.

'Smile, pretty girl!' a random guy at breakfast demands while I'm pouring myself a cup of coffee.

I turn to him, eyes cold. 'I'll smile when I feel like smiling,' I snap back. 'It's *my face.*'

Still simmering, I run through the script with the director – trying my best to stay polite – then I'm taken to a hotel room for prep. The stylist gives me the same outfit as the last two days, except this time clean and new. I'm given fresh, cute make-up: no blood, no scratches, no sweat. We're going back to the beginning, to the scene where it all started.

*Figures.*

Then I'm driven to the new set. Another bare field with a wooden hut stranded in the middle: half falling down, holes in the roof, ancient swing set outside, classic creepy. The crew is trying to squeeze as many cameras and pieces of lighting equipment into a ten-metre-square shed as physically possible.

'Frankie!' Christian Ellis waves me over. 'Let me introduce you to your kissing co-star! This is—'

'Fred,' I say shortly.

'My name's Ambrose,' a very good-looking blond boy says, holding his hand out. 'But, yes, I'll be playing your boyfriend.'

'Hooray,' I sigh. 'Another one.'

He blinks and I turn to Christian.

'So.' I just want to get on with this. 'Where do you want me to—'

'Hello, Effie.'

Something heavy drops in my stomach. I spin round.

'Ah!' my director shouts. 'Perfect timing! Faith, this is Patricia Allerton, one of the best acting coaches in the business. Today's going to be tricky – don't we already know, haha! – so she's here to give you some extra guidance.'

It's the older lady with tortoiseshell glasses from my auditions – the one I recognised but couldn't name. With a smile, she takes my hands gently in hers and squeezes them.

'We know each other, don't we?' Her voice is kind. 'Do you remember? I used to coach your mother, so I knew you when you were a little girl.'

There's a sudden lump in my throat. Because I *do* remember her, watching us in the marquee at my parents' party, standing next to a huge vase of orchids. I remember us in white, in red, in blue, in yellow, in green, in purple. I remember my parents smiling and I remember the audience and the lights and my overwhelming fear.

I remember everything, and my anger abruptly softens.

'I know I haven't been in touch,' she says quietly, squeezing my hands again. 'And for that I am so sorry. I wasn't sure what to say, although that's no excuse.'

I nod and swallow.

'Effie, I know that you've never found performing easy. I was there for that show at your parents' anniversary party, remember? But we're going to find a way to work this scene together. Does that sound good?'

I suddenly feel nine years old again, wearing my mother's shoes.

'Yes, please,' I say in a little voice.

'Nice!' Christian interrupts. 'Now, Frankie, in the hut with Fred, please? Patricia, go with her, yeah? Let's get this opener nailed!'

My hands are starting to shake again. My face is stiffening. My shoulders tightening. My stomach spinning. Hardness is rushing through my body, turning me – organ by organ – to ice. A living, breathing statue.

I've trained. I've rehearsed. I've read this script

dozens of times. I've even *acted* this scene before. I know that Frankie loves Fred; there are strange noises outside; he's going to leave the hut though she doesn't want him to; she's scared; they kiss . . .

So why am I freezing up and icing over again? What's *wrong* with me?

'You can do it,' Patricia says as my eyes flicker wildly, looking for an escape. 'I'll be here if you need me.'

I nod, blinking back tears. Then I walk into the hut.

Christian Ellis positions me on my mark, briefs us on angles, then stands outside, watching through a glassless window. I smile apologetically at Ambrose – *sorry I was rude* – and he smiles back.

'EVERYONE QUIET ON SET!'

'Sound?'

'Sound speed.'

'Camera ready?'

'Camera rolling.'

'Scene one, take one.'

'And . . . ACTION!'

Noises sound outside: frightened animals, branches breaking, footsteps. Fred turns to me with wide eyes, and my line is:

406

*Fred! What was that? I heard something – there's someone outside*

and his line is *There's nobody there*

and my line is *We've made a mistake – we should go*

and his line is *It's just a sheep or something*

and my line is *but sheep don't sound like that*

and his line is *A cow, then*

and my line is *Don't go* and we kiss we kiss we kiss.

I stare at Fred in silence.

*I can do it. I just don't want to.*

'No.'

'Ummm.' Fred blinks at me, at the crew, at the camera and at me again. 'That's not your line.'

*Actually, it is.*

'I don't want to act.'

I turn to the director. My voice is clear and grey and calm. 'I have never wanted to act. I don't like it. It doesn't make me happy.'

My body has been screaming NO at me for nearly a year, I just wasn't listening. I was so busy worrying that I wasn't *good* at acting that I never really asked myself if I *wanted* to be. And I don't. That's what I'm now sure of.

407

I need to move my circle right now, before it gets superglued to the floor.

'I'm sorry, Mr Ellis, for taking the job and for . . .' I pause. 'Actually, I'm not that sorry. I'm only sixteen years old, but you used me for headlines. That is not OK. I'm sorry your crew wasted time filming me, but I'd rather waste three days of your life than the rest of mine.'

He stares at me blankly.

'So I'm saying . . . no.'

A steady, quiet roar spreads from my toenails to my ankles to my knees to my hips to my stomach to my chest to my shoulders to my elbows to my fingernails to my neck to my cheeks to my eyes and, when I finally smile, I can feel it in my whole body.

There isn't a single dimple to be seen.

'Right.' Christian looks at the glaring sky and pinches his nose. 'Yeah. That's probably a good decision. I don't really have to be coaching my lead through every scene when I can get a professional who knows what she's doing. We'll get the standby flown over this evening.'

I blink in surprise and then relief. 'Thank you,' I say warmly.

Patricia smiles at me. I smile back.
And I go outside and I breathe

I breathe

I breathe

I breathe

I breathe

I breathe.

Then I pull my phone out of my bag and message
just one person:

YES.

## 55

What did the duck say when she bought a lipstick?

Put it on my bill.

Mercy is waiting for me.

As I climb through my window the next evening, she's already there, exactly where I knew she'd be. Huddled on my bed. Leaning against the wall, arms wrapped round her legs, chin on her knees, watching the door with huge, bottomless eyes.

My heart *twangs*. 'Hi, sis.'

She looks up, and the pain in her face takes my breath away. 'Hi.'

We gaze at each other.

'Mercy—' I start.

'It was me,' she says quietly. 'I kissed Noah.'

And the world should tip, it should spin, it should implode . . . but it doesn't.

'He didn't get you,' she says fiercely into the silence, her eyes glittering. 'You're not like us, Eff. You never have been. We need the spotlight to feel like we *exist*. To feel bigger and more real. To feel . . . *seen*.'

She blinks hard.

'With you, it's the opposite. Even when we were kids. The fame – it makes you *shrink*. And Noah never got that, not in a whole year. I couldn't just stand by and watch while you got smaller and smaller. Until you started . . . disappearing. But you were never going to leave him so . . .'

My sister flushes and her eyes dart away.

'. . . I stuck on a blonde wig and jumped in a cab. I snuck into the after-show, gave a guy fifty quid to take a picture, grabbed Noah and kissed him. He didn't even know it was me. Then I gave the photos to the press.'

*Faith, I'm so sorry.*

'I let the paparazzi into the grounds. That was me too,' she adds in a hard voice, lifting her chin.

I know this expression. It's the one Mercy always wore when she trashed Max's new bike or broke

411

Mum's best vase or ripped Hope's favourite T-shirt during a game of Bulldog: chin up, jaw set, eyes defiant.

She's still there, the little girl inside the big one. And my rush of love for my sister is so raw and sudden it feels like an animal cry. I want to hug her and kill her and kiss her and hurt her and rip her apart and put her back together again.

Mercy doesn't crawl into my bed every night to annoy me, or because she can't be bothered to find her own. She climbs into my bed because she still has nightmares and doesn't want to be alone.

Because she knows I still have them too.

'OK,' I say simply.

Silence, and then Mercy's head whips round as if I've slapped her. '*OK?*'

'Yes.'

'Did you just say *OK?*'

'Yes. I underst—'

'STOP!' My sister leaps off the bed: fists clenched, breathing hard. 'DON'T YOU DARE SAY YOU UNDERSTAND, FAITH! Don't you *dare* try and see it from my side! Don't you dare love me this much! Don't you *dare!*'

412

Mer whacks my arm, hard.

'SCREAM AT ME!' She whacks me again. 'HATE ME!' Whack. '*HATE ME!*' Whack. 'WHAT I DID WAS UNFORGIVABLE! I am *your sister*. *YOUR SISTER!*'

She starts crying.

'Mer—' I reach out and try to pull her towards me. 'You just wanted me to be happy, you—'

'NO, I DIDN'T!' She tugs away, shaking all over. 'I DID IT BECAUSE I'M HORRIBLE, FAITH! Because I *break* things! Because I want to rip and smash and destroy everything around me until there's NOTHING LEFT.'

Mercy wraps her arms tightly round her stomach. Her eyes are wet and shining.

'I *hurt* you, Faith. I let them all in and I made it *worse*. I made you run away. I should never have – had no right to – can't believe I—' Her voice is thickly wet. 'I made a *huge* mistake,' she sobs, holding a shaking hand over her face. 'And I'm so sorry. Please don't hate me, Faith. Don't hate me, don't hate me, don't hate me—'

My heart is roaring so loudly I can't move. Pain surges up my throat until it shuts with a click.

413

Two years ago the Valentines didn't just detonate, they exploded into a million tiny pieces.

'I can't . . .' Mercy crumples to the floor, sobbing into her hands. 'I can't— Please forgive me, Eff. Please. I can't lose another sister.'

## 56

*Eight years ago.*

'Lights! Camera! Action!'

'That's *not* what film people say,' Max points out loudly from the side of the stage, swishing his mustard skipping rope over his shoulder. 'Total urban myth.'

'Oh, you are *such* a damp squid,' Hope sighs. 'Just leaking your water everywhere. Leak, leak, leak.'

'Damp *squib*. Squids are always damp. Obviously.'

'What's a squib?'

'It's a firework!' somebody calls out from the back. 'That's why it's a saying – you can't light a wet firework.'

Beaming, Hope turns to face the famous audience. 'Oh hello, I forgot you were there! Thanks very much!'

There's general laughter.

'Ladies and gentlemen!' My sister holds her hands out wide. 'Highly steamed members of the industry of Hollywood! WELCOME to your entertainment! Tonight, to celebrate our mother and father's *ten-year wedding anniversary,* we – the *infamous and celebrated* Valentine children – will be inraptoring you with our very own, specially written performance!'

She twirls round in her bright turquoise sweater and starts flapping her arms. We shrug at each other: *What's she doing? Does anyone ever know?*

'Prepare yourself for a state of *mesmi– mesima– mesme—*' My little sister pauses thoughtfully. 'Amazement! And *please* feel free to collect my business card from the table to the right. I shall be available for all good actressing parts in just over eight years. I thank you.'

Po gestures dramatically at a pile of scribbled-on scraps of cereal box to a warm ripple of laughter.

'Innnntrrrooooduuuuuucccing – *Murder on the National Express*!'

She retreats to loud claps.

As Mercy and Max squabble over who gets to

blow the trumpet, I tuck myself further in the corner of the marquee. Everything's so beautiful – the flowers, the food and the dresses – and there are so many people I recognise here, movie stars stretching across generations.

My parents stand at the front, shiny and happy. Mum looks curvy and luminous in her green gown while Dad, so handsome in his tux, is grinning at her, one arm holding her tightly to his side. They're both laughing a little too loudly.

'Jeez Louise,' I hear Dad say. 'Juliet, do you see what we've done? Why do they crave this much attention? Do we need our parenting skills re-evaluating?'

'I think so.' Mum smiles radiantly. 'Little thespian show-offs.'

'Sorry, guys,' my father announces to the A-list crowd. 'Consider this payment for a generous selection of vol-au-vents.'

More laughter. Everyone loves the Valentines.

'*Go*,' Mercy whispers, shoving Max. '*Go*, idiot.'

My skinny eleven-year-old brother swaggers onstage, twirling his skipping rope, and fear inches through me. We'd rehearsed for weeks, but it wasn't just the six of us any more. Suddenly it feels very real, very . . . public.

'That is *not* my best side,' Hope explains to Ben, pointing to the left side of her face. '*This* is my best side.'

Ben – wearing huge glasses and a big green scarf – turns her round and taps the back of her head. '*This* is your best side actually.'

'Oh my goodness!' Po tosses her hair, delighted. 'You are *so rude.*'

'*Faith*,' Mercy hisses. 'It's your turn next!'

My entire body starts to tremble and I clutch my hands together. The stage is somehow getting closer, the crowds louder, the lights brighter, my voice smaller and I can't do it, can't do it, can't—

A soft hand lands on my arm.

'Be the Orange, Eff.' A husky whisper. 'And, if that doesn't work, try a clementine. Smaller. Fewer pips.'

I turn to face Charity, who is dressed in purple.

Our eldest sister: older than Mercy by three minutes and physically identical apart from a tiny scar running through her left eyebrow. In character, the polar opposite. Where Mercy is impatient,

Charity is laid-back; where Mer takes everything seriously, Tee is constantly laughing.

*Everything* is a practical joke to her.

Clingfilm across the toilet seat and grass seeds sprouting in Dad's laptop and the white centre of Oreo biscuits replaced with toothpaste, the middle of a doughnut refilled with mayo.

Her music is always too loud, her bedroom always too bright.

'*Charity!*' Mum yells every hour. 'Lights!'

'Don't you get enough of that at work?' my sister calls back with a throaty laugh. 'Such a *diva*, Mother.'

Yet we gravitate towards her and somehow she balances us all out. Gives Hope strength, Max a comrade, Mercy softness, Mum playfulness, Dad pride, Grandma warmth.

To me, she gives laughter.

'Here.' Tee grins as Max swishes his skipping rope yet again and is gestured to get offstage by an impatient Mercy. 'Take this with you. For luck.'

My sister rips a yellow Post-it from the front of her script, grabs a pen, scribbles something and pushes it into my hand.

I look down.

*What happened when the bed bugs fell in love?*

*They got married in the spring.*

'Don't get it.'

My nine-year-old sister laughs: a goofy, ridiculous chuckle that causes Mercy to flash her a *Don't Even Think About It* look.

'I know,' Charity twinkles. 'You never do. Try.'

Frowning, I look back at the note. The funny is always tucked away in there somewhere, lurking where I can't see it. An answer to a question I haven't even asked.

'What does a bed have, Eff?'

'A mattress? Pillows? A duvet?' My eyes widen. '*Springs.*'

'*There* you go.'

We stare at each other – my sister's face so utterly like Mercy's in every way and yet totally its own – and then every muscle in my body starts shaking.

A snort pops out of my nose. And, before I can

catch it, I'm sniggering, chortling and squealing with laughter until every bit of my nerves evaporate, spun into the air like purple mist.

'Whenever things get too much, find the joke, Eff.' My sister ruffles my hair. 'Nothing is too hard to handle when you're laughing.'

I nod and tuck the joke into my pocket.

'Love you, Tee.'

My big sister, the eldest Valentine girl, puts her purple arm round me.

'I love you too, Effpot.' She nudges me towards the stage. 'Now go get them, my funny little sister.'

## 57

In one motion, I drop to the floor.

I wrap my arms round Mercy as she sobs into my neck, my knees against hers. 'You haven't lost me,' I whisper fiercely. 'Mer, I'm not going anywhere. I promise.'

Finally, she hiccups into stillness.

'Except for right now,' I clarify, kissing her tenderly on the forehead. 'Meet me in the hallway in five.'

Because enough is enough.

# 58

One by one, I collect my family.

It's the second anniversary of Charity's death, and we've all come back here automatically. I find Hope in the cinema room, Dad in his armchair in the living room, Grandma in the library, Max in the kitchen, Mum in her darkened bedroom.

Together but achingly separate.

'Where did you come from?' Max blinks at me from the hallway. 'I thought you were in Alaska.'

'You're *home*!' Hope leaps up the stairs and throws her arms round me in relief, covering my cheeks with little kisses. 'Eff, you're home, you're home! I *knew* you'd come back! *He* said you'd emigrated, but I *told* him that's only for birds.'

Mum's bedroom door creaks open; she sees us and hesitates. Then she takes a small step out.

'Mum!' Po unwraps herself from me and rushes

over to her. 'You're here too! Oh and *so* pretty, I *love* your nightgown, is it designer? Can I borrow it, please, please, please?'

Mum starts slightly, then puts a hand on top of Hope's head. 'Of course, baby.'

'Hello, Juliet.' Dad dwarfs the hallway.

Mum nods, her eyes watery and bright pink. Nobody's going to mention that she ripped the house apart two days ago, looking for a baby blanket to donate to the auction. *For Charity.*

'Could *somebody*,' my grandmother puffs, hauling herself on to the landing with her walking stick, '*please* explain why I am being *summoned* to the top floor of a three-storey building like some kind of *performing monkey*?'

My bedroom door swings open. Mercy's face is clean and puffy, scrubbed free of make-up. Without it, she looks so young. She's in black jeans and a black jumper: still in perpetual mourning.

She blinks once at me – *thank you* – then holds her head down.

I think this might be the first time we've all been in the same place since the funeral.

I pull a key out of my pocket.

424

'There's something I want to show you,' I say, unlocking the door that sits directly between Mum's and Mercy's. The room that used to be so bright and full of light and is now so deafeningly quiet.

We enter in silence. Then Mer makes a small, guttural noise and puts a hand over her mouth.

There are yellow Post-its stuck everywhere. Around the dusty mirror and over the walls; on the edges of posters and across a dresser still covered in spilt make-up and open lipsticks. Over the doorway and on the headboard and on framed photo-collages of all of us.

Why did the two 4s skip lunch?

They already 8!

What do you call a snowman with a six-pack?

An abdominal snowman.

Why can't you hear a pterodactyl go to the toilet?

The P is silent!

Joke after joke. Mostly terrible, all cheesy, the vast majority copied from the internet or cheap books I found. Every single one I wrote when it became too much, when I needed to laugh, when I needed to feel closer to my sister.

*Make me one with everything.*

'Crikey,' Max says eventually with wide eyes. 'Faith. You OK?'

'No,' I admit. 'Obviously not.'

Hope's drifting round the room, gently touching Charity's books and old teddy bears, and Mum keeps blinking, as if everything's too bright for her to focus properly.

Dad picks up a still open magazine.

'Nobody—' He breathes out heavily. 'It's exactly the same . . . We didn't . . . ? I thought we . . . I mean, didn't Maggie tidy everything away?'

'No,' I say quietly. 'Mum asked her not to.'

Grandma sits down sharply on a dusty armchair.

'I don't understand.' Mercy picks up a yellow Post-it. 'Did you write these, Faith? There are . . . *hundreds.*'

'Two years' worth of comedy.'

'But—' There's a wet click at the back of her throat. 'We never talk about her. None of us. We always change the subject. I thought everybody was . . . forgetting.'

'No,' Hope says, trailing a finger along a shelf. 'We don't talk about her because we all remember, all the time.'

I stare at my little sister in surprise.

Then I look round the bedroom that Charity painted primrose yellow: cheerful, sloppy brush-marks on the ceiling. 'All she wanted was jokes. She'd hate all this misery.'

I pick up a toilet roll from her bedside table.

'This is *fake.*' I hold it up and pull the top layer of paper off: underneath it's plastic. 'Our dumb-ass sister *made a fake toilet roll* so she could hold us hostage in the loo while she giggled outside.'

Max laughs loudly. 'I'm scarred for life, the little dirtbag. I had to carry tissue in my pockets for *years*.'

'Mer.' I grab a long red wig from Charity's desk.

427

'She used to pin this over your bed so you'd wake up and think a ghost was climbing through the ceiling.'

'Yeah.' My big sister shrugs. 'Never worked.'

'Erm, you screamed the house down. And this?' I pick up a scrap of paper with *Voice Activated* typed on it. 'Remember when she put this on our new toaster and Hope spent hours shouting at it to make breakfast?'

'Hey!' Po says indignantly, opening a curtain. 'We are very rich and very famous. If anyone is going to have a magic robot-servant-toaster, it should be us.'

Dad booms with unexpected laughter as a ray of sunshine pours into the darkness and hits the yellow walls. Dust spins and bobs like millions of tiny lights.

*Hey, sis. There you are.*

'Charity was an idiot,' I say, pulling open the other curtain. 'She was annoying and ridiculous and spent most of her allowance on whoopee cushions.' I tug open the window. 'And we loved her and that love made us brighter. I want to remember that. I want to talk about her. Laugh about her. Get on

428

with our lives. Instead of . . . locking ourselves away in the dark.'

Everyone looks down.

I go to the next window and fling both curtains open. The room is glowing gold as if we're standing inside a buttercup. My mother quietly walks over to stare at the garden, her back rigid.

'There's just one more thing,' I say, swallowing. Grandma looks up sharply.

I still haven't spoken to her since the auction. Now I take a deep breath and meet her grey gaze directly.

'I don't want to be an actress. I don't want to be famous. I don't want to do interviews or give fake answers or have my photograph taken or have my life dissected every single day. I want to be *private*. Normal. I've been trying so hard to make you all happy, I forgot that I'm allowed to be happy too.'

My grandmother's hands grip her walking stick tightly. 'What on earth are you saying, child?'

I look at the family I love with my whole heart, each part tugging me in a different direction.

*The world is my oyster.*

'I don't want to be a Valentine any more.'

## 59

Silence. Then—

'NOOOOOOOOOOOOOOOOOOOOOOOOOOOOO OOOOOO!' Hope drops to her knees and shakes her fists at the ceiling. 'I KNEW IT! I KNEW YOU WOULD DIVORCE US EVENTUALLY! I KNEW THIS WOULD HAPPEN! NOOOO! I DIVIDE YOU, STARS!'

Laughing, I pull my little sister up by the armpits.

'I'm not *divorcing* you,' I explain gently. 'I'll still be part of the family. I'll just be living somewhere else. Doing something else. With . . . a different name.'

OK, that *does* sound a bit like a divorce.

'But—' Max chimes in. 'Eff, *everyone* wants to be us. Why on earth would you want to be *them*? What are you going to *do* with –' he pulls a grotesque face – '*ordinariness?*'

430

'No idea.' I grin. 'That's the point.'

Because the mist has gone and when I look down I can see my feet and I can see the ground and I can go in any direction I want.

Even if I don't know quite where that is just yet. *Especially* if I don't.

The warm roar spreads through me again and I look with tenderness at my mother. Did she ever get to choose?

She remains at the window – still fragile and curled in on herself – and my heart squeezes. I'm not even sure if she's been listening. It's not going to be easy for her to come back to us. Losing a sister is unbearable, but a daughter? How do you recover from that kind of grief? Where do you even start?

As if she can hear me, Mum turns round and her tearful eyes meet mine. *I'm sorry.*

I smile sadly. *Me too.*

Without a word, Dad walks over and wraps Mum in a giant bear hug as she returns her empty gaze to the trees outside. Then he turns to me and asks, 'So, Effie, if you're not going to be a Valentine any more, who *are* you going to be?'

'Faith Rivers,' I say simply.

'But—' My father looks genuinely stunned, bless his massive socks. 'You're taking *my* surname? Wait – is that even allowed?'

'People do it all the time,' Hope says, patting his arm. 'It's called *gender quality*, Dad.'

I glance over at my grandmother. She hasn't said a single word since she entered the room, and she's so stiff and velvety she's practically indistinguishable from the armchair.

She leans forward on her walking stick and slowly pushes herself up.

'Faith.' Her gaze is steady. 'Do you know why I trained you every Wednesday for a year?'

'Yes.' I nod and swallow guiltily. 'And I'm sorry, Grandma. I am. I know we're a dynasty a hundred years in the making. I know I'm throwing away an extraordinary opportunity. I know I was the future of the Valentines, but I just—'

'I trained you,' she says, 'because you needed it.'

I flush. 'Yes, *I know*. I'm a terrible actress, but—'

'No. Not because you're a terrible actress. God knows, Hollywood has been built on the faces of

432

beautiful women who couldn't act their way out of a paper bag. I was training you to *keep you private*.'

I stare at her. 'Huh?'

'You think I don't know what your favourite colour is?' She's watching me carefully. 'Or your favourite ice cream? You think I gave you pre-written answers and Genevieve's social-media posts because the real you *doesn't matter*? Darling girl, I gave them to you specifically because it *does*.'

My mouth drops open. I wasn't being trained to be known by the entire world. I was being trained *not to be*.

After six decades of fame, my grandmother was trying her very hardest to give me a shell and make sure that nobody could prise me open.

Like they did my mother.

'But if you don't actually *want* to act –' Dame Sylvia Valentine leans further forward – 'then, for goodness' sake, don't take all the other nonsense that comes with it. For that would make you utterly miserable indeed.'

There's a sudden lump in my throat. 'Thank you.'

'Although,' she adds drily, 'I very much enjoyed

your little takedown at that auction. Even if the old master you sold for pennies *did* belong to us.'

'Wait,' Hope pipes up. 'Which one?'

*Oops.*

And slowly the room starts to fill with noise and colour. Dad is looking fondly at an old photo of him and Charity, Hope's reading some of the jokes and giggling, my mother has walked away from the window and is now tenderly stroking the clothes in Charity's wardrobe and Grandma is watching her with soft eyes.

The Valentine family is slowly recalibrating: finding our places, remembering our lines, resuming our positions. Only this time I've got a role I've chosen.

'Mercy,' I say suddenly, picking a yellow Post-it off the wall and turning to face the only shadowy, silent corner. 'Do you remember how Tee thought this was the funniest ever—'

But something tells me this corner has been empty for a while.

My sister has gone.

## 60

Why did the crab never give to Charity?

Because it was shellfish.

Just a few things left to do.

Quietly, I return to my empty bedroom and stick the final (terrible) joke next to my bed so I can see it every morning.

*Go get them, my funny little sister.*

Then I stand in front of the cracked mirror. I lift my heels off the floor and watch my reflection as I gesture to the side with my left hand: *grand plié*. Flatten my foot and hold my leg up and back: arabesque. A single-leg *relevé* to stretch my foot. *A la seconde.*

The White Swan didn't have to drown herself, you know.

*Battement fondu, battement frappé; quatrième devant.*
*Glissade.*

She had wings; she could have just flown away.
*Entrechat.*

Smiling, I stand on tiptoe, lift one leg and slowly pivot in a circle with my arm in the air. I chop a few bats. *Kapow.* Then I laugh and curtsey at a thousand versions of myself in the mirror. Because what I can see now is all the women I am, all the women I want to be and all the choices I'll make.

And they are going to be . . . *mine.*

With a final flourish, I lean forward and kiss the mirror. Then I shove on my neon trainers, grab my mobile and headphones and slip back down the stairs.

'—*do!*' Hope's lilting voice carries into the hallway. 'Seriously. They sent me a *hundred* yellow roses and *fifty* heart balloons and they did it all anonymously! They must be *crazy* for me. Love at first sight, I reckon.'

Curious, I pause outside the cinema room. The door is ajar, so I can get close enough to see a film playing and the backs of two heads next to each other on the sofa.

436

'Clearly an oddball,' Ben laughs, elbowing my sister playfully. 'You were at school for less than three hours. I'm pretty sure *love* means introducing yourself in person, you know, face to face? Who even gave them your address? Also, your favourite flower's the poppy so *fail*.'

'*Pffff*.' She sighs. 'What do you know?'

'More than this bozo.'

'*Bozo?* Who even says *bozo*? What are you, a hundred years old?'

'Sure. Whatever. They got it wrong. That's all I'm saying.' Ben snorts. 'Yellow roses. *Lame*.'

There's a short silence, then suddenly Hope turns to him.

'Ben, are you *jealous*?'

'Umm, no.'

'You are! You're *jealous* of my secret admirer! And if you're jealous then . . . that means –' I can practically hear my little sister's cogs whirring – 'you must *like* me.' A pause. 'Ben-jamin-o, do you *like* me? You totally like me, don't you! Do you have a *crush* on me? Oh, you have *such* a huge, massive crush on me!'

The entire back of Ben's neck has gone bright red.

*About time, Po. Took you long enough.*

Smiling, I creep away.

As quietly as I can, I swing open the front door, slip my headphones on and stand calmly on the front step. There's nobody outside. No limousines waiting, no paparazzi, no ex-boyfriends, no Genevieve, no speeches to be made. Just a whole world full of fresh air and opportunities, ready to be cracked wide apart.

Pulling my phone out of my pocket, I tap on every single one of my social-media accounts and delete them all.

*Laters, Faith Valentine.*

Then I turn my music to full volume, stretch outwards, tilt my face towards the sunshine and breathe in.

Breathe out.

Breathe in, for luck and also for staying alive.

My phone *pings*.

Yo yo! Rehearsals going super well. If you get time off, wanna fly over here? Also, know anyone who might want to babysit my flat? Somebody has to look after my parties while I'm not there S xxx

Smiling, I text back:

**Yes and yes. I can probably think of someone**
**xx**

Laughing – feeling ever so slightly silly – I crouch down on the front door step and put my hands over my head.

*Make a circle.*

And I don't see Mercy in the garden, kicking the hell out of a tree. I don't see her pelting it with her fists and screaming. Because you know what? That's her story to tell.

I look to the sky and I blow my sisters a kiss. Then I bounce on my tiptoes on the edge of a world that is bright and open and waiting for me.

And I run.

# Acknowledgements

This is my tenth book.

That anyone has allowed me to write so many stories is frankly amazing; that I've been encouraged, motivated and supported to keep going, even more so.

My agent, Kate Shaw, has been with me for a decade (another anniversary!). Without her vision and fierce championing, I'd still be a terrible waitress. For that, I – and any potential customers I would have had – am beyond grateful. Likewise, my genius editor Lizzie Clifford has been with me from the start: from the little dinosaur GEEK biscuits she hand-made on our first meeting, right the way through every idea and nuance and wobble. To both of them I owe everything, and these words are just a drop in a giant bucket of love and thanks.

Without a brilliant team of talent, passion and hard work a book remains in the author's head (or in a box under the bed). I have been incredibly fortunate to have made a home with HarperCollins. Ann-Janine Murtagh, Rachel Denwood, Nick Lake, Samantha Stewart, Michelle Misra, Yasmin Morrissey, Jess Dean, Lowri Ribbons, Jane Tait, Mary O'Riordan, Elorine Grant, David McDougall, Elisa Offord, Beth Maher, Alex

Cowan, Geraldine Stroud, Jo-Anna Parkinson, Louise Sheridan, Sam White, Robert Smith, Carla Alonzi, Sarah Mitchell, Aisling Smith, working with you all has been a joy and an honour. And to Jessie Ford, thank you for yet another utterly beautiful illustrated cover.

Ten books in, and I fear the novelty of being mentioned in acknowledgments has somewhat worn off for my nearest and dearest. But Mum, Dad, Tara, Autumn, Grandad – all this is because of, and for, you. To the rest of my enormous family – Caro, Louise, Adrien, Vincent, Vero, Charlie, Simon, Ellen, Freya, Robin, Lorraine, Romayne, Dixie, Grandma, Judith – thank you for all the love, the hugs and for reading this far.

A big thanks is due to my dear friend Emma Jane Unsworth, who gave me a role in her brilliant film *Animals* and thus allowed me to experience a real movie set for myself (and confirm that I, like Faith, have zero acting talent). Also to Maya, Alice, Ben, Steve, Steven, Lucy, Nina and Helen: thanks for keeping me sane, happy and frequently dehydrated this year. It made it all so much more fun.

Finally, thank you to my readers. Without you, these stories wouldn't exist – I'd just be talking to myself (which I do, but not for money). Your kind words, your support, your affection and your loyalty make this the best career in the world.

So keep reading, and I promise I'll keep writing.

Here's to another ten.